LOVE
LIES
SLAIN

LOVE
LIES
SLAIN

L. L. Blackmur

St. Martin's Press ● New York

DESIGN BY JUDITH STAGNITTO

Library of Congress Cataloging-in-Publication Data

Blackmur, L. L.
    Love lies slain: a romantic mystery / L.L. Blackmur.
      p. cm.
    ISBN 0-312-03388-5
    I. Title.
    PS3552.L3426L6 1989
    813'.54—dc20   89–35109

10 9 8 7 6 5 4 3 2

To my parents

LOVE
LIES
SLAIN

1

It was just before ten when Galen Shaw descended into the breathless night washed in the cool light of a three-quarter moon, down a boarded path to the beach. The scrub pines gave off a sweet smell but not so much as a whisper. An anemic Atlantic Ocean weakly licked the hard sand; a black-crowned night heron passed unseen overhead, its raspy squawk like someone hawking to spit. But no other sounds disturbed the cloying stillness that had raised sweat between the woman's breasts and driven her from her cottage and out into the night.

The breeze she had hoped for was still somewhere far out at sea, but the sand at water's edge was cool and the black water, into which she waded, was achingly cold. Knee deep, she stooped to draw it up her long slender arms, filled her hands, and doused her face. With a wet forearm she dragged back a ripply tangle of wheat-yellow hair. Watching skeptically from dry land was a small caramel-color dog with pop eyes, a golfball-size lump for a tail, and a nose the color of goose liver pâté. A long pink tongue hung six inches out of its mouth.

"Lily, come!" Galen ordered. Lily continued only to look and to pant. "Suffer, then," she said, and after pausing a moment to let the chill penetrate her skin, began wading slowly south down the invisible edge of Bassing's Bay. Except for the 1-4-3 pulse of Quicks' Light a mile and a half out (I L-o-v-e Y-o-u or I H-a-t-e Y-o-u, depending on one's frame of mind), there was no other evidence of human life. It was early in the season yet and the rest of the summer cottages were boarded up and dark.

This side of the bay was cupped by a mile-long stretch of dove-gray beach looped between outcroppings of ledge that rose lumpily out of the sand like half-inflated zeppelins. Dark hulks by night, they were pink and orange in the sun, draped to the high-water mark with black clots of dried kelp and fading to yellow and finally white at their rounded peaks where herring gulls shattered their crab and clam shells or huddled together like a collection of gray-and-white weathervanes.

To cross from one segment of beach to the next, woman and dog made for the low spot along the ledge. Several generations ago one of the old summer families had put in steps and later traced them with a now-thickly rusted section of handrail sunk in blocks of concrete. Galen groped for the rail in the darkness. As her hand made contact, a voice not three feet from her ear said, "Good evening."

Her short scream shattered the silence, triggering an inelegant howl from the dog. This, in turn, was followed by a vigorous curse as Galen faltered, missed her step, and drove her shin into the leading edge of the concrete stair.

The voice was not really threatening and her scream was not exactly one of fear. But screaming when spoken to unexpectedly was an unfortunate habit that had embarrassed Galen in libraries, airplanes, museums, and anywhere else that concentration had suspended her sense of the world around her. (All the same, she suspected that if ever actually menaced and called upon to employ "a woman's best weapon," she would be incapable of more than the desperate breathy wheeze of dreams.) But this the speaker could scarcely have known. The voice that was formal to begin with was now ravaged by regret as Galen, having tumbled muttering to the sand, alternately rubbed her shin and peered blindly at the palm that had sacrificed itself for the good of her nose and teeth.

"Oh, I *say*, I am *terribly* sorry, I didn't mean to alarm you, are you *quite* all right?"

The man sounded elderly and in that way of Americans of a certain generation and social standing, British.

"Yes, yes, I'm fine," she said, finding a seat and trying to make out a body to go with the voice, which because of its decorous tone lent a decidedly ludicrous aspect to the circumstance.

"I was afraid I might startle you, but I rather do need your assistance." He moved just enough to allow her to distinguish his presence from the skirt of black seaweed at the base of the ledge. She was quickly at his side.

"Are *you* all right?"

A small man was propped stiffly against the rock as if seated at the head of a silver-set banquet table. The dog had finally stopped barking and was cautiously sniffing the knee of the stranger, who reached to pat her stubby head as if it were glass and the weight of his large knuckly hand might break it.

"Well, to be perfectly truthful, I'm afraid I've injured my ankle," he said contritely. "Coming down these miserable steps I caught my heel on the last one and landed up here. I think it's just a sprain but I've had no luck at walking or crawling. I was hoping I might trouble you to help me back to my cottage."

He was old, after all, and happily quite light, and Galen had little trouble helping him to his feet. The man was also as stiff as he was wounded. He had been sitting

against the clammy ledge with the patience and certitude of
ascetics and the elderly since the sun went down over three
hours ago, confident that someone would come across him
and fully prepared to wait out the night if no one did. Earlier that afternoon he had opened up the lovely, trellised
butter-yellow Cape House just down from Galen's cottage.
He said his name was Henry Louis and that he had come
out for the summer.

She told him hers.

"Yes, well, the pleasure's all mine, I assure you. Now
then, shall we?" He placed a hand on her shoulder and
they started gingerly up the sand.

The boards were off the windows; however, assuming
he would be back before dark, he had not left on any lights
before going down to the water's edge "to see in the night,
or as I like to imagine it, watch the 'wild team . . . arise and
shake the darkness from their loosen'd manes and beat the
twilight into flakes of fire.'"

"Tennyson!"

"Right you are."

Galen smiled smugly—it had been a good guess—as
she groped into a blackened room that smelled like the
pages of an old book. Her fingers found the lamp he said
would be on a table by the door, and with a *click* a vintage
New England den—primitive antique chests and tables
bearing their original paint, velvet chairs, oak wood boxes,
glass lamps, ceiling-high shelves overflowing with leather-
bound books and black-and-white photographs—mate-
rialized around her. The walls and floors were a soft blond
wood worn warm and smooth by generations of use. A
hum of satisfaction escaped its visitor.

The light also provided the first view of its resident,
whom Galen saw to be in his late sixties. The frailty of his
body and tremor in his voice had belied a vitality in his
face. A handsome man still, his square jaw and brow were
accentuated by the line of his unruly hair, which lay gray

and wiry and badly in need of a cut well back of the crown of his forehead. His mouth, full and creased deeply at the corners, was sensitive, once sensual, now subdued. But the pale-blue eyes, wet and sparkling in the lamplight, were genial, if not blithe at this moment. Galen eased him into a dark-blue leather sofa that was worn to a polish and cold to the touch.

"Do you have any ice?"

"Hm? Oh, yes—swelling up nicely, isn't it? You'll have to look and see. I was sufficiently prescient to fill the trays this afternoon, but it may not have occurred to me to plug in the fridge. Honestly, I can't remember."

Galen left the room in the direction of Henry's nod and found herself in a large kitchen with red-brick linoleum floor, glass-paned cabinet doors, and a huge black cast-iron wood-fired stove that covered nearly an entire wall. Cluttered with wooden lobster-pot buoys, glass flotation balls, and other combings from the beach, its current use seemed only as a backdrop for a vintage collection of flotsam and jetsam. Most impressive of these was a three-foot-long profile of a roughly carved and thickly painted eagle's head, whose grotesque yellow beak rested heavily on the mantel.

"That gruesome thing is from the transom of the *New Hampshire,* sunk off Quicks' in 1902," Henry Louis called, as if on cue, from the other room. "It washed up with most of the cargo a few days later. My father found it. It and five hundred pairs of boots."

"I want one," Galen called back.

"You like it! What a find you are! Not only literate but with a refined taste in art to match. What a lovely neighbor you'll make."

"This is a family house then?" she asked on returning to the living room, dishtowel ice bag in hand. She laid it gently against Henry's blue-white ankle.

"Yes, my grandfather built it in 1892, the year my father was born."

"It's perfectly beautiful. I've often wondered what it looked like inside. And you're a painter?"

To Galen's surprise, the man seemed almost to start at this and gave her an odd, inquiring look, arched brow drawing wavy lines across his forehead.

"I thought—the easel," Galen said quickly, nodding toward the door where a well-seasoned easel, filthy white apron, bouquet of brushes, and brilliantly splattered box of paints were piled.

"Oh, yes!" he said with a quick, comprehending laugh. "I do paint—a little."

Henry, as he asked to be called, told Galen that he had been coming to Bassing's Bay for nearly fifty years. First as a child, later with his wife, Phoebe, and their two boys. He ordered Galen to bring him pictures from their various posts in the room. Tapping the dust-powdered glass with a thick fingernail, he traced the decades of his marriage to a black-haired woman who maintained an august beauty throughout the thirty-odd years he had preserved her likeness in photographs. He also showed her their sons, who grew from leggy lads of six and eight into gangly teenagers posing with studied nonchalance at the fender of their first car, a '48 Plymouth, into elegantly handsome men with comely wives.

Most revealing of the life Henry had provided his family was an early color photograph of a much younger Henry and his handsome wife, each with a son on a lap, posing with a gracefully careless gaity in high-backed wicker lawn chairs in front of what was obviously a very large stone house.

Perhaps most revealing about his boys—Galen guessed—was a picture taken some twenty years later. What it was in its filmy grays that she found strangely moving, she could not have said for sure, but it was taken here at the beach. It was of two men close in height and build; one fair like his father, the other like his mother, dark. They were standing naked to the waist, knee deep in the froth of a broken wave, frozen in time, beautiful in youth. The light-haired son appeared to be telling a story, gesturing grandly, the humor of the moment glittering in his clear eyes and the unbridled energy of the man caught in his broad, bold smile. The darker brother, whose wet hair was slicked back off his brow, was watching the other with hands on narrow hips, head cocked indulgently. His pose was more reserved, but his large, intent black eyes, like his slowly curling mouth, radiated unalloyed delight in the figure they beheld and spoke of a love that touched Galen as she grasped the silver frame in her hands. She returned it to its shelf feeling, for whatever it was worth, as if she knew something essential about them both, and that she might have liked them had they met.

For the last eight years Henry had come to the beach house only with his dog Tiny, a swaggering blue tick hound he described as "blasé but fundamentally loyal," as his wife was dead and his sons had lives of their own. Now that Tiny was dead, this would be his first summer completely alone.

"The rest of the year I winter—don't you love that expression?—in Stover, a pastoral hamlet about a hundred miles west of Boston that has the dubious distinction of being the hometown, or so I'm told, of Troy Donahue's childhood sweetheart—or first wife, I don't remember which. In all honesty, I don't remember who Troy Donahue was, but my housekeeper seems to think it's significant."

Besides the long Brahmin *a* that distinguished Henry as an Old World Bostonian, there was a dryness in his humor and delicate flourish in his turns of phrase that

Galen would have been content to listen to for the rest of the night. However, his résumé complete, the man abruptly turned the focus on his guest, insisting she refill the sopping towel with the last of the ice and return to tell him what had brought her to East Cutty. He seemed genuinely interested, and there was something in his bright gentle gaze as he absently nursed a pipe he had clamped at the corner of his mouth that reminded her of her father. She found herself talking easily.

Since she was twenty-nine, unmarried, and childless, Galen's story was not so elaborate. She told him that after almost five years as a metropolitan reporter and a tour of duty as African correspondent for the *Boston Post*, she had grown dissatisfied with newspaper work and had taken a leave to co-write a biography of the South African dissident Helen Joseph, an antiapartheid activist in the fifties and sixties. What she was going to do after this, she could not say.

"So you've taken the Blight for the summer to write your book?"

"The Blight?"

"Did I say that? Oh dear, well, yes, it's a nickname the boys gave your cottage many years ago. Just a snotty little family joke. Silly really, as it's a perfectly nice place. . . ."

Galen reflected: Artless and rundown, it was at best a careless afterthought to the impressive collection of graceful old homes with which it shared the beach. She smiled.

"In answer to your question, I have it through July, by which time I should have finished the book."

"By yourself?"

"This half, yes."

"No, I mean you are staying by yourself?"

"Yes."

"Do you enjoy it?"

"Being alone?"

"No, writing."

"Ahhh—yes. Most of the time. The tyranny of the

blank page is some days more oppressive than others, if you know what I mean."

The old man's eyes lit briefly on his easel.

"Yes," he said. "And do you like be alone?"

"Yes. Well, for the most part. I love it here, I love the sea, but it gets a little quiet sometimes. I don't mean quiet, exactly—"

"I know."

"It's that I don't have a television or telephone or even a radio—"

"I know."

"Or anything that generates man-made noise of any kind."

"And you talk to yourself."

Galen looked at him suspiciously. "Yes . . . I do, in fact. Constantly."

"I heard you coming down the beach."

"Oh, no."

"You were talking to someone named Lily."

Galen looked at her pop-eyed dog. "What was I saying?"

"Don't look so distressed, my dear. Tiny was a good listener, too."

"Yes, well, according to Dr. Friedl Guftersen, whose classic work *Your Neurotic Pet* I found among the complete works of Helen MacInnes and Rex Stout in the extensive library at the Blight, as you call it—according to him, talking conversationally to one's pet undermines one's authority with it."

Henry smiled. "This would explain Tiny."

"Authority is not the word that springs to mind in my relationship with Lily." Galen sighed. They both gazed for a moment at Lily, whose marbley eyes gazed expressionlessly back. "I've caught myself talking to the furniture," she went on, still looking absently at the dog, "the food I'm about to eat—'Sorry Mr. Chicken but in you go.' This is not the sign of a healthy mind. Mara, the woman I share a place with in the city, and who was strenuously opposed to my taking a beach house alone, gave me two weeks before I went completely bonkers. I'd hate to think she was right."

"Listen, my dear, a little madness simply goes with the territory. Solitude is like Limburger cheese: It has its rewards but it takes getting used to."

Galen rose to leave but Henry did not seem eager to have her go.

"What do you think you'll do after you finish your book?"

"It depends," she said, sitting back down. "Mow lawns maybe."

"Ahhh."

"Probably not newspaper work."

"You seem a clever girl. I'm quite certain you could do anything you want," he said, pulling a favorite catechism from her father's Doctrine for Right Thinking. He was smiling gently now and Galen had to stop herself from reaching out to smooth his wild hair.

"What do you like to do best? I'd use the word 'hobby,' but like poor 'dilettante,' it's been so brutally trivialized."

Galen's gaze, which had been roaming the room as they talked, had come to rest on a tiny oil painting, smoky with age, in a large walnut frame. Heavy-bellied brood mares grazed in the shadows, possibly the moonlight. She nodded toward the picture.

"I do love to ride."

"Of course," he rejoined with obvious sympathy.

"Do you ride? Is that you?" Galen asked, indicating an old-looking, badly focused black-and-white photograph of a much younger man leading a flashy black colt.

"That? No, no. That's my son Colin, with a favorite horse."

There was with this something new in the old man's

voice that discouraged Galen from asking more about the picture. Whether it had to do with the horse or with his son, she had no way of knowing, but after a brief, awkward pause, she changed the subject, asking him instead about a teak Buddha squatting improbably between two pieces of ivory scrimshaw. Looking very tired all of a sudden, he began a story about a trip to the Orient he and his wife had taken when they were first married.

It was almost 2 A.M. by the time Galen and Lily got back to the Blight. By the time one was balled up in her wicker chair and the other was sprawled naked on her bed, a cooling breeze was just beginning to come in off the ocean.

The east wind strengthened steadily throughout the night and by morning had cleared the air of haze and humidity, buffing the day to a crystalline shine. A sapphire sea glittered with a light chop and the gulls soared the ledges without beating their wings. Rising late, Galen had time only to shower and dress before racing out the door to collect Henry, as she had promised, and drive him to the clinic by nine.

His driveway was two tire-wide strips of tar with grass growing up in between that, after a long winding run, ended abruptly, dumping her onto a lawn of closely cropped crabgrass. Here a very old white Volvo station wagon and very new forest-green Jaguar sedan sat side by side. Pulling alongside the new car, she wondered which one was Henry's. Catching her reflection in the Jaguar's tinted window, she hoped it was the Volvo. Her appearance might have charitably been described as casual, rather as if she had just come in out of the rain. Her slicked-back hair was still wet and had soaked the shoulders and back of a faded-green Celtics T-shirt. Her worn khaki shorts bared a generous expanse of brown leg that gleamed with oil. Rubber thongs added to the hosed-down effect by making loud plopping noises as she walked. The only thing remotely upscale within reach was the pair of designer sunglasses Mara had left in her car. Galen went back for these.

Still with half a mind to go home and change, she knocked tentatively on the back door. Hearing nothing, she was just turning to go around to the deck when a silhouette appeared behind the screen, its features blurred by the bowed wire mesh. With the added height of the back step it seemed to tower over her.

"Yes?" The voice was deep and faintly superior. Somewhat taken aback by the whole presentation, Galen said she had come for Mr. Louis.

This produced a momentary silence, and then, to Galen's further surprise, a mildly irritated "Mr. Louis?"

"Yes. He's injured his foot and I am supposed to take him to the doctor." Galen was beginning to feel somewhat irritated herself at being scrutinized in this manner, particularly at the physical disadvantage of the inquisitor being able to see her while she could not see him, when the voice warmed, if only slightly, to say "Oh, you must mean my father."

She smiled toward the upper part of the shadow, fully expecting to be let in at last, only to hear its voice cool again with a dismissive "Yes, thank you, but there's no need, I will see to it."

Galen hesitated a moment, wondering whether to persist and try to see Henry, or at the very least convey a message, when the old man's voice reached them from a front room: "Galen! Julian, for heaven's sake! Bring her in here! She's the girl who rescued me."

The screen swung open now and glaring down with a look of forced tolerance was a face she knew. It belonged to the dark-haired brother she had seen in the photograph. But if that day on the beach was no more than a few years ago, the halcyon moment the camera had frozen was light-years past. Galen felt only a brooding coldness where she had seen mirth, and the eyes whose passion had moved her were now occluded and remote. So struck by the difference between the photograph and the flesh, she did not immediately appreciate that the man was holding the door for her. After how long, she had no idea, he reminded her with a canned "If you'll follow me."

Reaching for her hand, Henry was bubbly and solicitous.

"My dear, come in, come in! Was my son growling at you? He's been abusing me all morning. Julian, this is Galen Shaw; Galen dear, my son, Julian."

There was an obvious tension in the room that Henry's chatter did nothing to dispel. Galen had the unmistakable impression she had interrupted a confrontation of some kind, and it seemed forever before she could gracefully inquire whether her services were still needed.

"We were just talking about the weather," Henry said boisterously. Judging from the sharp look between father and son, Galen found this hard to believe. "I was telling Julian that I came down to the beach early this year because of this unreasonable heat, though it seems this morning to have abated somewhat, hasn't it?"

"It would have been nice had you told someone of your plans, that's all," murmured the son.

"Dear boy, you were in Europe, or so I thought" was his father's cheerful response, which he punctuated by swinging around to Galen, who had affected a just-passing-through pose at the edge of a chair next to him, and asked her how she had slept.

Stealing a glance at Julian as she and Henry exchanged pleasantries, Galen saw that he had plainly disengaged himself and, seemingly unaware of them both, was fixed on some point outside the room. She saw also that the lines of his face were, like Henry's, powerfully drawn, yet the creases in his cheeks seemed deep for his age and the eyes too dark with shadow. A vein bulged at the temple where the black hair was swept furiously back. Bored or irritated—she could not tell which—the man was waiting for her visit, a momentary irritant, to play itself out.

Disliking him at once, Galen could not have been happier to oblige. She finally found her opening in Henry's suggestion that she join them for coffee. She almost laughed.

"No, thank you, Henry, but what about your ankle? I'm happy to take you to the clinic if you still need a lift."

"That's so good of you, my dear, but Julian will see to it. However, there's no need to run off."

"I really must," she said, jumping up, her gaze involuntarily sweeping the room for the silver-framed photograph that had somehow captivated her the night before. "I'm seriously behind in my work and really ought to get back to it." Her eyes found it but the brothers were only two thin shadows from where she stood. "Another time, though." She quickly added, "I can find my way out" as the black-haired man appeared to be rousing himself from his reverie. She was out of the room before he had raised himself to his feet.

The back screen door crackled open and as it clapped shut she stepped into the blinding spotlight of June's morning sun. Her sunglasses! Damn! Turning back to the house, she had her hand on the knob when she heard the older man's voice rise in anger.

"I *am* careful!" Then after a small silence. "Oh, stop, Julian! If anything you should be grateful! I'd be washed away by the tide by now if the girl hadn't come along."

The glasses, she decided, could wait.

2

By the end of Galen's fourth week at Bassing's Bay, all of the houses on the beach were occupied and the high-pitched cries of children playing in the water and hunting for crabs in the kelp along the ledges mixed naturally with the cackle of gulls. By ten each morning, half a dozen mothers or baby-sitters had erected command posts in the warm dry sand above the high-water mark and, reinforced by numbers 6, 8, and 12 sunscreen, coolers and Thermoses, folding chairs, straw bags, beach towels, and inner tubes, presided over their broods, which would already be hard at play. By eleven the body count would have doubled.

Galen heard rather than saw most of these felicities because she generally swam before breakfast and walked the beach only late in the day. The air this morning was as yet devoid of human sounds as she shivered at the writing table she had set up on her porch, waiting for the early yellow sun to dry and warm her.

Before her was a letter she had begun the night before. It was to Mara:

June 30

My Dear M.,

I'm told by those with contact with the outside world that the temperatures in the city are life-threatening. I couldn't be happier for you. It's what you deserve for abandoning me on the Fourth. (Alone on our nation's birthday once again.) They say if you shut all the windows and turn on the fan you can actually cook yourself. Why not give it a try?

Work is going a little smoother now that I've finally finished excavating our lost empire of notes and begun to lift out the life that's buried there. I've (typically) overresearched, and the transition to writing is always a trial. I'm also (typically) way behind schedule and am at this point thankful I don't have a phone. Have I gotten any calls from *Boston Post Books*? How about the newsroom? Alex Taylor is not going to like hearing that I've decided I'm not going back to the paper in August.

You'll be happy to know I haven't completely stopped talking to Lily, my furniture, or the comestibles (Mr. Potato and Mr. Thresher Shark send their best, poor dears), but I've made great strides. Thanks mostly to my neighbor, the old gent I mentioned a few weeks ago. He brought your sunglasses back the next day, incidentally, just after I mailed your letter, so don't lose any more sleep.

He's clever and kind and lovely and we've become quite good friends. I think he must be as lonely as I am because he flags me down for tea and beer whenever I'm on the beach. He's fluent—and effusive—on the problems with the Middle East, the national debt, the Red Sox bull pen, and wives who drag their husbands into Fi-

lene's Basement (though how he knows about
that is a mystery to me as he's Brooks Bros. head
to toe). He's even had me to dinner a few times.
I'd hoped to introduce you. Alas, another time.
Happily, we've seen nothing of his doleful son
since that first day. I was delighted to hear he lived
in France.

Galen now scrawled at the end:

July 1
I trust your show is coming along and that you've
managed not to fold, spindle, or mutilate any
priceless Renoirs. (Fine by me if you do, I think
the man is highly overrated.) Which week will you
be in Paris and will the Vermeer exhibit have
opened at the Petit Palais yet? I want the poster.
Oh, I almost forgot to mention, Henry's a
painter. I've only seen sketches and a few water
colors but "I do paint a little" is certainly the understatement of the year. In fact, I've been sitting for
him. This one an oil, which he's refused to show me
till it's done. (Fully clothed, of course. I've never
much fancied myself a grande odalisque.)
Love, G.

By ten-thirty the coffee at the bottom of her porcelain
shaving mug was cold and all that remained of her bran
muffin were crumbs. Galen was perched in profile on the
wide railing of Henry's deck in a gauzy white sundress and
loose turquoise turban that made her skin look coppery
and her green eyes Mediterranean blue. Her lips were
burned to an almost burgundy red. A stripe of zinc oxide
blazed down the bridge of her nose. Across the deck atop a

burnished wooden stool, shielded from the sun by a faded denim umbrella his wife made him twenty years ago, Henry was painting her portrait.

This was the last of six days of posing for him (he had promised to paint out the sunscreen), and they had returned to the topic of the day before, forgery of great works of art, which was clearly shaping up into something of an obsession with Henry. Galen had hoped to find out more about his family and life in Stover but, as loquacious as the old man was, and as easily as he talked about the safely distant past, she discovered that he was surprisingly private about the present and eased aside any questions about his life outside the beach house. She noticed too that as happy as he was to reminisce about his wife, mention of his sons, except as boys, tended to leave him morose. Galen never dared ask why, but could easily imagine that Julian, for one, was a boorish and difficult man and a source of irritation if not anguish for his father.

"The museums are loaded with fakes," Henry was muttering as he worked. "The big museums, mind you, the ones with the resources to authenticate these things. The Getty! The richest of them all and the worst of the lot. The art world is as crooked as Lily's hind leg. Yes, hello, Lily, now go lie down. The dealers are the lowest of the low. Vile, depredatious cutpurses." He stopped painting and looked up. "Inflating prices is one thing, but buying and selling *known* stolen works is completely unfathomable. They're slitting their own throats! We are talking about avarice of biblical proportions, my dear."

"Henry, you're beginning to sound like my ninety-three-year-old socialist great-aunt who thinks money causes cancer."

"I'm sorry, but I find the whole business very disquieting. Now, Galen, you are squinting. Is the sun too much for your eyes?" He had put his palette aside and was digging at a pipe with the pointed end of a brush. "Why don't you shut them for a while? I'm going to fetch some iced tea, wouldn't you like a glass?"

"That would be wonderful," Galen said, closing stinging eyes on the sun's glare.

"It will just be a few minutes more. Can you stand it?" His voice trailed off with the bang of a screen door behind him. The sun was hot, pouring over her like warm liquid, while the onshore breeze brushed against her skin with a feathery chill. The combination raised gooseflesh on her arms. She listened to the sound of the waves collapsing lightly onto the sand, the breaking notes of gulls, the unworldly screech of a solitary tern. Presently she heard the screen door creak and slam and the sound of Henry walking slowly back across the deck. He said nothing and Galen saw him in her mind's eye frowning at his canvas as she had seen him do many times before, lips puckered in thought.

After several moments, however, she began to wonder what had become of her drink. Waving a long brown arm in his general vicinity, she tried to prompt him with a raspy *"Water . . . water."*

"Excuse me?" replied a languorous voice that was deep and cool and clear as ice.

Gasping, Galen swung around and opened her eyes, which the sun quickly blinded, but not before they made out a tall figure standing in front of the easel, his hands in the pants pockets of a dark-gray suit, looking for all the world as if he were waiting for a train. Henry's son Julian was gazing intently at the painting. If, when he finally raised his dark eyes to Galen, they seemed marginally less hostile than she had remembered them, they were no less arrogant. Her distaste for the man was instantly revived, nevertheless—and to her great annoyance—she found herself stammering as she slipped off the railing. "I—I'm sorry, I thought you had my drink."

A black eyebrow arched at this and his mouth moved

as if to speak, but he said nothing, instead stared silently at her with a look as inviting as a barbed-wire fence. Having recovered her poise, she glared wholeheartedly back. At which point Henry came to the rescue.

"Julian! Wherever did you come from!"

Dragging his gaze slowly off Galen, he swung on a heel without taking his hands out of his pockets and said warmly but with a measure of reserve, "Hello, Father. I came from the top of the driveway—Carla dropped me off. She had an errand to run in town, but she'll be along in a moment."

Henry, obviously used to his son's ways, let the explanation stand, embraced him with several vigorous pats on the back, and asked with more amusement than surprise, "And what brings you to these parts? Checking up on me?"

At this, Julian's eyes lighted briefly again on his father's model but he said only, "We've come for the weekend, if that's okay with you. Carla wanted to surprise you, but perhaps we should have phoned."

"Don't be silly—what a nice surprise," Henry said, ignoring his son's inference and pointedly holding out a sweating highball of iced tea to Galen, who had begun slipping her things into a straw bag. "But I thought you were in Paris."

"Prague," said his son. There was a pause. "Beautiful portrait, Father. This is. . . ?"

"Surely you remember, Galen Shaw, the girl from the Blight."

"Of course."

As if he didn't, Galen thought hotly, having missed neither the sarcasm in his voice nor the insinuation in his glance. She returned his frigid smile. While it struck her that there was something rehearsed about the whole encounter, about the curious thrust and parry between father and son, it was not something she felt compelled to learn more about.

Before she could make her getaway, however, the screen door was flung open yet again and with a cry of "Henry Louis!" an extraordinary-looking woman, with a flaxen mane bulging from behind red-framed sunglasses and skin tanned to an unnaturally even bronze, burst onto their tepid little scene. Squinting and grinning into the sun, she hurled toward them with outstretched arms, bracelets tinkling, full mobile lips painted fire-engine red. Translucent blue eyes held Galen's and, to her surprise, lingered in them, even while the woman embraced the older man.

"And who's this?" she asked as soon as the first round of salutations were through, flashing a brilliant, empty smile at Galen. She might as well have said "And what have we here?"

"My neighbor, Galen Shaw," Henry answered. "Galen, my daughter-in-law, Carla."

"How nice," the woman said with a disparaging look at Lily, who had come over to press a wet nose against the woman's sleek bare calf. But then, suddenly as disinterested as she had seemed keen, she swung back to Henry and went on emphatically, "Darling, I hope you didn't mind our little surprise. It was my idea, really . . ."

Galen did not hear the rest; rather, she took advantage of the diversion to gather the rest of her things. Dismissing a perfunctory protest from the new arrivals ("We're not interrupting anything, are we?") and a ludicrous dinner invitation from Henry, she made her escape. With Lily at her heels, Galen gained the driveway in a state of mild agitation.

The forest-green Jaguar sat between her rotting Alfa Romeo and Henry's disintegrating Volvo wagon. Passing between them, she caught her likeness in the new car's window once again. For an instant she did not recognize it, so at odds were her self-image and what was reflected in the glass. Having completely forgotten the costume Henry had draped her in, it came as something of a shock to find gaping back at her a flushed face under a blue turban that sagged like a picked flower in the sun and with a shock-white streak down its nose like the stripe on a skunk.

"You may have misread that scene," it murmured to her, then added with heart-felt sympathy and slow sheepish grin, "Oh, you femme fatale."

Galen steered clear of Henry's cottage for the rest of the weekend. With the painting unfinished, she fully expected him to pay a call on Monday, but by Monday afternoon Henry had not come and she had to assume that the couple stayed on an extra day. By evening her curiosity got the better of her and she decided to walk down the beach past his house. If no one was on the deck, she would pass close enough to hear, if not see, whether his company was still in attendance.

It was dusk when the butter-yellow Cape came into view. To her surprise, it was dark. How strange, she thought. But, coming closer, she realized that it was more than dark. It was abandoned. Its deck, which Lily began to browse for scents, had been cleared of furniture. Its windows and doors were boarded so resolutely shut they looked as if they had never been opened at all.

3

"I *hate* this city in August," Galen hissed, slamming the apartment door to dramatic effect and kicking off her high-heel shoes with a vengeance. Her yellow silk shirt clung to her back, the short curly hairs at her hairline lay flat on her forehead. There was a wash of heat in her cheeks.

Mara James waved from the couch where she was curled around a telephone receiver in a white terry-cloth bathrobe, smiling at Galen and painting her toenails peach.

"How'd it go?" she asked.

"Same."

Into the receiver: "No, I'm talking to Gale, she just came in." To Galen: "Ginny says hi."

"Hi to Ginny."

Into the receiver: "Gale says hi." To Galen: "She asks how it went."

"Tell her he offered me nights and weekends, no benefits, no sick days, a fifty-percent cut in pay, and I took the job."

"D'you hear that? She says she's crumbling after two

weeks of job hunting and is going to sell out and write 'Gram Bakes Baby's Buns' stories for metropolitan Boston's sleaziest tabloid."

Ginny said something to Mara, who let out a guffaw.

"I'll tell her." Mara giggled, but their conversation swerved back to whatever plot was unfolding when Galen had walked in—most people waded through life: Mara conspired from one point to the next—and Galen limped into the kitchen. Poised in front of an open refrigerator, she was trying to decide between cold spaghetti and boysenberry yogurt when Mara buzzed up beside her.

"Don't do it," she said.

"I didn't have lunch."

"No, I mean don't take the job. You don't want to go back to work for a newspaper. Why did you even go to the interview?"

"I know the city editor, *he* called *me*," Galen said wearily, lifting out the pot of spaghetti.

"You're panicking. You've interviewed only at newspapers and that's exactly what you don't want to do. You're not going to heat that up?"

"It's better cold," said Galen, standing at the counter, forking a mouthful out of the pot. "I told you, they've been calling me. Don't worry, I'm not going to take the job."

"You haven't made one call yourself, have you? You're a gutless coward."

"Don't beat around the bush, Mara. What do you really think?"

Mara yanked a fork from an overstacked dish drainer, which loudly rearranged itself all over the counter as a result. Oblivious, she went on:

"Listen, two things: Alex Taylor called, I think he's going to try to get you to come back to work for him, and there's a big opening at the MFA I want you to come to with me tonight. Don't say no. Pass me a root beer, will you?"

"I'm too tired."

"Oh, Gale! *Please* come, it's going to be a fabulous show. You've been a screaming bore since you got back from the beach and it will cheer you up. We'll get snazzed up, break out the party pumps. It's très exclusive, a big artistic happening. Come!"

"Who is it?"

"H. L. Baugh, all new work. And the first sight of him, let alone his paintings, in public in over two years. There was some kind of tragedy in his family and the word was he'd stopped working. Everyone's *dying* to see what he's been doing. This is a *very* big to-do."

Galen affected a pleading tone. "Mara—"

"Oh, for crying out loud, don't be a pill!"

"All right! I'll go! What time is it?"

"Seven, seven-thirty. I have to go to my office first for about half an hour but I'll catch you up. Wear your blue dress."

Galen had known Mara since they were freshmen in college, at which time Galen had been suspicious of the short but handsome Long Island girl who energetically commanded the center of an enormous circle of friends. Brainy, clever, supremely ambitious, tirelessly charming, and irresistibly catty, Mara was also arrogant and overbearing and not obviously trustworthy. But she grew on Galen, and by their senior year the two had become intimate friends. They had been sharing a small two-bedroom brick-and-fern affair on Beacon Hill since Mara took the job as assistant curator of twentieth-century art at the Boston Museum of Fine Arts a year and a half ago. With Mara traveling two weeks out of every month and Galen working nights, they had hardly had enough time to get on each other's nerves.

Mara was right about Galen's having been on the sullen side since getting back from the beach three weeks ago and that she had been less than aggressive about finding a job. But having finished her chapters of the Helen Joseph book, she was uncertain what to do next. Anything but newspaper work, she told herself as she slipped a cobalt-blue silk dress over her head, sashing it across her slender hips. She piled her sun-washed hair on top of her head and fastened a string of pearls around her long, graceful neck. Definitely no newspaper work. No more deadlines, no more third-edition rewrites, no more Christmas Eves spent in the lonely green glow of a computer terminal, no more newsprint stains on her fingers, her face, her clothes.

Galen darkened her eyelashes, pinked her lips, and made a face in the mirror. Another book, maybe. She sighed. Something will turn up. Satisfied with her reflection, though no more in the mood for an artistic happening than she had been three hours before, Galen went out into the sultry evening to hail a cab.

Mara was right about something else. The Baugh opening was indeed a happening, and by 7:45 the floor on which the artist's work was hung was a glittering pool of cultural luminaries. Black-tied, besatined, and bejeweled museum heads, artists, critics, and benefactors, like suns in their own spinning solar systems of hangers-on, generated waves of party noise that oscillated with the distinct rhythms of exclusive and inbred groups. Mara, a rising star in her own right, would arrive shortly with the subtlety of a snow goose splashing down. Galen, for her part, was happy to go discreetly in ahead, slipping like a stream into a pond and flowing naturally to its outer edge.

It was in a quiet corner populated only by the inevitable fica tree and guests on their way to somewhere else that she saw the first H. L. Baugh painting. Galen knew some of the artist's earlier, highly popular work, but the huge bold oil of shimmering colors and simple, powerful lines was vastly different from anything she had seen before. It was a stark but vivid seascape. Three bands of color so brilliantly lighted by an invisible sun she wanted to squint.

The next was also a beach scene: a band of glowing silver-yellow sand meeting a blue-black sky, textured with the smells and sounds of that moment, the quivering heat of the day, the distant chill of the ocean. The next, a pink ledge topped with snow-white gulls slicing into a glassy gray calm, smooth as a puddle of mercury.

They were more than powerful; they were personal and evocative. But they were more than that, too. To Galen they were somehow familiar. That one, with a red ledge jutting out of a surging navy-blue sea, could have been Bassing's Bay. She peered at the title. *Seascape VI* was all it said. But she was transported to her bay and her beach, her sandy cottage, her solitude, and with a minor pang of aging anger, she recalled her mysterious neighbor who had fled without so much as good-bye almost two months ago and vanished without a trace.

"Ga-len!" A familiar voice jolted her back to the present.

"Oh, hello, Ginny," Galen said warmly to a tall, gawky red-haired woman in a tight black dress and white satin jacket with a red carnation pinned to the lapel.

"Where's Ma-ra?" Ginny had a way of breaking words into two distinct syllables, rolling each separately off her slow-moving tongue.

"She'll be along any minute—she had to stop in at her office. How's Renoir coming?" Galen always liked Ginny, whose awkward movements and absent manner—she always wore the pained, unfocused look of someone breaking in a new pair of contact lenses—reminded her of a big orange stork. Mara, who had hired Ginny as a research assistant for the Renoir show she was hanging in Paris, swore the girl was exceptionally bright, though Galen had never seen any sign of it. Still, she found her sweet.

"Oh, we'll be up on time. How about these, though?" Ginny drawled, rolling her sore-looking eyes to indicate the wall of paintings. "Aren't these incre-dible? He's never done any-thing like this. I think it's just ama-zing. There's so much energy for such an old man."

"I never thought of him as old," Galen said, though she had never seen a picture of him. "How old is he?"

"I dunno. That's him over there, though." Ginny nodded toward a shoal of tuxedoed men standing in identical poses amid a larger, looser crowd of onlookers. All eyes were fixed on a balding, pink-faced man with a prodigious cummerbunded diaphragm who appeared to be building to some sort of climax, gesticulating wildly with one hand and in the other trying to balance a full glass of champagne. But Galen barely saw him: A perilous arm's length in front of the speaker stood a diminutive, gray-haired man with sun-freckled forehead and watery blue eyes.

Henry.

So startled by his appearance in this context, Galen momentarily forgot herself and the last of her anger. She bore her way through the large crowd around him and landed with a flourish directly in his line of focus. This, she noticed too late, had the effect of stopping the fat man's recitation in midsentence as if she had tripped on a wire and pulled his plug. Thus was provided the silence into which she spurted a boisterous "*Henry!* Hello! What are *you* doing here?"

A look of polite shock spread across the old man's face, accompanied by a collective gasp from the attending entourage. But to Galen's immeasurable relief, Henry's scowl passed like a cloud's shadow and behind it a broad smile creased his cheeks and lighted his eyes. He snatched both of her hands in his.

"Galen Shaw! *Dear* girl! What a lovely sight you are!"

"Henry! I can't believe I've found you! What *are* you doing here?"

"They insist on trotting me out for these things," he answered, voiced lowered, sounding almost coy. "But you, my dear, how are you? How extraordinary you look. And how is it I haven't heard from you?"

"Heard from *me?*" She was confused. "How was I supposed to find you? There are no Henry Louises in Stover."

Henry, looking a little confused himself, frowned. In the brief but excruciating silence that followed, Galen was suddenly aware of the many eyes on her. Losing her footing under a surge of embarrassment, she backed away, murmuring, "I'm sorry, Henry, I seem to have interrupted, I—I was just so surprised to see you here."

"You were?"

Something in his voice made her stop. Feeling suddenly that she was even more out of step than she thought, she answered with a confused laugh. "Yes, I was. Why wouldn't I—"

Galen did not finish her sentence. Her eyes had just now come by chance to light on a small painting over Henry's shoulder that she had not seen before. Like a blow to her midsection, the sight of it took her breath away. It was of a figure in the sun slightly blurred by its heat, a white dress glowing like snow, long brown arms cradling a draped knee, a brilliant turquoise turban wound loosely atop a coppery face with blue-green eyes and burgundy lips. The stripe, as promised, was gone.

Galen's eyes, widened by the struggle to orient herself amid the turbulent swirl of things foreign and familiar, swept back now to Henry, who took her hand and, squeezing it, said gently, "I'm beginning to see now." As he spoke a flush reddened Galen's cheeks and the pieces of the larger picture crashed into place.

"So am I." She pulled her hand out of his.

"Come talk to me for a moment and I'll explain," he said, excusing them from their large, rapt audience and drawing her to the side of the room.

"You didn't trust me? What do you think I was going to do, ask you for your autograph? Steal one of your paintings?"

"You have every right to be angry, but don't be hurt."

"I'm not hurt, I'm insulted."

"No, you're hurt." H. L. Baugh was speaking to her with the abrupt certitude of a man of specific experience: This was not his first time saying this.

"My dear, you mustn't take this personally. There are certain inconveniences that come with—notoriety. A scarcity of privacy is just one of them. You must see—"

Struggling with a mix of embarrassment, anger, and wounded pride, Galen interrupted him here and said coolly, "Henry, I'm sorry, this is all a little strange. But don't say any more, you don't owe me any explanations, I'm just surprised, that's all. And I was a little stung by your not saying good-bye."

His expression changed completely at this, from a paternal frown to surprise and finally a half smile of recognition.

"You didn't get my note." It was not a question.

"What note?"

He laughed heartily. "Which I'm now beginning to see was lost. Dear girl, no wonder you're angry. I explained all of this in a note I left on your door the Sunday morning we left."

"You left a note?"

"Yes, yes. I couldn't understand why you hadn't called. I thought you were mad at me for having played this silly game." Henry laughed again, loudly, and took her hand. "Poor girl. *Will* you forgive me?"

"I didn't know," she said quietly, glancing again at her strangely beautiful portrait.

"Yes, I can see that."

Galen looked back into the warm sparkle of his smiling eyes. A heart of granite could not have resisted the appeal there.

"Yes, I forgive you," she said with a half laugh of relief. "But can I sue you for hanging my portrait without my permission?"

"Probably, but will you accept something else in payment? Not, however, the painting. It's one of my best, don't you think?"

"They're all spectacular, Henry. The *H* is for Henry, isn't it?"

"Yes, of course, and the *L* for Louis. I may lie by omission from time to time, but rarely do I invent."

"Spoken like a true con man."

"My dear—"

"I'm kidding, Henry. You owe me at least a little of that."

It was in this state of relieved merriment that Galen looked up to see a stony-faced Julian Baugh making his way through the crowd toward them. The sight had the effect—at least on her—of rain on a picnic.

"Julian, you remember Ms. Shaw," Henry announced grandly. "Galen, my son Julian." Julian nodded his head slightly, black eyes impassive but with what looked to Galen to be irony in the half smile raising the corners of his mouth. Before he could speak, however, Henry was forced to amend his introduction.

"And my daughter-in-law, whom you met earlier this summer," he said as Carla appeared, as baroquely beautiful as before. Smiling like a benign dictator over a crowd in the square, she slipped one arm through Julian's and extended the other in Galen's direction.

"Why, yes, how *nice*," she said mildly, but, Galen thought, not without surprise.

"I was just apologizing to Galen for the charade I played on her this summer and"—Henry turned to Galen— "urging her not to think me pretentious."

At this point the rotund storyteller Galen had interrupted some minutes before, having floundered under the glare of H. L. Baugh's inattention and grown pinker in the interval, saw a chance to wrap up his narrative. With a booming voice he now swept in upon their party with the pretext of introducing a Wagnerian-looking woman in an unfortunately loud gown. Relieved of the spotlight and the prospects of a stilted conversation with Henry's son and daughter-in-law, Galen stepped quickly back from the group and turned to slip into the crowd. Julian, however, caught her elbow.

"Ms. Shaw, if I may have a word with you?" His request had the unpleasant ring of an executive order. He did not wait for a reply. "I trust you understood about my father's need to protect his privacy."

"Mr. Baugh," Galen said coolly, hoping to bring a quick end to the matter, "as I told your father, it is his affair and no explanation is required."

Ignoring her protest, Julian went on deliberately as if leading to a point. Galen could almost hear the tectonic grumbling beneath the immaculately controlled surface. The man was not to be trifled with. But, if it came to that, a willingness to roll over was not one of Galen's strong suits. As it was, she was growing increasingly annoyed.

"Anyone who becomes even slightly well-known has to find ways, however crude, to protect their personal lives," he said, his tone matter-of-fact. "This is particularly true for the artist. I'm sure my father explained this to you. You may or may not be aware that he has had unfortunate experiences with"—he stopped to choose his words carefully—"self-interested acquaintances who have taken advantage of his generosity in the past. We have all been concerned that this sort of thing not happen again."

If an apology was inferred in this, Galen also heard a warning. Her eyes flashed with anger. Pulling free her elbow, which he had continued to grip, she had been about to assure him that she had not known until a few minutes ago who his father was and that in any case it would not have mattered one way or another. Before she thought better of it, however, she changed her mind. Loudly, she shot back:

"I'm not sure just what your problem really *is*, Mr.

Baugh, but my relationship with your father is simply none of your business."

Exactly how this hit him, she could not be sure, as she stayed only long enough to see the initial surprise ripple across the smooth veneer. Before Julian could speak, she had wheeled and stalked away—unfortunately not in the direction of the door.

A study in nonchalance as she navigated a 180-degree swing through the crowd, Galen was already regretting what she had said by the time she found the coatroom, where she then realized she had not left a coat. Sitting down on a red-velvet bench and feeling the sobering chill of marble against her back, she let out a long breath and asked herself *why* had she allowed herself to be so easily provoked by this man. Julian Baugh's tony brand of arrogance would naturally irritate her, but even if he *was* convinced she was after his father's money, there was no point in inflaming him. Henry seemed to be clear about her integrity; why should she care whether or not his son was? His animosity toward her could only make life more difficult for Henry. No, she resolved as she got slowly to her feet, it was not an encounter to repeat.

Trying to appear as purposeful leaving the coatroom as she had entering it, she ran head on into Henry, who was just rounding the corner, evidently in search of her.

"So you *are* in here! Well, good, I was hoping I'd catch you before you sneaked off. I want you to come for lunch this weekend. Saturday, come at noon."

"Henry, I really don't think I can—"

"Nonsense, I insist. Carla has business at her gallery in New York and Julian is returning to Europe tonight." He was, after all, not oblivious to the tensions around him. She gave the kind old man a resigned smile.

"Good, it's all settled then," he said with a satisfied air. "Here's my number. Stover is easy to find. Call when you get there and I'll direct you. Now I must get back to my party."

Giving her hand a pair of farewell pats, he added gently, "Julian's had quite a rough time of it lately and can be a little abrasive sometimes. But he doesn't mean to be. You won't let him upset you, will you, my dear?"

"No, Henry, not in the least."

4

"Don't I take you to all the best places?" Galen said to Lily as they wound through Stover, an affluent New England town hidden at the base of the Berkshire Hills and dotted with ivy-covered brick mansions and Revolutionary War houses with ripply twelve-over-twelve paned windows. Its hills were heavily forested in maple, birch, ash, and pine; its hayfields were lush and sweeping. A frenzy of birdsong met their ears as Galen cut the engine halfway across a rattly covered bridge to look down into the steep gorge that it spanned. A narrow silver river incongruously named Swift lazily flowed below.

"I should have given you a bath, yes a bath, a baaath," Galen taunted as they neared the end of the bridge. ("Bath" and "supper" were the only two words she was sure her dog knew.) "Don't you think—" she started to add, but never finished her sentence. Having just broken out of the dark tunnel, she was momentarily blinded by the blast of sunshine. Before she could recover there was an angry blare of a horn as a big silver Cadillac swerved sharply to avoid her front end—which she suddenly realized, to her horror, was over the faded yellow line into his lane. The Cadillac spewed up gravel from the narrow shoulder and vanished into the shadows behind her, its horn echoing like a banshee's scream.

Galen pulled over and stopped the car. Her hands felt as if they were shaking but when she held them out they looked steady. Perhaps they would start in a minute. "He wasn't kidding," she murmured to Lily, who, wiggling her hind end stupidly, remained aware only of the car ride's promise of fun.

This was the turn Henry had warned her about. Here River Road flung right at a ninety-degree angle only ten yards from the base of the bridge, and immediately began its ascent up a thirty-degree escarpment, falling back over itself like a half-coiled snake. It was nothing if not a treacherous curve, and Galen's eyes searched automatically for signs of earlier accidents. It came as no surprise that the guardrail tracing the left-hand swing onto the bridge was scarred and misshapen. It was, at least, still standing and roughly intact, although she could easily imagine the rusted skeletons of a host of vehicles strewn at the bottom of the gorge. Perhaps they replace it every year, she thought as she started the engine.

Galen was considering the various disasters open here to a careless driver as she made her way up the steep incline. But with the anticipation of her meeting with Henry growing, her alarm quickly began to fade. Two miles later, with the road straightening out, parting a billowing hayfield and gliding into a copse of mottled sycamores, she had forgotten the incident completely.

The "stucco-styled thing" Henry had told her to look for turned out to be another of his understatements. Whitewashed, with a roof of red clay tiles and surrounded by carriage houses, grain bins, and grooms' quarters, the stable was worthy of the Spanish Riding School and held, she guessed, more than a dozen large box stalls. The central courtyard, she saw as she swung left onto the driveway under a sign that read THE WINDS, was cobbled and centered around a dry fountain. On her right was a pasture the size of two football fields that sloped away from the road. Four or five mares, one clearly in brood, grazed, flipping their tails under a stand of trees that bordered a small stream. They reminded her of the oil painting she had admired in Henry's summer house.

However, any thought of other pictures she had seen there were, like her near miss at the bridge, far from her mind. The sight of horses always excited Galen, and she was almost giddy greeting Henry on the steps of the nineteenth-century stone manor house that commanded the high ground of the estate, looking through a line of towering sugar maples over the distant stable grounds.

"Nice little fixer-upper you have here, Henry," she called with a grin. "Bet it keeps you busy."

"I married well," he said, beaming, both hands outstretched, an expansive smile making slits of his sparkling eyes. He was dressed in a coat and tie but a disheveled look somehow prevailed. "Welcome, dear girl, to my demesne."

Leaving Lily outdoors to tour the gracefully overgrown grounds, Henry led Galen into a long cool hall lined with black-framed tintypes that emptied into a spacious sitting room littered with furniture. Their arrangement suggested several rooms within a room: a desk and bookshelf in one corner; a card table with straight-backed chairs in another; a cluster of yellow satin armchairs here; a pair of green velvet ones there. The haphazardness of the overall placement of things suggested a man several years without his wife.

Struck by this, Galen was just wondering how he managed the solitude when she realized that at the farthest corner a red-faced man with a smooth wash of creamy-yellow hair and thick white walrus mustache was waiting to greet them.

"Galen Shaw, this is my very old and dear friend Francis Mole," Henry said with a sweep of his arm as if unveiling a statue.

"Franny, please," the gentleman said with an equally gallant bow. "Lovely to meet you. H. L. tells me you're a newspaper woman. How thrilling."

"*Was* a newspaper woman—I quit my job."

"Oh really, my dear, how splendid." This from Henry, who showed Galen to a velvet davenport under a tall French window. Having seated himself across from her in an incongruous, plastic-covered sitting chair that looked as if it were once a favorite of unwashed coal miners, he began stuffing one of a dozen pipes that crowded a tin like a brood of periscopes.

"Why don't we have a drink and eat on the patio in, say, a half hour?" An enormous red-haired woman with thick stockinged legs that hissed against each other under her nurse's uniform had swaggered in and was standing, one meaty hip outthrust, at Henry's elbow. "Miss Shaw will have a—"

"Club soda with lime," Galen said with a polite smile. The woman, scanning the molding as if for cracks, gave no sign of having heard.

"And Franny and I will have Bloody Marys, that's all right with you, Fran? Yes. Thank you, Mae. We'll eat in thirty minutes?" He might have been asking if he could borrow her car.

"Right" was all she said as she lumbered away.

Seeing the look on Galen's face, Henry said in a low voice, "Mae's been with us for almost twenty years. She more or less runs the place. Her bite is in this case every bit as bad as her bark, but she's ultimately forgiving. She knows I'd be quite lost without her."

*   *   *

Returning a drained teacup to its saucer and patting his cherry-red lips with an oversized linen napkin, Franny stated emphatically, "Marvelous luncheon, H. L., as usual, but"—leaning forward to lightly touch Galen's hand—"a particularly charming guest. You must insist she come again."

The party had for the most part indeed been gay, with Franny exhibiting an agile sense of humor and an inexhaustible collection of facts, theories, and anecdotes collected over decades of travel around the world as a consultant to the World Bank. Throughout lunch Henry and Galen provided a Parliament-like audience, offering, alternately, rapt attention and boisterous dissent. The day wound down in roughly the same key, but there had been a discordant strain at a point in between that Galen was at a loss to comprehend.

After lunch the three had walked down to the barn where, to Galen's great delight, Henry had had a mare lunged, tacked, and waiting for her to ride. Henry had directed her to a musty tack room over their heads that, out of half a dozen trunks of gear, bore up a yellow buttondown shirt, a pair of white britches that were tight but not obscene, and high black boots stiffly creased at the ankles but that perfectly fit her foot.

As she tripped excitedly down the stairs, however, she had been met by a silence and unavoidable sense that something was amiss. The atmosphere in the barn had become suffocatingly heavy, like the air before an electrical storm, though she could tell nothing from Henry's face, which was turned away. She had thought perhaps the two men had had words. It was under a shadow of something intangible, a morbid gloom, that a dark-skinned, black-haired, blue-eyed boy of about twenty-three had led up a tall gray Thoroughbred and wordlessly handed her the reins.

Soleil was a long-strided ten-year-old hunter with luxurious gaits and no ambition to speak of. Galen had worked her in a sand ring while Henry and Franny looked on. Adequately trained and extremely cooperative, she was, in Galen's words, "a push-button horse." She had noticed, however, that after twenty minutes, the horse was breathing hard and had brought her to a walk.

"She is lovely, Henry, but not terribly fit."

"She's the fittest horse in the stable," Henry had said apologetically. "Except for Ming, whom I've kept up. Nobody has had the time." Though the storm had seemed for the most part to have passed, a graveness had returned to his voice when he added to no one in particular, "I'm afraid the Winds has gone to seed." They had walked back to the house in virtual silence.

The sunlight was slanting through the trees now, thickened by the evening's dampness like a beam through smoke, and Galen rose with Franny to leave. As the three started across the great Oriental rug that covered the expanse of floor nearly end to end, Henry put a hand on Galen's arm and asked her to remain behind while he followed Franny the rest of the way to the door. He had long since regained his good humor and Galen had all but forgotten his curious sullenness at the barn. She was reminded of it now and thought perhaps their private talk would shed some light. She could see, however, by the carelessness of his smile as he dropped back into his chair that it would not.

"If you're not in a rush, I've had an idea and I want to see what you think of it," he said cheerfully. "Have another cup."

"No, thank you, but go ahead, I'm all ears."

"Several years ago I signed a contract with Scribner's to write an autobiography, though I have since wondered whether I was of sound mind at the time. Regardless, I did and with the help of"—he paused, poking at his pipes with a finger—"a writer who was assisting me, I wrote about three-quarters of the thing. About two years ago I lost my writer, the project bogged down, and I haven't looked at it since. Now, with the show up, I have decided finally to get it finished. What do you think?"

"I think that's great," she said cautiously. "Of course you should finish it."

He hesitated for a moment. "What do you think about helping me?" he asked slowly, assuming she had missed his point.

"Me." Galen had not misunderstood.

"I hope you don't mind, but I've looked up some of the stories you wrote for the newspaper, and judging from that and what you showed me of the Joseph biography, you're certainly a fine writer."

"Of course I'm flattered."

"It had crossed my mind in East Cutty, but I wasn't sure I really wanted to tackle the beast again. But now that I have the time . . . I was hoping I might interest you."

"Henry, I—I don't know."

"You did say you were out of a job."

"It's a very interesting idea, but—"

"But it would depend, of course, on what I paid you."

"Well, yes, and—"

"Julian."

"Yes. That, too."

"So H. L. Baugh wants you to come live in his bungalow in the pines! Wait till *Vanity Fair* gets wind of this!"

"Oh, please, Mara! Climb out of the gutter for a minute, will you?"

"You know I'm just teasing," Mara said, topping off their wineglasses and stacking Galen's dinner plate on hers.

"And jealous. No, Galen, I think it's fabulous. Selfishly I'd miss you, but I think it's the perfect answer."

"You won't miss me. I'll be here on the weekends and we never see each other during the week anyway. It just doesn't make sense to commute when there's this beautiful little guest house standing there empty. I can't wait for you to see his place—it's nothing short of baronial. He must have ten horses, though I can't see why as they're never ridden, and he said I can ride any of them whenever I want. It's like dying and going to heaven."

"What about the son?"

"I was worried about that but Henry assured me he wasn't expected back at least until Thanksgiving. And I should be out of there by then."

"You've signed the contract?"

"No, but I looked it over yesterday and it's very generous. I don't know what happened to the first writer—Henry was very mysterious about it—but I can't imagine it was the money. Anyway, we'll sign something this week, and I thought I'd take Henry up on his offer for me to go out next weekend and spend a couple of days riding before we dig in. Why don't you come?"

"I can't," Mara said. "I have to be in New York. Business with the Carla Baugh Gallery, if you can believe it. But talk me up anyway—I want to hang H. L.'s next show."

5

At eight-fifteen a pair of teenage boys, who had introduced themselves implausibly as Pat and Mike, were three-quarters of the way down the center aisle with two wheelbarrows rounded with a mix of grain, sweetfeed, and pellets. The long cavernous barn echoed with the cannon shots of horses kicking the wallboards of their stalls in impatient anticipation.

Dressed in her own yellow britches and worn brown field boots that wrapped around her slender calves like a glove, Galen was going through a long-closed tack room just off the center aisle in search of a different bit to use on the mare she had ridden the weekend before. Above the battery of tack trunks and saddle racks, molding satin ribbons lined the walls. An army of tarnished silver trophies covered a bank of file cabinets. Undisturbed long enough for a woolly blanket of dust to lie heavily on every surface, the room appeared to have doubled as an office. A leather sofa faced a stately oak desk and high-backed swivel chair that looked out onto the indoor ring through a filmy bay window.

The desk had been cleared of everything but an old-style black telephone. Idly curious as to whether it was still connected, Galen raised the receiver to her ear. She heard a flat silence, then a gasp. Galen jumped, partially stifled a cry, and wheeled around to see the black-haired, blue-eyed boy standing in the frame of the door. Paling under his coffee hue, he looked for all the world as if he had seen a ghost.

"Jesus! I thought— You scared me," he said, relieved but obviously shaken. "I didn't expect anyone to be in here." Henry had said his name was Caetano da Silva and that he managed the barn.

Galen apologized and began to explain that she had been looking for a gentler bit for Soleil, but he seemed not to hear. After taking a moment to recover from some sort of shock, he seemed to have grown uncomfortable and was slowly backing out the door.

"Caetano, wait," Galen said.

He stopped, eyeing her suspiciously. "What is it?"

His voice was deep and melodious and his accent distinctly Brazilian, with its elongated vowels and loping, almost musical rhythm.

"I was just wondering . . ."

"What?"

"Why—what happened to the Winds?"

"What do you mean?"

"I mean, the barn is full of unfit show-level horses not one a day over ten and there's more tack in here than I've ever seen in one place, but for what? It looks as if nothing's been used in years."

If she had delayed his retreat, she had not opened the floodgates exactly. He regarded her through narrowed eyes and said nothing for a slow count of five, during which time he seemed to be weighing his choice of replies.

"I don't know," he said finally, and after another long pause added, "Nobody cared anymore after the accident."

"Accident? What accident?"

His regret for having chosen this one was obvious. "The plane crash," he said eventually.

"What plane crash? What happened?"

He looked around him at the door, whether concerned at being overheard or contemplating a quick escape, she could not tell. When his light eyes turned back, they narrowed again—it looked to Galen almost like a wince—but this time to sweep the dust-grayed room as if it were a house in which he had once lived.

"When Colin and Johanna were killed," he said.

"Colin? Colin Baugh? Henry's—"

"Son."

"Johanna?"

"His daughter-in-law."

"Were *killed*! My God! When did this happen?"

"Two years ago."

With much prodding, Caetano told her that Colin and Johanna Baugh had been flying in Colin's private plane and had crashed fifty miles south of Stover. Both died instantly. No cause had ever been established. Colin, two years older than Julian, had been thirty-seven. He also told her that the entire family were riders but that Colin and Johanna rode competitively and the earlier success of the barn, which was Colin's pride and great passion, was due to them. Johanna was a writer and Colin, like his brother, an international financier.

In the course of the interview, Caetano had become increasingly ill-at-ease. Finally Galen decided she ought not pursue it any further. But enough had become clear. The death of his eldest son and daughter-in-law was the tragedy that had sent H. L. Baugh into isolation. It must also have been what Henry had referred to when he had said Julian had been through a "rough time." Galen could see the laughing, fair-haired man in Henry's photograph as plainly as if it were in front of her. She saw, too, the look in his younger brother's dark eyes and shivered suddenly in the stifling heat of the airless room.

But why, if Henry trusted her enough to work on his autobiography, had he gone out of his way to avoid even allowing that his son was dead? Surely after two years the wound would have healed enough for that. Two years . . . What had Henry said? That two years earlier he had "lost" his writer and the project had come to a stop. Had Colin's wife been ghostwriting for her father-in-law? Whatever the answer to that and the dozen other questions Caetano's sparse sketch loosed on her brain, one thing was clear: As even the art world knew no more than that a tragedy of some sort had taken place, the family had gone to great lengths to keep the accident under wraps. What was not at all clear, Galen reflected as she walked slowly back through the barn, worrying the cool steel bit she carried absently in her hands, was *why*.

Labor Day weekend came in like a Serengeti afternoon, dry heat loud with the buzz of flies, whine of cicadas and katydids, and the flutter of sparrows bathing in the dust. The horses Pat and Mike turned out headed straight for the trees, swinging their heads like dashboard dogs and propelling themselves with furiously whipping tails. Galen had spent the week reading the uncompleted manuscript and going through Henry's notes and those of his assistant. She had not asked him about the writer or said anything to him about her conversation with Caetano. Knowing his book would have to address his son's death in some fashion, Galen would wait and let Henry broach the subject in his own time.

She planned to drive back to Boston after lunch but there was one thing she had to do first. The morning before, she had seen Caetano leading a black Thoroughbred she had never noticed before out of a separate barn. The horse was dancing beside the boy, nearly lifting him off the ground each time he threw his elegant head. Galen had been transfixed by the animal's beauty and by the power and grace of his movement. Leaning against the fence at the far end of the turnout they were heading toward, she had watched as Caetano slipped the halter off and the horse erupted in a series of bucking leaps and careened wildly toward her, trumpeting, his thick blue-black tail erect like a flag. "Who is he?" she had called, standing back from the fence as the horse slid to a frenzied stop in front of her, snorted, wheeled, and raced back up the dirt. Caetano had looked up but did not answer. "Caetano—" she had called again, but he had turned his back and was walking toward the barn. The plaque on the stall in which she found the black horse Saturday morning read BUTTONS; the brass plate on his halter bore the name DUROMETER. She had little trouble deciding which belonged to the stallion.

The stable grounds were deserted, as was usual for weekend mornings, and as she led Durometer through the main barn and into the indoor stadium, still clammy with the night's air, Galen felt like a thief in Cartier's. Henry had put no restrictions on her riding, and she decided to err on the side of literalness—at least until she had ridden this animal just once.

She lengthened the stirrups to get as much leg on him as she dared and, struggling with her own nerves, pulled herself cautiously up onto his back. She had expected him to fight her right away, but this horse, she could tell immediately, was a slow fuse. Even at the walk, which was rangy and fluid, Galen could feel the power of his broad chest and well-muscled haunches, the spring of his pastens, and a dangerous, nagging boredom.

After only one lap Durometer began to twist his hindquarters toward the center of the ring, throwing his head with rattly snorts, and sprang into a jog. One, two, three paces of this; then suddenly he ducked his head, slammed his two front feet on the ground and, taking his weight in a half rear, spun around with a speed that came perilously close to unseating her. Incredibly (to her), she recovered before he could bolt, landed hard on his back, and with a furious snarl yanked his head back around the same way it had come, booting him as hard as she could with her heel.

The fuse was very short now as Durometer continued to jog, head up, ears back, fishtailing in a haughty display of independence. He planted his front feet and tried to whirl again, but this time Galen was waiting. She snatched him in the mouth before he found any momentum and dug her heels rapid-fire into his sides. "Get up, you bastard!" she growled between her teeth. Dancing almost in place, Durometer was clearly put out but showing a budding respect for this new rider. It took a full turn around the ring before he would walk again, but his head had begun to ease down. She now relaxed her hands and asked him to trot. "Easy, handsome, this is not a race, whoa . . ." she cooed in a steady stream of conversation directed at the flattened ears. Throwing his stately head, he sprang into a choppy canter and fought her until she broke his stride with an ever-tightening circle. "Let go . . . bend . . . relax . . ." She turned him until slowly, responding to the left-right pulse of her fists, his neck began to round. "Atta boy . . . easy now . . . don't anticipate . . ." She loosened the circle, eased him out onto the rail, and, after a few more turns at the trot, urged him into a rolling canter that was as luxuriously smooth as satin sheets.

After forty-five minutes Durometer's chest was polished with sweat and spattered from the beard of white froth rimming his mouth. But the horse was now responding to her subtlest commands. Their swan song was a perfectly executed flying change, and a wide grin lighted Galen's face as she gathered her reins in one hand and slapped his wet neck and puffing side with the other. "Not bad, not *bad*!" she said exuberantly, eyes sparkling with emeralds, as she dropped from a collected canter to a jog and finally to an exaggerated walk that threw her hips forward and back like a rocking chair. Her bare arms shone with a hint of moisture, her throat and brilliantly flushed cheeks glistened with sweat. Her hair, which she had piled on top of her head, had loosened and she wiped her wet hairline with a forearm. Swinging Durometer around to face the barn, she reined him to a stop and looked up to see Julian Baugh languishing against the frame of the door as if he had been there all day.

Caught off guard, an involuntary "Oh, hell" escaped her, followed by a twitch at the corner of her lips—the grin had evaporated—that could not quite pass for a smile. That vanished quickly, too, as she struggled to suppress an irrational feeling of guilt, as if she had been caught fondling the family silver.

She leapt lightly off, slid the stirrups up, and busied herself loosening Durometer's girth, defensiveness flowing naturally in to replace remorse. She could not see Julian but she could feel his stern gaze boring into her back. Fumbling with the girth, which was made no easier by Durometer's ill-timed fussing, she tried to collect herself. She had known it was unlikely that she could avoid seeing him again—though she hardly expected him so soon—and had promised herself not to let him provoke her again. She was not, however, off to a good start. The abrasive texture of their last encounter, which she had, regrettably, chosen to make all the more memorable with her parting remark, was still fresh in her mind. Judging from the look Galen had glimpsed at the door, she could be certain it was also fresh in Julian's.

Determined to avoid a confrontation, Galen told herself she would say a mild hello, smile amiably, and simply lead Durometer by him. If the *bloody horse* would stand still!

Her plan, however, suffered something of a setback

when, just behind her, Julian suddenly snatched Durometer's bridle. With an authoritative "Whoa!" and short sharp jerk on the reins, he froze the animal in place.

"Thank you," Galen murmured from under the saddle flap.

"That was quite impressive," Julian said, his voice as slow and cool as ever, but lacking the sardonic edge she had expected. He sounded instead distracted. "I don't remember when I last saw this horse under saddle."

"Thank you," she repeated without looking up. "He is very talented. It seems such a waste that he's never ridden."

When Julian did not respond to this, Galen glanced up and saw he was studying the lines of Durometer's head with the absorbed concentration of a jeweler holding a diamond up to the light. Whether the animal's beauty, or images evoked by it, held sway, the man was consumed in thought. Lingering herself on Julian's profile, Galen could not help noticing that his head was about as finely sculpted for a man as Durometer's was for a horse. His nose was strong and straight, his brow and jaw—like his father's—powerful. His lips were full and, though severe, quite sensual. She had to admit that he was, if nothing else, a good-looking man. But she saw also silver strands in his thick black hair, a hollowness in his cheeks and a fatigue about his eyes. She was reminded of the troubled weariness she had seen once before, and could not help thinking with a begrudging impulse of compassion of his brother's tragic death.

But the sentiment was short-lived as the face became shrouded again and Julian turned suddenly and caught her staring at him. Wherever he had been, he was very much present now.

"You seem to be something of a Renaissance woman, Ms. Shaw," he said. "Besides being an accomplished equestrian, I understand that you are a talented writer as well. My father tells me that you're helping him finish his biography."

"Yes, we started this week," she said, meeting his gaze boldly enough but wishing very much that he would let go of the bridle. She reached for the reins but he ignored the obvious suggestion in her gesture. As disengaged as he seemed in every other respect, Julian Baugh's eyes were fixed on her face, and he seemed to be in no hurry to end their encounter.

"Tell me, where did you learn to ride like that?" he asked now. Braced for a grilling about her new station at his father's estate, Galen was surprised that Julian seemed content to let the subject drop.

"I studied with Joe Macklin for a little," she answered.

"I see. Perhaps you'll be joining us for our evening ride?"

"I'm afraid I'm leaving for Boston as soon as I put Durometer away," she said, hoping Julian would get the hint. However, he made no move to release the horse.

"A pity," he said. Galen visibly bristled at what she took to be sarcasm, and he added simply, "I mean that."

Beginning to lose balance on the shifting ground of this curious conversation, which Julian seemed intent on prolonging, Galen was almost relieved to hear a mellifluous "*Jooo*-lian" echo through the arena, even to see that Carla Baugh was wading through the thick sand toward them. She was wearing a baby-pink chamois belted over the top of loose white trousers that narrowed and stopped just below the knee.

Her country wear, Galen mused.

"*There* you are," Carla puffed as if she had been searching for some time. "Whatever are you—Miss *Shaw*! How nice to *see* you again." Her affected delight was not entirely convincing. "Have you been riding?"

Galen did not have a chance to answer as Carla looked beyond her at the horse. "Isn't that—?"

"Indeed she has," Julian said. "In fact, I was just telling her how well Durometer was looking."

For an awkward moment, nobody said anything as Carla looked long and hard at Julian. Whatever passed between them was not meant for Galen to understand, but he evidently communicated something to Carla. The woman fell visibly back into step and in the overdone tone she had first addressed Galen began to complain about the heat, the flies, her hay fever, the hay fever of someone called William.

At a gap in her string of banalities, Julian excused himself and left them. Galen tried to ease herself into his wake, but Carla was not ready to let her go. Galen wondered: A changing of the guard?

"I understand you're living in the bungalow," Carla said, cutting across her move to leave.

"Only during the week. I was just telling Mr. Baugh that I was heading for Boston this morning and in fact really ought to be on my way."

"And you just quit your job?" Carla went brightly on, ignoring Galen's attempt to end the exchange. She was smiling warmly enough, but the tenor of the question made Galen's jaws tighten.

"I didn't have a job at the time. Didn't Henry tell you?"

"No. Only that you were going to help him finish his book."

It occurred to Galen now that the couple's unscheduled appearance this weekend might have something to do with her own arrival at the estate. She was, on second thought, about to dismiss the notion as hysterical, when Carla went on.

"He said your coming to his show was entirely by chance. What an extraordinary coincidence, and how fortuitous!" The woman was anything but subtle, Galen thought. But then maybe she was not trying to be. Either way, the chat had clearly turned into a grilling. Angry as well as impatient to leave, Galen did nothing to disguise the irony in her voice.

"Yes," she said. "Imagine my surprise."

If Carla noticed, she did not let on. "Miss Shaw, there's something you should know." Her tone was hushed and intimate now, as if preparing a friendly piece of woman-to-woman advice. "H. L. is an extraordinarily generous man and, as a result, he has been badly taken advantage of by—"

"Mrs. Baugh, Henry and I have been all through this and there's no need to say any more." Galen tried to sound brisk, but something inside her was beginning to give way. "Now if you'll excuse me, I'm afraid I just don't have the time."

She led Durometer quickly from the stadium and, not seeing Julian standing inside the stall of a horse called Teton, thrust him at a surprised Caetano, who had just arrived and was talking with his employer's son. Calling angrily to Lily, Galen stormed out of the barn, unaware of the gaze that followed her to the door.

Galen drove the quarter mile to the bungalow in a state of distraction. She was fighting the sinking feeling that Henry's family would make her life here miserable, her work impossible, or both. She had dealt with left-wing zealots, right-wing maniacs, bomb-throwing anarchists, and the inimitable Rick Davies, her former night editor who, like an incubus, still haunted her dreams, but she had rarely if ever lost her composure. Galen was losing it now. Carla was an irrepressible vulture, but it was her husband who was going to be trouble. His civility at the barn just now notwithstanding, there was something smoldering about Julian Baugh that Galen found utterly unnerving. Powerful, driven, and uncompromising, he was the kind of man who would try to mow down anything in his path, which in this case she suspected meant her. So much for dying and going to heaven.

The phone was still ringing by the time she made the kitchen door. Mara's voice at the other end was like an explosion amid her thoughts.

"Slow down, for God's sake," Galen said as she worked off her boots, scattering small bricks of mud over the glossy parquet. "I've missed everything you've said. Can't this wait, I'm on my way into town now."

"No, it can't! I had to tell you right away, you won't believe it. Can you talk?"

"What do you mean can I talk? Who would be here? Mara, what is it?"

"I just got off the phone with Ginny in New York. Well, she ran into a friend of hers who's an art dealer and does a lot of business with Carla Baugh. Get this, Ginny's friend says that two years ago, H. L. Baugh's oldest son Colin—"

"Right, I know, was killed in a plane crash," Galen cut her off.

"You *knew* and didn't tell me?"

"I only just found out yesterday."

"Isn't that something? It sort of makes sense why they kept it secret."

"Well, it doesn't make any sense to me!" Galen erupted. "So they are a famous family. But accidents happen and it's not like it's someone's fault."

"Well, it's not so much a question of fault—"

"In fact, I'm convinced all this secrecy is unhealthy in the extreme. It's cast this sickly shadow over everything out here, you can almost feel it eating its way into the core of this family like some disease."

"Gale, honey, you sound upset."

"Well, I am. I've just had another encounter with Julian Baugh and his adorable wife and it's left a very bad taste in my mouth."

"His wife?"

"Yes, your friend Carla is here, too, and putting Alexis Colby to shame."

"Carla! *Carla's* not Julian's wife!"

"Sure she is, Henry's introduced her as his daughter-in-law two or three times."

"Some reporter you are! Gale, Carla Baugh was his *brother's* wife! *Julian's* wife died two years ago—in the plane with Colin!"

6

Galen idled the car for several minutes before turning into the Winds gate. It was Monday evening. The heat wave had not broken and the wind, which flashed through the silver beech trees at the mouth of the driveway, was gritty and dry. Her hands were wet on the steering wheel. Lily gave her a meaningful look: It was not as if they had someplace else to go.

Galen had been fighting a mix of macabre fascination and dread most of the drive out from Boston. Mara had the tenacity of a pit bull when it came to scandal, and for two and a half days Galen had been listening to her theories about Johanna and Colin's fateful plane ride. Their last conversation was on her mind.

"There's no other explanation for the secrecy," Mara had repeated over lunch. "If their little sojourn was so innocent, why did the family handle it in the guiltiest fashion possible?"

"To try to protect their good name against boorish rumor mongers like you."

"Don't be naïve! Face it. Julian's brother was *shtupp*ing his wife. But what inquiring minds want to know, given that you say widower and widow are as cozy as white on rice, is which came first, the chicken or the egg?"

"You're mixing your metaphors. Do we have any decaffeinated coffee or is this espresso it?"

"I bet they've been unfriendly to you because they don't want the press nosing around."

"The *press*, Mara? Yes, I'm sure that's it."

"For Christ's sake, Gale, don't try to tell me you're not intrigued in the least."

A horn blared and a pickup truck swerved around her car, jolting her out of her daze. She put the Alfa in gear and turned into the driveway, telling herself what she had tried unsuccessfully to convince Mara of—that she was not interested in Baugh family secrets; that her only concern was finishing the book and getting out of everyone's way. But a hundred yards into the estate, the car came to another stop, at the entrance of the stable yard. It was half-past five: Henry would be out on his nightly ride and it would be a simple matter of counting empty stalls to know whether Carla and Julian had stayed on.

"So, I lied," Galen murmured, catching Lily's interested look, but in the end did not pull in. She resolved instead against setting such a precedent and continued on, veering off from the main drive to the mansion and following the road across the back of the paddocks and into a stand of pines. She emerged a half mile later in the small clearing where the squat white one-story bungalow stood. Encased on two sides by a wide wooden porch and smothered in lilac bushes, the house looked like something out of a storybook.

The interior, on the other hand, resisted a single theme. Its kitchen, a caricature of a woodland cottage's, was disproportionately large, with a walk-in fireplace hung with huge cast-iron pots and pokers worthy of the witch

who went after Hansel and Gretel. Behind it was an unrea-
sonably large, virtually empty pantry, and on the other side
of that, a living room with a bear rug and only slightly
smaller fireplace. Its walls were covered with a battery of
the most gory prints in the Audubon elephant folio. A
small dining room with midnight-blue wallpaper and
drapes that belonged in a medieval castle ran off the living
room, which provided its only, roundabout access to the
kitchen. Why there was no connecting passage to the pantry, let alone the kitchen, Galen could only guess. On the
other side of the house were three textbook colonial bedrooms with muslin curtains, petit-fleur wallpaper, and antique hooked rugs. The long sunny study at the back of the
house was done in straw mats, bamboo furniture, and
jungle art. For all its airy smartness, Galen never used it. In
fact, when she was not sleeping, she was rarely in any
other room than the kitchen. On a hot night like this she
would make herself a drink, slump into the cool leather
sofa there, and read.

Not, however, tonight.

As she let Lily out of the car, Galen realized immediately that something was wrong. The dog was weaving
with uncharacteristic zeal back and forth over the front
steps, stopping periodically to drive her nose against the
crack under the door. Someone or something had been
here.

Or still was, Galen considered as she lifted a ski pole
off a nail inside the screened porch and let Lily into the
shadowy cottage ahead of her. Stopping just inside the
kitchen, she listened as Lily, making short piglike grunts,
trotted deliberately about the house. After a moment there
was silence. Galen called "Lily" and got no response—she
never did, but it seemed the thing to do. After a moment
she went in after her dog. Pointed end preceding her by
three feet, Galen found her in the bedroom, still as a statue,
ears cocked, head askew, body poised for a strategic retreat.

Her attention was fixed on the closet door. Galen's nerves tingled.

"Hello?" she called feebly. Getting no answer, she poked the door twice with the pole. Lily grunted. Galen felt suddenly hot. There was a moment when nothing stirred; then suddenly the room exploded into chaos. The closet door blew open with a crash and a figure erupted from her wardrobe as if it had been shot from a cannon. Galen gave a little shriek and dropped her ski pole. Lily ran out of the room with a menacing bark. It was not until the intruder was almost at the window that Galen realized he was barely three feet tall.

The boy was frantic with fear and kicked wildly when Galen grabbed him by the leg. She remembered reading somewhere that an effective response to dog attack was to lift the animal off its feet, at which point it could be expected to release its hold. Dragging the flailing child back into the room, Galen tried this, holding him against her a foot off the ground. To her amazement, he went as limp in her arms as if she had knocked him on the head. He was in fact so still as she carried him to the living room that she began to wonder whether she had hurt him in their struggle. As she set him down between her feet, she saw tears in his eyes.

"Are you all right?" she asked gently, pushing a drop off his cheek with the flat of her thumb. There was no reply. With a large head that was too big for his slight body, he looked like a baby bird. His skin was miserably pale and his features small, which combined to make his round, teal-blue eyes appear unnaturally large. His hair was bright orange, his lips were wet and scarlet, and his ears stuck out. Dressed in a crisp white shirt, navy-blue shorts, knee socks, and dress shoes, he looked like something out of an English boarding school. She guessed he was six or seven. He had stopped crying but his breath still caught his chest.

"Don't be afraid," she said softly, tugging gently on his

arm. "You scared me a lot more than I scared you. Are you a spy or just a robber?" He looked at her for the first time but did not return her smile. She let go of his wrists.

"What's your name?" She asked. He looked away.

"Larry?" No answer.

"Barry?" Still nothing.

"Harry?"

"Nooo!" he said with surprising force and the hint of a smile. "It's William." His voice was deep and husky.

"I see. Well, my name's Galen and this is Lily. You can pat her, she doesn't bite." William was lifting his arms away from the mauve nose as if it were a rising tide.

"Honestly. She doesn't even chew her meat."

A smile tugged again at the corners of his red mouth. The boy was still unsure of the extent of his guilt.

"Where's her tail?" he asked.

"I don't know. You didn't come across it in my closet, did you?"

Whatever smile was there vanished with this. Drawing on some hidden pocket of courage or anger, the child lifted his head and responded imperiously, "It's not your closet! It's my mother's closet!" His ears turned bright pink.

Galen tried to maintain her casual tone. "I see. Where do *you* live, William?"

"There," he said, thrusting out an arm.

Galen looked at him with some concern, but in a moment realized that the television console, at which he was pointing, lay roughly on a line between her living room and Henry's house.

"What's your mother's name?" Galen asked.

"She's dead!" William Baugh retorted, as if this was the more important thing to know about her now.

"I'm sorry, sweetheart. And your dad?"

"We live in France." Galen could see that the boy's brief moment of courage was already beginning to pass and that timidity was fast reclaiming lost ground. "But he's in Boston today."

"Well, I'm very glad you came to see me, William,"
she said, getting up from the couch. "Did you come
through the woods?"

He nodded.

"There's a path?"

He nodded again.

"Will you show me?"

It was no more than a slight depression in the carpet of
yellow pine needles and a crease across a field of blackberry
brambles and immature cedars. But William obviously
knew it by heart and escorted Galen with an air of of-
ficialdom. He had relaxed as soon as they were out of sight
of the bungalow. By the time they broke out onto the open
grounds of the estate he had told her everything he could
remember about the airplane in which he had flown from
Paris and translated into French the words for boy, girl,
dog, bird, tree, grass, house, and grandfather. Also, "I am
six years old" and "The cook is going to have a baby." He
had taken her hand to jump a small stream halfway between the two houses and was still holding it as they approached the edge of Henry's broad flagstone patio.

"When are you going back to France?"

William held up eight fingers.

"I hope I'll see you again before you go. We can take a
walk down to the barn. Do you know how to ride?"

For the second time Galen saw terror contort the
child's features. His entire body seemed to flinch, almost as
if she had raised a hand to strike him.

"You're not afraid of horses, are you?" she asked
quickly. The look in William's eyes answered her question.
She knelt in front of him. "Sweetheart, what happened?
Did you have a fall?"

But before she got her answer, the sound of footsteps
on the patio drew his gaze around her and brought a look
of relief into the ashen face.

"Grandpa! Uncle Franny!" he shouted.

"Well, there you are, William, and I see you've discovered our Ms. Shaw, how lovely. I bet if you asked her
nicely, she'll agree to have dinner with us. We are in the
midst of a scintillating debate, and the larger the audience
the more clever we become. Cocktail? What's your pleasure?"

"Gin and tonic. What's the fight about?"

"The playoff game between the Yankees and Red Sox."

"Is it the playoffs already?"

"Not this year."

"Oh, no."

"In 1978."

"Oh, boy."

Drinks in hand, the party retired to four cast-iron
chaise longues arranged on the terrace shoulder to shoulder
like lounge chairs on the deck of a cruise liner. The sun had
just set and a pink film was beginning to spread across the
pale sky.

"If Boston was such a paragon of courage," Franny
was saying, "how is it they piddled away—excuse me,
Galen, William—a fourteen-game lead?"

"That's not my point. All I'm saying is that they played
the finest game of baseball ever played."

"Is that why Carl Yastremski popped out with the
tying run on third?"

"Who's Carl Yaskremski?" William asked.

"You see that!" Henry sat up in his chair. "There's a
French education for you. What a criminal waste. *William*,
my dear boy, Carl Ya*stremski* was one of the finest baseball
players—Francis, I'm warning you—of our time."

"Don't listen to your grandfather, William, he's
positively puerile in these matters and such grand,
groundless ipse dixits should be set gently but firmly and
permanently aside."

"What?"

Galen wondered how many times this same point had been through this mill.

"Are you quite through?" Henry came back, and with this their debate quickly deteriorated into a contest of baseball trivia and was soon over William and Galen's heads. Leaning over to the boy, she asked him in a whisper whether he would not like to show her his room. He was on his feet at once.

"You deserved what you got for selling Babe Ruth to the Yankees," they heard Franny saying as they disappeared into the house. "And don't say you weren't born then."

At the top of the wide, gradual front-hall staircase, a long hallway ran to the right, back over the central living room, jogged left over the ell, and ended in a large, airy bedroom enclosed on three sides by latticed glass. William said it was his grandfather's bedroom and pointed out items of interest: a stuffed hawk, a model ship, an African mask, a recent photograph of William and Henry playing croquet, an ivory pipe carved in the shape of a bear's head. If none were so open and well lighted, the other five bedrooms along the hall were at least as stately, with fireplaces, inlaid furniture, four-poster or canopied beds, large-print wallpaper, and heavy draperies half closed on regal views of either the stable grounds to the front or the velvety field encircling the back of the house. But they all had the same unused feeling of the rooms downstairs, as if they had outlived the generation for which they had been built. Only echoes of their gay parties, weekend guests, and running children remained.

The rooms on the back shared a stone balcony that ran the length of the house. William led Galen down this to the last room on the tour. Except for a papier-mâché castle set about with hand-painted Britains lead soldiers, there was little that distinguished it as a child's room. In answer to "Where are your toys?" he opened the door of a cavernous closet, really a small room, where a staggering collection of playthings were arranged meticulously on shelves like arti-facts from an archeological dig. Every generation appeared to be represented, with skates, footballs, baseball gloves and bats, bow-and-arrow sets and dartboards dating back fifty years or more.

"So this is where Baugh toys go to die," Galen said without thinking. But William did not seem to have heard. He was half leaning, half sitting on his bed, gazing absently at a silver-framed photograph on his dresser. It was of a woman cradling an infant in her arms. The baby's face was pink and puckered but there was no question as to who it was. Johanna Baugh's hair was long, thick, and auburn, her skin smoothly pale, and her round, deep-blue eyes the image of William's. He seemed to want Galen to see it.

"That's my mother and me when I was a baby," William said when she lifted the frame off the bureau.

"She's very beautiful," Galen said, squatting at his side.

"I know," he said matter-of-factly. Overcome with pity, Galen reached out to embrace the boy. Instead of fall-ing tearfully into her arms, however, he erupted with a joyous squeal of "Daddy!" and bolted from the room. Galen was left sitting on the floor in a state of bewilder-ment. It was only after several moments that she heard the muffled commotion in the front hall and finally the voice that had shot through William like an electrical current. As she got slowly to her feet, she glanced again at the photo-graph. For just an instant it looked to Galen as if the red-haired woman were laughing at her.

Not only had Julian and Carla returned from Boston a day earlier than expected, they had brought with them a portly middle-aged gentleman in khakis and a duck-print tie and a tall white-haired woman in topsiders, white cable-knit cardigan, lime-green slacks, and an impressive display of gold jewelry at her ears, neck, and wrists. Both had leathery tans. They were introduced as Margaret and Richard Bowdoin, old friends and neighbors whom everyone had thought were in South America.

"I'm flabbergasted," Henry exclaimed. "I thought you weren't due back until Thanksgiving! Why didn't you write? Julian, where ever did you find them? Peggy, you look as if you just got off a boat."

"In the lobby of the Ritz Carlton," Julian said with a light smile. "They were being evicted for vagrancy."

"He's absolutely right," the white-haired woman said in a whiskey baritone that cracked with laughter. She had one hand on her chest, the other on Carla's arm. "They'd lost our reservations—can you stand it? The Ritz? And we *were* on a boat. You'll get the postcards. We decided to come home early so we hopped a liner. Very spontaneous. Not like us at all." Margaret Bowdoin threw back her head and released a sonorous belly laugh.

Mae was told there would be eight for dinner and the group took their drinks on the terrace. There was something remotely familiar about Richard Bowdoin, but he was not the kind of man one would forget. Having allowed his wife an early lead in the salutations, Richard quickly found his stride and dominated the conversation from then on. Margaret's participation was reduced to punctuating his soliloquy with "That's the truth," "Can you stand it?" and "Couldn't you just die?" As bombastic as the man was, the Baughs seemed a surprisingly willing audience.

Galen for her part wished she was somewhere else. The evening was cooling and darkening into a soft summer night, but its promise of an intimate supper had proved grossly false and had left her feeling very much let down. Taking a seat at the farthest acceptable edge of the goings-on, she tried not to appear uninterested, but could find nothing to say. Consumed as they were in their own unanticipated reunion, Baughs and Bowdoins did not seem to notice, or if they did, happily were making little effort to draw her in. Even William, who was leaning against his father's knee, was entranced by Richard's discourse, though Galen wondered if he was capable of following its cluttered, erratic course. Richard was at this point digressing from his story about a great score in Andean art.

". . . By God, H. L., you'll never guess who we ran into in Lima! A horrendous little man, but you liked him, Bimmy Railsback's brother, the poet, oh, what's his name? Anyway, I thought he had died, didn't you, Peg? *Gerald!*"

"Gerard?"

"Yes, that's it, that's it. A crackpot if you ask me! He's shacked up in a hut on a mountain with a virgin goatherd in quest of the artistic fountain of youth. What a pontifical horse's rear end he has become. Anyway, he asked for you . . ."

His voice trailed away as Galen's mind wandered halfheartedly back to the selection of excuses she had devised to leave, none of which, she knew, she would use. Looking down at the limp skirt of her drooping yellow shift, she wished she had at least managed a shower before Lily had found William in her closet. Her cheeks were flushed with the heat, her skin felt sticky, and her hair, which had not been brushed since before she had left Boston, had gone wild in the humidity. She glanced across at Carla, who looked like a skin-care ad in her fashionably minimal black-and-emerald strapless dress. Perfectly composed, not a hair out of place, the woman was as fresh as a mountain stream. It was hard not to feel underdressed. Galen told herself it was just as well she was being ignored.

Beyond that, she felt distinctly uncomfortable in the bosom of the Baugh family, which even before the revelations about Johanna and Colin, Galen found collectively about as cozy as a damp cave. Even in the exuberance and frivolity of this apparently happy reunion there seemed to be something else, a curious undercurrent she could not quite put her finger on. She looked up and caught Carla's fantastic catlike eyes on her. The smile that followed was broad and beautiful. Galen smiled back. It was perhaps just her imagination. Resigning herself to an evening among them, Galen thought in turns of Mara's crack about the press and of the red-haired woman in the picture upstairs, whom she tried to imagine in their midst.

"I understand you've met my son," a voice said just beside her. Galen, who realized she had been staring off into space, looked up to see that Julian had come up and was standing at her elbow. He was not smiling but there was an unmistakable lightness in his dark eyes. Whether she was or not, he seemed to be enjoying the party.

"Yes, I did," she said, glancing over at the red-haired boy who had taken a seat at his grandfather's feet. Henry was absently stroking his hair. "He's a darling child." Galen drew Julian a quick picture of their first encounter, revising it slightly so as not to expose William to any possible reprimand, staging their surprise meeting on her front porch.

"He was very informative, very proper," she said at length about his tour through the woods. "I was thoroughly charmed."

"I assure you the feeling is mutual. He's normally quite shy around strangers, but I get the feeling that won't be the last you'll see of him."

"I hope not."

"I hope not, too."

"Yes, well . . ." Galen's voice trailed off and her gaze went back to William.

Julian's eyes had followed hers and were resting now on his son.

"That was very sweet of you," he said after a moment.

"Not at all, he—"

"No, I mean for covering up for him. He confessed his transgression to me just now."

Galen's face swung back to him. "Oh."

A half smile touched the corners of Julian's full lips as he turned to look at her, but whatever he was about to add would have to wait. Mae had come to the door and announced that dinner was served.

By the third course, Richard, who somehow managed to eat and drink as energetically as he spoke without falling behind, was showing no signs of fatigue. He had been describing their South America trip.

"But Brazil was far and away the most fun," he said, taking a prodigious swallow of wine. "Wonderful people, wonderful people, wonderful. The warmest people in the world. Isn't that right, dear?"

"Oh, these people are *charming!*"

"You've all been there, of course. Carla, Julian, I know you have, but not you, H. L? Fran? I'm incredulous. It's a man's dream world down there. (Forgive me, ladies.) Copacabana, Ipanema, Carnaval. It's a bacchanalian paradise!"

"It's also very poor, Uncle Dick," Julian interjected.

"Well, of course, but name one country south of the Tropic of Cancer that isn't. Besides, Brazilians—the ones that aren't filthy rich—are poor but never destitute. These people are so"—he searched for the word—"*spiritual.* You can see it in their eyes—there is a light there, I swear to God—you saw that, too, didn't you, Peg?—and in their walk. Their *walk.* These people have the straightest backs of any national group I have ever known."

Julian dropped his napkin beside his plate with a chuckle.

"I'm surprised at you, Uncle Dick," he said with gentle mocking. "You may be the worst cultural chauvinist I know but I've never known you to try to sell the benign poverty line before. You visited the *favelas*, I suppose?''

"I refuse to feel guilty for the world's troubles tonight, Julian—now be quiet and let me finish. After Rio we took a side trip up to a city about a thousand miles to the north called Bahia. It's the oldest city in the country, once the capital, you know, utterly charming, very quaint, very charming. *Gorgeous* women, my, my, out of this world. Cobblestone streets. *Most* interesting, this city is the center of the African cultism in Brazil. They called it . . . Peg, do you remember the name?''

"No, darling, sorry.''

"Wait a minute, I'll get it—''

"Macumba," Julian said.

"Candomblè," Galen corrected him.

She had barely mumbled the word, but the way the seven heads whipped around she might have thought her chair had spoken. It was true she had hardly said a word the entire evening.

"Yes! That's right," Bowdoin went on with only a slight pause, during which he seemed to take note of her for the first time. "That's right. They have the most extraordinary rituals, eat powdered toad's eyes and bat wings, that sort of thing, quite exotic stuff, really, and then go to Mass by the *drove* on Sundays. They have a term for it—oh, bother!''

Richard looked at the ceiling for the answer. Julian looked at Galen.

"Syncretism," she offered. This time only Henry's face turned back to Richard, the rest lingering on her in various poses of interest.

"Just so," Richard had continued, nodding in Galen's direction. "The country's extraordinary in that way, the blending of the races. People come in all colors, black-black skin with yellow hair, brown skin with auburn hair and green eyes. It's virtually a nonracial society. Interbreeding is rather a time-honored tradition there, starting with the Portuguese slaveholders themselves. Nothing like their North American counterparts. Brazilian slavery was a far more humane system."

Here he stopped to lean forward to peer down the table at Galen. He asked in a challenging voice, "Isn't that so?"

Galen looked around her. A smile was fading unevenly from Carla's red lips. Margaret Bowdoin looked as if someone she was anxious not to offend had just served her a bowl of eyeball soup. Julian, who was leaning back in his chair with his arms folded across his chest, was clearly amused. He gave her a nod of encouragement. It was not needed.

"Not necessarily," Galen answered as mildly as she could. She had had this conversation many times before and it was all she could do to restrain her irritation.

"How's that?" To his credit, Richard Bowdoin seemed genuinely interested. The rest of the dinner party, appeared, forks suspended in midair, at least as much so.

"Statistics suggest," Galen continued, "that it may not have been quite the slaves' paradise the Brazilians would have everybody believe."

"Go on. Go on."

After a pause, she added, "Take, for example, the fact that for some reason Brazilian slaves died faster than they reproduced and that Brazilian slavery thus depended on the African slave trade long after the American South was being supplied solely by natural increase. While Brazil received perhaps ten times as many Africans as the North American colonies, the Brazilian slave population in say, 1860, was only about half as large as here."

"Go, team," Franny muttered under his breath, and Julian let out a bellow of a laugh. Galen got the feeling Dick Bowdoin was not often contradicted.

"What a revoltingly clever thing you are," he barked,

indignant but with a gleam in his eye. "Quiet, Julian. Now tell me, young lady, is it or is it not true that the Portuguese allowed their slaves to marry and were careful not to break up families?" He winced as if expecting a blow.

"It depends on who you go by," Galen said, surprised and a little impressed by the retreat. "There was no law prohibiting the separation of families until 1869—that's three hundred years after the first Africans were transported—and many families were in fact broken up in the internal slave trade. As to this idea that slaves were allowed to marry—the vast majority were not."

"I think that's a no, Dick," Henry said with a grin.

"Wait, H. L.," Bowdoin said, putting up a hand. To Galen he said, "And now?"

"Excuse me?"

"What about now? You've dispensed with each of my points but one: the racial situation in Brazil today."

"And now there is, as you say, a higher degree of intermarriage in Brazil than in this country, certainly, but racism is firmly, if somewhat more discreetly, rooted in the economics of the country. It is a rigidly class-conscious society and the classes get blacker the lower you go. You could, however, say that in Brazil, money whitens."

With that, Dick Bowdoin slapped his hand down on the table and demanded: "All right, young woman, who *are* you?"

"She's a newspaper woman, Uncle Dick," Carla said with a slow, ambiguous grin. "You've been tangling with the press."

"My father lived in Brazil for many years," Galen corrected her, not missing the echo of Mara's words.

"What did he do?" Dick asked.

"He was an anthropologist."

"What's his name?"

"Geoffrey Milton Shaw."

"Good God!"

"You knew him?"

"Rather well."

Dick Bowdoin and Geof Shaw had met in 1962 in Nigeria, where Bowdoin was conducting a land-use survey for the World Bank and Galen's father was studying Yoruba religious traditions. They had done, according to Dick, "a bit of drinking together." This was, Galen knew, a difficult period for her father, and "a bit of drinking" was undoubtedly a delicate understatement. Knowing this, Dick had avoided the subject of his death until the dinner party adjourned to the living room for coffee. As her private conversation with the man revealed a reservoir of intelligence under the thick layer of pomposity, Galen began to be able to picture a friendship between her father and Dick Bowdoin. He was at any rate a heartfelt man.

"I must tell you how sorry I was to learn of his death," he told her as soon as they were alone. "How awful it must have been for you."

"It was, I suppose."

"You poor girl. He was a brilliant and a fine man, Miss Shaw. I respected him greatly."

"Thank you, Mr. Bowdoin."

"Dick, please. He talked about you all the time, you know. I should have known you from your picture."

"It's been several years, I've probably changed."

"He loved you very much."

"I know that, but thank you."

"When we get back in our house, you'll come and have dinner with us. There's so much I want to ask you about. I believe I still have some letters, if you'd care to see them."

"Of course. I'd love to."

"So much tragedy," Dick Bowdoin said, laying a fat hand on hers and looking around the room. "Dear lord."

*   *   *

Galen was halfway across the driveway when she heard the front door close behind her. She turned around and watched Julian stride quickly toward her, hands in his pockets as if he were cold.

"A vote has been taken," he said, affecting a formal tone, "and it has been unanimously agreed that you should be driven home." It was too dark to see his expression clearly, but she could hear a smile in his voice.

"Thank you, but as I told Dick and Henry *and* Franny, there's a moon and I really would prefer to walk."

"In the words of my father, 'Moon, my arse! It's black as ink out there.'"

"It is not. There's more than enough light."

"It's also one o'clock in the morning."

"This is not exactly Avenue C."

He laughed. "Are you always this stubborn?"

Galen looked at him. Julian's manner toward her this night had not exactly been as she had expected. The irony, and the challenge, seemed to be gone. It was perhaps the wine and brandy, perhaps Dick Bowdoin's public embrace, but Julian sounded almost gay. Galen could see that she was not going to get her walk without a struggle.

"You're not going to let this go, are you?"

"Please, Galen," he said with a smile, "indulge us this once."

She gave in with a sigh, let him lead her to his car, and slipped into the leather bucket seat of the Jaguar. She leaned her head back against the headrest and closed her eyes. It had been a long day and night. It would not be so terrible to be driven after all. Julian slipped in beside her, the engine turned over and with the confident throaty purr of expensive cars, they started down the driveway. Galen's mind went back to the morning she first caught sight of the car in which she was now being escorted, but whether out of fatigue or under the influence of Henry's wines, she let the image go and evoked instead a picture of her father.

They were halfway to the bungalow before Julian spoke. When he did he seemed to be reading her mind.

"I gather Uncle Dick and your father were quite good friends."

"Yes, well, they knew each other in Africa during the sixties."

"You had never met him yourself?"

"No, I was here, in school."

"Where is he now?"

"He's dead."

"I'm sorry."

"It was a long time ago."

As they glided into the clearing, the headlights came to rest on Lily, who, having long since quit her vigil at Henry's front door, was gazing at them from the bungalow porch. Illuminated by the beams, her eyes looked like a pair of tiny electric lamps. Julian turned the engine off. Darkness fell like a black drape, and he turned in his seat to face her.

Galen reached for the door handle.

"You were quite young?" he asked.

"No. Twenty."

"How do you know so much about Brazil?"

"I lived there with my father and helped him with his research. He was writing a book on African cultures in the Western Hemisphere, in slaveholding countries."

"Your mother—"

"She left him—us—when I was young."

"Do you have brothers or sisters?"

"No. Why?" Julian's persistence was beginning to make her uncomfortable.

"I'm sorry, I don't mean to be personal. It's just that

that seems early to be completely on your own. It must have been awfully lonely."

"No more than for someone in a family of ten, or a city of ten million," she said in a tone meant to put an end to his line of questioning. "There's a word in Portuguese, *saudade*, that has no direct translation in English. It means the feeling of missing someone you love who is gone. One feels this for the dead, but it has little to do with loneliness. Loneliness—"

But here suddenly she stopped, aghast. What had she been thinking of? Could she really be lecturing on death to a man who only two years before had lost his wife and only brother? How sensitive can you get? She had somehow for a moment forgotten. A wave of heat rushed to her cheeks.

"Go on," he said kindly.

"I—I don't know, it's really a matter of personal perspective, I didn't mean to sound—"

"You didn't."

"Well, I do sometimes . . . You see, my father was an alcoholic. I don't think that it was that bad when he and Dick knew each other, but he was very sick by the time he came back to the States and took me out of boarding school to live with him in Brazil. I took care of him until he sent me back to go to college, then just during the summers. We were on one level very close, but he grew worse and more difficult to live with until one night, in a drunken fit of depression, and, as I understood much later, self-hate, he crammed handfuls of my clothes into a suitcase and threw it and me out of the house. He was shrieking and crying. We both were. That was the last time we saw each other. I took a plane to New York the next day. Six weeks later I received a telegram from a colleague of his saying he was dead, that he'd shot himself in the head."

For a long moment, her words seemed to Galen to hang in the air between them. Why had she told him all this? Julian Baugh of all people. She had meant to atone for her indelicacy, not to strip herself bare.

"I'm very sorry," he said.

"Yes, me, too . . ." Galen fumbled with the handle of the door.

Julian leaned suddenly forward and would have kissed her—as it was he barely brushed her cheek with his lips—had Galen not maneuvered skillfully out of range and fairly leapt from the car. She murmured good night, threw the door shut, and was on the porch before the Jaguar's lights could splash against the bungalow to show her the way. She was halfway through the house before she heard the big engine start up again and the sleek car speed away.

Galen found her bedroom littered with shoes and the pieces of clothing that had accompanied William on his charge from her closet. The closet itself was a disaster. After slipping her shift over her head, she crawled in on her hands and knees to dredge it of its tangled contents. She was much too agitated for bed.

The incident with Julian had left her feeling exposed and a little angry, but whether more at Julian or at herself she was not sure. Several voices in her head were speaking at once. They were going something like this: It's bad enough that you went on about your father to a man you do not particularly trust, let alone like, but then to have him make a pass at you when you're done! Not only has he barely spoken a pleasant word with you until tonight but he's practically married, and suddenly he's trying to kiss you in the dark in his car? The nerve of the man! Yes, but why? Because you couldn't resist showing off during dinner. And how about that pathetic scene you drew of a father and daughter's last meeting? *He was shrieking and crying. We both were.* How could you *tell* him that? That was much worse than the kiss. You've never told anyone about that! Why *him*? So what if you were insensitive about his own personal loss, have you no sense of *proportion*?

Halfway out of the closet with a load of dresses and shoes, Galen had paused to listen to the dressing down that was running its course in her head. By the time the phone rang just behind her she was so absorbed in it that she jumped as if someone had spoken. It sounded horrendously loud at this time of night and, suddenly conscious of being half dressed, she looked quickly around. Half thinking it might be Julian, her voice was carefree to the point of hilarity.

"What's the matter with you?"

"Mara? Do you know what time it is? Is everything all right?"

"Yes, I'm sorry, but I knew you were up because you weren't home fifteen minutes ago. Are *you* all right? You sound a little off the wall."

"Thanks. Yes, I'm fine."

"Where were you?"

"Dinner at the Baughs'. Are you sure there's nothing wrong?"

"Absolutely. We just got back from Ipswich. Serge is circling the block trying to find a place to park. I just wanted to make sure you made it back okay."

"You were at the beach? At twelve o'clock at night?"

"We had drinks on the way home. I got scorched. You should have come. How was dinner?"

"Okay. Oh! Guess what—I met someone who knew Dad." Galen described her exchange with Richard Bowdoin as she continued to pull things from the closet.

"And were Scylla and Charybdis there?"

"As a matter of fact, yes, but we barely spoke. Carla ignored me completely and Julian was . . . civil." She did not tell her about the kiss. "He has a lovely son, though, which makes up for a lot."

"I don't know how, considering his mother died in the arms of his uncle and his father is making a play for his aunt. Gale, *what* are you doing? You sound like you're giving birth."

Cradling the receiver with her shoulder, Galen had crawled back into the closet for another load.

"Sorry—cleaning out my closet, if you can believe it."

"I bet they used the bungalow for trysts. You haven't found any paraphernalia, have you? I *miss* you, honey, when are you coming back?"

"I dunno, Friday I assume—I wonder who this is?"

"Who are you talking to? Lily, no doubt."

"No. I just found a photograph in the back of my closet. I wonder how long it's been here . . . There's a book here, too. Verse. Swinburne, don't you know . . . And a box."

"Locked with no key."

"No, open and empty."

"Sounds like the makings of an O. Henry story. What's it of?"

"Wood."

"No, the photograph."

"A man with a horse. I've seen this somewhere before . . . Huh. Let's see, nothing on the back. Nothing in the box. Nothing in the book. No money. No microfilm. No mateless emerald earring. Not so much as a map."

"Too bad. Hi, sweetheart! I'm talking to Gale. Listen, honey, I've got to go. Serge just got back and sends his love. We've got to eat."

"It's quarter to two in the morning."

"He's on Tokyo time. Call you later. Bye."

After hanging up the phone, Galen decided to leave the replacement effort for the morning and, soft leather-bound book in hand, dragged herself up into bed. Propping herself on a pillow, she opened it at random.

Life treads down love in flying,
  Time withers him at root;
Bring all dead things and dying,
  Reaped sheaf and ruined fruit,
Where, crushed by three days' pressure,
  Our three days' love lies slain;
And earlier leaf of pleasure,
  And latter flower of pain.

She turned to the first page. There was an inscription: "To CB, ever your love, JF."

Galen closed the book slowly and turned out the light. As tired as she was, sleep was a long way off.

7

In honor of the Bowdoins' arrival, Henry had declared Tuesday a day of rest. Galen and Lily were at the barn before the boys had finished their grain rounds. It seemed, however, that Galen was not the only one with a morning ride in mind. She counted six horses groomed and saddled in their stalls. If she hurried, she could be gone before they arrived, she thought. Group rides were not Galen's thing. She pulled Durometer's saddle off the wall, then hurried out of the barn and headed toward the annex where the black horse would be waiting.

After dropping the saddle by his stall she trotted down the aisle, with Lily at her heels, to fetch a hoof pick and brushes. She rounded the corner at the far end of the barn and stopped dead in her tracks. The scene that spread before her was the last thing she had expected to see.

"Oh! Hello" was all she could think of to say.

Lounging in the sun on a bale of hay with a plastic cup of coffee in one hand and an unlighted cigarette in the other was Caetano. This in itself was not so odd. But sitting

beside him in shirt sleeves and the pants of the suit she had
seen him in the night before was Julian. His jacket hung
from a nail on the wall. Judging from the heaviness of his
eyes and dark shadow on his jaw, he had slept little since
she had seen him last.

"*Bom dia!*" the boy hailed her gaily. "*Como vai?*"

"*Todo bem,* Caetano," Galen answered cautiously, "but
if you don't mind my saying so, you look awful." The boy
had obviously been up all night, as well. Her eyes went
involuntarily to Julian. She did not say "you, too," but she
might as well have. Julian let out a short, mirthless laugh.

"It's been a long night" was all he said, pulling at the
back of his neck and looking up at her with an ambiguous—was it ironic?—half smile.

Galen looked at them dubiously. If Julian had spent
the night carousing after dropping her off at the bungalow
last night, surely he would not have included Caetano.

"It appears so" was all she said.

The teenager quickly answered her question for her.

"Fair Lady colicked and we took turns keeping her on
her feet," he said with more than a touch of pride. He was
clearly relishing the sense of camaraderie with his boss.
"We only just put her away."

"Really," Galen said with some surprise. Fair Lady was
a once-beautiful, now-sagging twelve-year-old Thoroughbred mare stalled in the annex at the opposite end from
Durometer. Like Durometer until Galen had arrived, the little dapple-gray was no longer ridden, but for different reasons. According to Caetano, she had foundered four years
earlier during shipment from a show in Kentucky. It had
been the driver's fault: The temperature had been in the
nineties and he had never stopped to cool the horses out.
At any rate, Fair Lady had arrived home lame and had
never fully recovered. For the last four years she had done
little more than brush flies and luxuriate on the fine offer-
ings of the Winds. The mare could not even be bred. And

now she had kept not just the barn manager but the master up all night with a case of stomach cramps. Galen was singularly impressed.

"Is she all right?" she asked, looking hard at the man in the dress shirt and gray flannel pants, now smeared with dirt and barn dust. Spending an entire night nursing a lame horse that anybody else would have put down years ago was not something she would have expected of him.

"We think so," he said wearily. "She does this now and again. Coffee?"

"No, thanks. What happened to Pat and Mike? I mean, surely . . ." Galen's voice trailed off.

If Julian appreciated the fact that his personal attention to such a routine barn matter might strike Galen as strange, he evidently did not feel compelled to clear the mystery up.

"There was no point in dragging them over here for something we could do," he replied, laying a large hand casually on Caetano's shoulder. "How are you this morning?"

There was that look again.

"I'm fine. You, on the other hand, look like you could use some sleep."

"I've had a few hours, thanks to Caetano. You're joining us on our ride?"

Galen looked at him skeptically. It had not been lost on her that the big hunter Teton was among the horses saddled, but Julian did not look exactly fit for an outing.

"I wouldn't miss it for the world," he said, draining his coffee cup and getting slowly to his feet. He had obviously read her expression. "Particularly if you're joining us. Please come."

"I think I'd rather not—I'm not wild about group excursions."

"You're sure?"

"Yes."

When Galen went back into the main tack room for the running martingale she had forgotten, the first of the riding party could be heard trickling down from the house. His pear shape accentuated by an ill-fitting riding habit, Dick Bowdoin looked as if he had waddled out of a cartoon. He was pink-faced and puffing and expounding on something to poor Franny, who, Galen could see by the gentle, inattentive smile, was less than absorbed.

"Ahh, Ms. Galen Shaw," Dick said decorously on catching sight of her. "How lovely to see you this morning, and that you will be joining us for our ride. We tried to phone you but you must've come down already."

"I'm afraid—"

"Oh, my, *yes*, it's a long-standing Baugh-Bowdoin tradition! And, like Francis here, you're practically family."

"I don't think so, but I'll bridle your horses if you like. The boys seem to have done the rest."

"Nonsense, Galen, don't be a snob." This from Henry, who had appeared from the courtyard with Carla and Mrs. Bowdoin close at heel. "But be advised, there will be a race. Dick was a pony express rider in his last life."

Galen could just imagine.

"Do come," Peggy Bowdoin said with not a shred of conviction as she passed them on the way to find Gem, a docile chestnut mare reserved for Henry's less aggressive guests.

"Yes, Julian says you're a beautiful horsewoman," Carla added. Dressed for the Lord Beauford Hunt, the woman stood with her weight on one hip, absently tapping her gloved palm with the flat tail of a leather bat. "How lucky you are to be so talented at so many things."

Galen looked quickly at Carla, who was grinning serenely and blinking like a cat in the sun. Where, she wondered, did Carla think Julian had spent the night?

The two women gazed at each other for a long moment before Galen said anything. Her reply was finally a simple, restrained "Yes."

Franny gave a little cough. "You appear to be on your way out anyway," he suggested pointedly. Galen looked at him blankly, then realized what he was saying. And that it was true: Her refusal to join them was becoming more awkward by the moment.

"So you're going after all! Great!" Caetano said, fastening Durometer's bell boots and running a body brush over the horse's glistening flank. He grinned at Galen conspiratorially, then, cupping Durometer's ear with his hand, spoke into it in a low voice:

"They'll be eating your dirt, *amigo*."

"That's dust, Caetano."

"Don't you let this nice pretty lady down."

Galen laughed. Caetano had spent long hours helping her retrain Durometer and was as fond of the big bold horse as she. He also appreciated that this would be their grand debut, for both horse and rider.

"You are nutty in the *cabeça*," she said warmly, knocking on his black head as if it were a door. "You need some sleep. I can't believe you and Julian . . . Caetano, has he. . . ? Is this the sort of thing he *does*?"

"What do you mean?"

"Well, I can't believe Julian stayed up all night for Fair Lady. I mean, isn't that what he pays you and the stable boys for? I can see his *maybe* personally supervising something like that with Teton—besides his being a twenty-thousand-dollar animal, he's Julian's own horse. But Fair Lady was never even his."

"No, she was his wife's."

"Oh—I see," she said, but in point of fact she most definitely did not. The fact that it was Johanna's horse made the least sense of all.

Galen sat deeply, her hands working but her long legs and erect shoulders perfectly still, as Durometer sprang into a supple, sidestepping jog at the first sight of the other horses assembled in the courtyard. Her white T-shirt and britches dramatized the blackness of his body, which gleamed with the finish of satin under his bunched and rippling muscles as they danced around the corner of the main barn into full sun.

If Galen had a vanity, it was about her riding, and she knew her training had paid off and that she and the young horse showed each other off to good effect. The reaction from the riding party was, however, nothing like what she had expected. Heads turned to stare, but the cheerless silence that descended on the group gave Galen the impression that they looked not so much in appreciation as in astonishment, and for the second time in two days she had the vague sense of having stepped outside the bounds of some privately prescribed code of conduct. Or did she only imagine that Carla and Margaret Bowdoin exchanged meaningful glances? Perhaps she was not expected to come after all, she thought. Perhaps her entrance was overdone, or perhaps her britches were too tight. Perhaps she was becoming paranoid.

Julian's reaction as he emerged from the shadows of the barn at this point was at least as unsettling. Looking up at her for the first time, he stopped so suddenly that the big bay he was leading had to throw his head to avoid bumping him. But the look of—it was more than surprise—on his face was quickly replaced by a weary but genuinely warm smile as he called, "Hello, again! I'm glad you've changed your mind."

Henry led the way out of the stable yard, followed by Carla and Mrs. Bowdoin as a pair, Franny and Dick, who had resumed their earlier discussion, Galen, Lily, and finally Julian. They walked as far as the pine trees on the far side of the hayfield that lay across the street from the barn. Here they picked up a well-groomed bridle path and broke into a trot.

The needles muffled their footfalls in the way of freshly fallen snow and, except for the unintelligible chatter of women's voices and jingle of curb chains, the group moved almost silently through the trees. The air was warm and fragrant with the sweet green smell of pine. Flecks of light splashed on them through the foliage. Overhead a squadron of jays jeered a solitary blue-black crow.

The beauty of the morning, however, was wasted on Galen, who was so consumed by the scene in the stable yard she was hardly aware of where she was. It was not until Durometer cut short her mental flight by leaning suddenly hard on her hands that she even realized that Teton had come abreast. Glancing over, she saw that Julian was studying Durometer. She also saw at once that the man was an accomplished equestrian.

"You and Durometer seem very well suited, Galen," he said, brightly, his gaze now on her. "You've devoted some time to him."

"Thank you, but the talent is all his." She looked over at him. Was it Julian's lack of sleep, or was it only in Galen's mind—knowing now how he had spent his night—that he seemed somehow a little more human? At any rate, she found herself feeling less self-conscious about having been so open with him the night before. As for the kiss—she glanced up at the undulating white-blond hair of the woman trotting ahead of her—it merely served her notice: Julian Baugh was still a man who believed he could have whatever he wanted, evidently whenever the spirit moved him. However, he would find in Galen a woman who took particular pleasure in having a say in these matters. She was no prude, but she was no man's trophy, either.

"Don't be modest," he was saying.

"Far from it," she said, echoing his self-assured tone.

"He's one of the nicest horses I've ever ridden, certainly the best horse in your barn."

A smile flashed across Julian's face, but not so much at her as if at some private joke. He looked as if he might be going to say something but seemed to change his mind. The group had slowed to a walk to cross a wooden bridge. Emerging in a blackberry field on the other side, they then broke in turns into a canter. Julian had gone ahead over the bridge but was now collecting Teton to fall back beside her. Relaxed but motionless, the man looked as if he'd been born in the saddle. He also looked particularly attractive in the tight, rust-colored britches and black field boots into which he had changed. They cantered side by side for a moment before he spoke. When he did, the subject was the same.

"You've been jumping him?" There was a curl at the corner of his lips; his eyes were laughing. He was driving at something.

"Indoors."

"High?"

"Four feet."

"Combinations?"

"Three-six, three-nine."

"Cross country?"

Galen looked over at him. "A little."

"So, Galen Shaw," he said after a pause, "you think Durometer is a better horse than Teton?"

Galen knew she was being baited but could not yet see the hook.

She answered cautiously, "Ye-es. Teton may be more polished, more experienced, but Durometer—" Before she could finish Julian erupted in the same short, deep laugh she had heard at the dining-room table the night before.

"Forgive me, but do you believe in ghosts?" He did not wait for a reply. "Durometer is simply a pretty face and he's turned your head." He was mocking her, but good-naturedly. The man might be arrogant but he had his charm.

"He's good-looking *and* he's a better horse than Teton."

He laughed again and said, "I challenge you to prove me wrong."

The hook.

Galen considered it for a moment. Hard-pressed to refuse a challenge of any kind, she found the chance to test her abilities as a rider and trainer against such an accomplished opponent almost irresistible. Her hand might never again be so strong. Durometer was not just any horse. What she had said to Julian was true, she had never known another like him. Warning bells where the man was concerned would have to fall for the moment on deaf ears. After all, Caetano would never let her hear the end of it if she turned him down.

"What," she asked at length, "must one do?"

The others had stopped at the top of a sagging field fifty yards wide and almost three-quarters of a mile long. It was imaginatively called the Long Field. Dick was about to have his race.

"Are you two ready?" he called to Julian and Galen, who caught up as the first four were spreading themselves out along an imaginary starting line. "Peg and Carla get a five-count jump then it's every man for himself."

"Jules, darling, come over here by me," Carla called melodically.

Galen slipped Durometer in between Franny and Dick Bowdoin and, knowing the kind of explosive effect such a thing was bound to have on her horse, began pulsing her hands to try to get the stallion's attention.

"Any time, *ladies!*" Henry shouted like a circus ring-master. With a squawk the two were off at a choppy canter. "One, two . . ."

"Whoa, Durometer," Galen murmured, flexing the animal's head left and right.

"Four . . . five and *go*!"

With a rumble of the earth, ripple of flank muscles, and hiss of belly-high grass, Dick, Henry, and Franny were off. Before they were two strides away, Durometer was up on his hind legs, fighting for his head and, not getting it, throwing his shoulder in the direction of the runaway crowd. He bucked and danced, but after several tight circles was quivering all over but back under control.

"You're all right?" Julian was sitting calmly atop an expectant but sublime Teton ten yards to Galen's right. "Okay, then, whenever you're ready."

When Galen released her hold on Durometer, he was off as if flung from a slingshot. So, she could see out of the corner of her eye, was Teton. After that she heard rather than saw him on her flank as they swept down the field. Lily, who had chased the other horses halfway across to the other end before she realized Galen was not among them and had started back, gave an exclamatory bark as they flew past.

The Well Gate, which Julian had chosen as their finish line, was the western entrance to the stable grounds, almost two miles away. She would have to pace Durometer. Three-quarters of the way across the Long Field she brought him down to a speed he could sustain. This brought Julian up beside her, but, having the same thing in mind, he did not pass. They were thus neck and neck when they swung right at the far end, through a break in the stone wall and into the abutting Ox Bow Meadow where the rest of the group had come to a flush-faced stop.

Here Julian put on a burst of speed and, with Galen just a length behind, tore through the riding party like a fox through a flock of hens. The rupture of squeals was only momentarily audible over the shuddering earth.

The meadow was small. In a matter of seconds they were across it and into the woods on a wagon trail that would wind back to the barn. Her mind racing ahead over the terrain, Galen remembered that the trail they were on forked around the next bend. The road to the left was smooth and flat and ideal for an all-out run. The path to the right narrowed, plunged down a hill, and cut through several fields. It would mean a series of walls and fences, three and a half feet or higher, but would take half a mile off the course. As they neared the turnoff, she could see that Julian, who had steadily increased his lead, was veering left. He knew his advantage and was counting on a test of endurance. Galen, however, knew hers and, with all her might, she drove Durometer sharply right.

She was barely at the bottom of the hill where the path swung left again to run briefly parallel with the main road, when she heard a resounding "Ha!" Julian had heard her turn off and was wasting no time (and sparing no safety) cutting his own path down through the woods toward her. Teton leapt on to the trail only twenty feet behind Durometer. In a burst of speed he closed the distance to a few yards, and they cleared a fallen tree trunk resting three feet above the ground almost in tandem. As she landed on the other side, Galen quickly realized two things. First that Teton needed more room for his fences, which forced Julian to pull him up before a jump, and took longer to recover his speed afterward. Second, that Durometer would do anything she asked. If Pegasus ever lived he was incarnate in this animal. Galen pushed their speed.

Neck and neck again, both horses had to slow to clear a big double rail into the apple orchard. Durometer was away faster, but Teton closed again and surged past her down the well-packed grass track between the evenly planted trees. The next wall would put them in the Ice Pond Meadows, two rectangular hayfields separated by an enormous vine-covered wall with a tractor-wide gap in the middle. The far field emptied out through the Well Gate. Entering the first field on the same side as the gate, they could leave the second only by running a long U around the wall. Whoever made it first through the narrow pass would surely be first across the finish.

Julian was at the stone wall/hedge combination at the end of the orchard ahead of her. Galen asked Durometer to take it early, and by the time the horses had cleared the jump and were back on stride, she had narrowed his lead a bit, but she knew it would not be enough. Durometer's surge in speed when she gave the stallion his head was matched by Teton's, and, glancing back over his shoulder, Julian's grin told her he knew it, too.

There was only one way to beat Julian to the Well Gate. Thinking back on it, she might not have done it again. It was not so much a question of risk as of fear. The wall was not impossibly high—at four and a half feet she knew intellectually that Durometer should have been capable of clearing it—but it was higher than anything she had asked him to do before. Wide and covered with a spreading tangle of wild grapevine, it was a menacing sight; had she been on another horse, steering him into it would have been unthinkable. But the black horse's fleetness and courage as they flew across the rows of mowed hay gave her a sudden sense of wind under her wings. Pulling on the reins until her shoulders ached, she turned Durometer away from the man and horse they were chasing and drove him toward the big wall. It took only a moment for him to understand. Then his ears shot forward, his head jerked up, and he hammered the ground with his feet. Galen picked her spot, rode him in, held her breath, and let him go. With arms outstretched, fists clutching his mane, and her body rounded over his neck, they rose together as if heaving themselves into flight. It felt as if they would never touch down.

When, after what seemed to Galen an eternity, they thundered back to earth, Julian had only just rounded the edge of the wall. He could never close their angle on the finish in time. With twenty yards to go Galen asked Durometer for more, and with a burst of speed she did not know he still had, they shot forward and through the Well Gate alone.

Slapping the black horse's drenched vein-embroidered neck, Galen turned Durometer in a slow arc to erode his speed. The wind had teared her eyes and made a complete mess of her hair. Her throat and arms glistened with sweat. She looked over at Julian with a brilliant grin. Cantering toward her with a graceful looseness that allowed Teton to toss him about in the saddle, Julian smiled back broadly. The dark eyes that so often shielded his thoughts were unnervingly alive. The man looked exhilarated and all at once unspeakably handsome.

"You cheated!" he cried as he pulled up beside her. "I demand a rematch."

"You wouldn't dare!"

They were both laughing. The horses puffed heavily as they dropped from a jog to an extended walk. Galen and Julian's stirrups clanked together. The air between them crackled like machine-gun fire.

"I'll grant you're the better rider."

"I am not! I am on the better horse!"

"All right then, Galen Shaw, you win. Rue the day, but Durometer is the better horse—but only under your hand." Julian had leaned over, taken up Durometer's loose rein, and stopped both horses. But whatever he had in mind to say, or perhaps do, Galen was not going to find out. At the rumble of horses coming at a gallop, Julian looked past her and dropped the stallion's rein. She turned to see the various shapes of the riding party scudding across the Ice Pond Meadow, hailing them as they came. They were quickly upon them and buzzing with questions. Julian did not look Galen's way again and rode home at Carla's side.

*   *   *

"What did I tell you!" Caetano grinned gleefully as he poured two cups of potent Brazilian *cafezinho* out of the child's *Wizard of Oz* Thermos he carried with him to the barn. It must have been the same batch he and Julian had been drinking earlier: It was no longer hot. But it hardly mattered.

"*O vencedor!*" the beautiful blue-eyed boy saluted.

"The victor!" Galen smiled, brushing her cup against his.

"*Saúde!*"

"To your health."

Squatting in the sawdust to massage liniment oil into Durometer's cannons, Galen recounted the details of the contest to Caetano over the stall door. As the rest of the horses had taken up the center aisle of the big barn, he was rubbing Teton down on the annex cross-ties.

"It's a wonder that Teton even kept up," she called. "I've had Durometer out regularly, but Teton should hardly be fit enough for what we just put him through."

"He should be okay. I've had him on a lunging schedule for two and a half weeks now. He and Jazz." Jazz was Carla's mare.

The ball of extension wrap froze in Galen's hand. "You have?"

"Yes, Mr. Baugh wanted them ready."

"Henry?"

"No, Julian."

"I see." She looked down again and slowly resumed wrapping the leg she had been working on. "So this was not exactly a spontaneous visit."

"I don't know."

Galen was silent for a moment. She could hear Caetano unfastening the cross-tie clips from Teton's halter.

"Caetano," she said slowly, "why is William so afraid of horses?"

There was infinitesimal pause.

"He fell into a stall once with one of them."

"Was he hurt?"

"No, no. Just scared."

"The poor child! How did it happen?"

"I don't know. I only found him there when I came in to grain. I heard this noise, I thought it was a puppy, you know that little sound they make? And there was the kid in a little ball in the corner of Mars's stall."

"Mars!" Galen stood up and looked over the door at him. Mars was an old stallion that proved to be such a menace, trying to bite or kick anyone or thing that came near his stall, that Galen herself had moved him to another barn her first week at the Winds.

"Mars," she repeated, shaking her head. "It's a miracle he wasn't killed. Wasn't anybody with him? What was he doing down here alone?"

"Mrs. Baugh—Carla—was taking care of him for his mother and he disappeared. She looked everywhere, the houses, everywhere. She told me about it when I came in and then went out looking for him in her car. That's when I found him."

"How did it happen? I mean, what did he say happened?"

"Actually, he wouldn't say anything. In fact, he didn't talk at all for a long time. I think he was climbing on the hay bales and fell in. The door was bolted from the outside."

"And you took him home?"

"Well, no, right after I got him out she—Mrs. Baugh—Carla came in, I guess to search the barn again. You should have seen the look on her face. She was pale as a ghost. I thought she was going to faint."

"Caetano, when *was* this?"

Galen saw a slight hesitation.

"A couple of years ago."

"Before the crash?"

"Yes. Well, actually, it was the day they left."

Squatting back down in the cedar chips in a stunned silence, Galen found nothing to say and presently heard the cross-ties clatter against the walls and then Caetano lead Teton out. For a long moment she just sat there consumed by the unthinkable image of William cowering in the corner of Mars's stall. It was several minutes before she resumed bandaging Durometer's legs and then only absently as she thought of the trauma that had been visited already on so young a child.

A man's voice spoke to her suddenly from directly overhead. "There you are," it said. It landed on her ears like a thunderclap and, even as she realized whose it was, she screamed. Durometer leapt away from her as if she had stuck him with a pin, snapping the chain on the lead shank and knocking her flat on her buttocks. From this vantage point, she looked up to see Julian's head roll back with a resounding laugh. Seeing her expression, he did his best to stifle it and, with a quick apology, let himself in and extended his hand.

"Damn!" Galen muttered, and got up to chase the bandage Durometer had trailed across the stall. Julian grabbed the horse's head and held him still while she untangled the mess. She was covered with shavings when she straightened finally to face him.

"I'm awfully sorry," he was saying. The laughter lingered in his bloodshot eyes. "I had no idea I'd give you such a scare. You must have been miles away."

"Not miles. But don't think anything of it. The truth is I do that a lot."

"Really."

For whatever reason he was standing there, Galen realized with a minor shock how much she had wanted to see him again before their extraordinary time in the fields was overrun by the plodding earthbound events of the day.

"I've come at the behest of my father," he said, holding the horse while she finished the unwrapped leg. "To convey an invitation to dinner. He insists on being able to toast you for putting me in my place. And Uncle Dick wants someone to talk to."

She straightened and glanced at him while she slipped off Durometer's halter. She could see there was something of their shared excitement still in his eyes. His hair was tossed. As tired as Julian clearly was, his face looked almost boyishly beautiful. It's not like he's asking me for a date, she told herself. It couldn't hurt.

"Thank you," she said.

"Seven-thirty then."

"Fine."

"Do you need a lift?"

"No! I mean, I'll drive."

"It's no trouble."

"I'd rather, thanks."

"Seven-thirty then?"

"All right."

With a half-dozen outfits lying like limp lettuce on the bed behind her, Galen stood in front of the mirror in a beryl-green rayon dress. It hung with elegant ease from her bare shoulders. She sashed it at a flattering angle across her hips. She shifted her weight. She unsashed it. Sashed it again. This, she said to herself, would have to do. She put her hair up. Took it down. Swept it to one side. Took it down again. She stared at her face in the mirror. What, she asked herself, *are* you doing?

Galen need not have worried. Not about her appearance, at any rate. Something of the day's excitement lingered in her face as well. Her cheeks were gently flushed with sun and exercise. Her sea-green eyes seemed almost to glow, as if lighted from behind. She was nothing short of radiant.

With a last glance, she turned her back on her reflection, dug a pair of sandals out of the closet, pulled a white linen jacket off a hanger, and threw a brush and lipstick in a handbag. She did not, however, head for the door. Rather, she sat down on the bed, pulled open the sidetable drawer, and took out the photograph of the man and the colt that she had found in her closet the night before.

Galen knew now why the picture had looked familiar. She had seen a copy of it at Henry's cottage in East Cutty. The light-haired man, who wore the same waggish grin she saw on his brother at the Well Gate today, was Colin. After bending up the metal clips on the back and sliding the picture out, Galen found what she already knew would be there. The frame had concealed the front foot of the young horse, which was now visible and clearly ringed along the pasten with a thin band of white. The colt, who Henry had said was Colin's prize, was of course Durometer. The strange reaction in the stable yard that morning was perhaps not so strange after all.

8

As was so often the case, Galen's draw in the first-round match-up of guests was easily the least interesting person in the room, and she found herself saddled with the onerous task of keeping her attention fixed on an excrutiatingly dull companion.

He was in this case a little man, shorter than she, with wide staring eyes and a small pouty mouth that barely moved when he spoke. His name was Jack Crocker but he could have been Peter Lorre's younger brother.

"My, my, so you're a newspaper woman," he was saying in a flat nasal voice. "A real live Brenda Starr. Now, my son worked on his school newspaper. *I* think he was very good."

(The conversation directly behind her was going something like this: "Gene is running a resupply operation to the African National Congress guerrillas through Angola . . .")

"His sister went to Stockbridge School of Agriculture at U Mass," Jack Crocker went on, "to study *shrubs*."

("... before he had to get out he was organizing student and labor strikes in Cape Town in the beginning of the eighties ...")

"At least she went to college. My nephew—that's my brother's son—took off to California right out of high school to open a health food store for *pets*."

("... He was also behind the first round of talks between the ANC leadership and South African businessmen a couple of years ago ...")

"Idiot pothead drove the whole darn way with his girlfriend in a Volkswagen beetle."

("... his wife was killed and he lost a leg in a South African bombing raid on an ANC camp in Mozambique.")

"Kids these days. So do you think you might find the time to talk with him?"

"Who?"

"My son. He sure would love a chance to talk to a real reporter."

"Oh, yes, of course."

Galen's fish-eyed companion was a fraction of the four middle-aged couples invited to celebrate the Bowdoins' early return to Stover. Cut from the same cloth, the Norrises, Crockers, Sherbrookes, and Blakes were weathered-looking mainliners whose fortunes had come from imports, investment banking, inheritance, and inheritance, respectively. The men had ruddy retiree tans from golf and sailing and liver spots from half a century of weekends at their summer homes on Cape Cod, Nantucket, and Martha's Vineyard. The women were large-boned and well dressed, with the kind of sturdy good looks that fell about halfway between Tippi Hedren and Margaret Thatcher. They wore magnificent engagement rings and sensible shoes and had the proud, healthy appearance of well-provided-for wives who spent their summers garden clubbing, grandparenting, organizing benefits, and meeting twice a week for ladies' doubles. Galen caught snatches of their conversation.

". . . I never think I'm really on vacation unless I can't drink the water . . ."

". . . You'd think there was something *else* they could do with all their millions . . ."

". . . Darling, he would have failed in the part if it was the ass-end of the Questing Beast . . ."

". . . She may have been a drunk in life but she was a *dream* in death—I've never *seen* a more serene corpse . . ."

There was something unidentifiable, like a tone or a hue, not too stuffy, never quite ribald, that tied them together. They had perhaps grown alike over the years of making money and raising children next door to one another. Maybe it was just the Stover look. Whatever it was, it seemed to Galen that the flock was as much the focus of celebration as the return of two of its lambs.

With the reunion gathering steam, Galen felt increasingly superfluous. As no one else seemed about to cut in, and without an excuse to interrupt, it appeared she was stuck with Jack Crocker, who was telling her now about his daughter's failed first attempt to landscape their front yard. Galen looked around helplessly. She had hoped to talk more with Dick Bowdoin about the time he had spent with her father but had seen right away that access to the guest of honor would be too limited for a private audience. Henry was similarly engaged. Franny had been detained in town. Carla, who had introduced her to Penny Sherbrooke as "our own National Velvet," was keeping a discreet distance, and Julian was nowhere to be seen. It was going to be a long evening.

At the point of regretting having come, however, an angel of mercy appeared at her elbow.

"Where's Li-ly?"

William was tugging at her dress. She could have kissed him. At the next break in Jack Crocker's limping monologue, Galen gave him a lovely smile, said "Excuse me for just a moment," and led William quickly out of the room. She hoped vainly that she had not appeared too eager.

William had guessed right: Lily was sitting on the front step staring expectantly up at the door as if she had just rung the bell. Happy to prolong their absence from the party, however, Galen and William agreed to walk to the wading pool on the west side of the house. It was just after eight. The night was overcast and only slowly cooling, but gray mist was beginning to rise off the fields in the distance and the lawn on the near grounds was already wet. They left their shoes on the steps of the western terrace, and William led Galen away from the house down a wide path between two overgrown beds of roses.

"My mother helped Grandpa Baugh plant all these flowers," he said with an all-encompassing sweep of his arm. "That was before I was born. They have prickers so you can't pick them."

"What kind are they?"

"Roses. Red, white, and yellow. She used to put one in my room every day."

"Did you spend a lot of time here growing up?"

"Yup. I lived here."

"You like it here."

"Uh-huh. Daddy said we might move back to the United States."

Galen looked quickly at the boy. "Did he?"

At the end of the path they came upon a walled garden in the center of which was a reflecting pool overgrown with water lilies. A stone madonna and child knelt at one end. They looked alabaster in the fading light. The child held a scaly fish in his hands that spurted the water that filled the pool.

"My mother said that this was her and this was me," William said, patting the softly rounded shoulder of the woman, then laying his small hand on the head of the child.

Galen sat down on the marble bench at the side of the pool and watched the boy. He had begun sidling along the pool's edge, peering into the water.

"But it doesn't really look like her or me. There are fish in here, you know. Goldfish. Big ones. You should see them."

Galen leaned back against the wall.

"And frogs sometimes. You can hear them."

"I'll show you how to catch one," she said, closing her eyes. But in the next instant she opened them again and got up in an effort to shake herself free of a train of thought that could only lead to trouble. She glanced back toward the house and sighed. "Sometime when I'm not wearing a dress."

"I have a net."

"You won't need it, not if you're very patient and quiet."

They were standing side by side now, stooped at the waist, hands on knees, staring into the blackening water as still as the statues at the other end of the pond.

"Like a leopard stalking a monkey," William said.

Galen threw him a sidelong glance. Henry, who forbade his grandson to watch television, had never owned a set, but Mae, she knew, kept one on in the kitchen and favored nature shows while she was fixing meals.

"We can pretend we're hunting monkeys," he whispered without looking up.

"There's an easier way to catch a monkey," Galen whispered back, peering again into the water.

"What?"

"You see, monkeys are very greedy, so all you need is a gourd and a string and some peanuts." William was looking at her now. "You cut a hole in the gourd—you know what a gourd is, good—just big enough for a monkey's hand and put the peanuts inside. Then you tie the gourd to a tree with the string. The monkey comes along, reaches inside for the peanuts, and grabs them in his fist. The problem is the hole is too small to get his fist out and he's too greedy to let go of the peanuts, so he's stuck."

"Really?" Apparently William had not seen this episode.

"Yup."

They looked at each other. There was no wind, no movement, no sound, until the voice came to them from the entrance of their enchanted enclosure.

"Have you two lost something or have the faeries cast a spell on you and turned you both to stone?" it asked, bringing them bolt upright. Something in his stance told her that Julian had been observing them in silence for some time before he spoke.

"Daddy! What are *you* doing here?"

"Looking for you. What are you doing here?"

"Looking for frogs!"

"Find any?"

"Not yet."

"Well, don't let me interrupt."

"I'm afraid it's grown too dark," Galen said. "Perhaps we've been away from the party for too long."

A wave of distant laughter reached them on a light breeze.

"I don't think so," Julian said. "But dinner is about to be served." Galen could not see his face but, judging from his voice, his spirits were high.

"I think it's time to go back," she said, laying a hand on William's shoulder. "We can look some more tomorrow."

William looked with disappointment at his father.

"Miss Shaw is right," Julian said firmly. "Now be careful you don't abuse her generosity."

The strange comment brought Galen's head around, but Julian's face was in shadows and she could only guess what he had meant by it.

"Come on," she said to William. Taking his hand, she led him toward the lights of the house. But as she passed by Julian, she felt a hand on her elbow and William's hand pulled gently out of hers. Holding her arm, Julian leaned over to his son and said quietly, "Run along to the house, William. Miss Shaw and I will be up in a minute."

Pulling her elbow free, she opened her mouth to speak but Julian cut across her protest.

"Please, Galen," he said in a low, earnest tone. William was looking at her now. She closed her mouth and gave him a little nod.

"I'll be up in a minute," she said.

With a reluctant glance at his father, the boy turned and trotted up the path. Julian watched his son's outline dance away in the light before finally turning to Galen, who had been watching him. Seeing her wary look, he smiled apologetically.

"I hope you'll forgive the intrusion," he said, turning away from her and taking a step back into the garden, "but I wanted to get a chance to talk with you. I was afraid you'd left the party. I realize we can be a little dull."

Galen said nothing but watched him as he strolled casually toward the pool. Whatever he had in mind, she was not about to follow him into the humid shadows of this summer night. As attractive, and sometimes charming, as he was, Galen had no reason to trust Julian Baugh. Or, for that matter, herself.

He paused at the edge of the pool, hands in his pockets, with the contented air of someone taking in a grand view.

"This is a lovely place, isn't it?" he said.

"Beautiful."

"I used to play here as a boy." Galen could not imagine Julian Baugh as a boy. "I imagined I was in a castle."

She said nothing.

"We had a different fountain then, a bronze lion, which no one liked but me. As you can see, its detractors had their way. Children are funny, aren't they?"

"Yes. But this is not what you wanted to talk to me about."

"No, it isn't."

He swung slowly around to look at her. She had waited at the edge of the garden and he began to meander back toward her. He seemed to be in a strange humor; he was perhaps suffering from lack of sleep.

"How is my father's book coming?" he asked, as one might inquire about the weather.

"Very well," she said cautiously. The elliptical approach she could do without.

He stopped very close to her. Here it comes, she thought.

"And how have you found living here?"

"Excuse me?"

"Have you found it in any way unpleasant being here?"

"What is it that you're driving at?" she asked carefully, taking a step back.

"Please," he said, catching her hand but dropping it before she had to pull it free. "What I've come to say is this: I've not always been very fair to you. I confess I was not entirely polite on our first meeting. It's not important that you understand why, but if I've never apologized I would like to now. I wish, in fact, to apologize for in whatever way I or any member of my family have not made you feel welcome."

"Is that what you meant by telling William not to 'abuse my generosity'? The comment was entirely inappropriate."

"Perhaps it was, but you needn't look like that. I'm quite sincere."

The merits of his apology aside, Galen was more interested in putting some distance between them. She turned away as she spoke.

"I appreciate the gesture," she said, walking toward the pool—he was blocking her way out of the garden—"but I assure you it's not necessary."

"I believe it is. But if you won't accept an apology, you've been a good friend to my father as well as a good writing partner, he seems to value you greatly as both, and for that I wish you would accept my"—he glanced toward the house—"our thanks."

"Your *thanks!*" This touched a nerve. Galen swung around to face him. "Julian, your father pays me to write for him, and as for my friendship with him, gratuity from you is misplaced, to say the least. Let's understand one another. It's in spite of you that I'm here."

"Is that what you think?" At first Julian looked taken aback, but then a smile began to spread across his face. Far from being defensive, he seemed to be enjoying himself. "I'll admit, at first I thought you might be trying to take advantage of my father."

"Yes," she said, smiling herself but giving no ground. "You made that abundantly clear."

"But you must know I abandoned that idea long before you even found out who he was."

"Is that why you bundled him off to Stover on your surprise visit to the beach? And, of course, you know nothing of the 'misplaced' note he left me saying good-bye and telling me where I could find him?"

"What misplaced note?"

"Tell me, did my coming to the Winds have nothing whatever to do with your sudden decision to drop in?"

"As a matter of fact, I came as soon as I heard you were here. But not for the reasons you think."

"Oh? Not to secure the family fortune?"

"No, Galen Shaw, the family fortune is safe from you."

"To what, then, do we owe the honor of your extended stay?"

"You don't know?"

She glanced up and caught the amused look. Galen had had several fantasies about telling Julian Baugh off for his insulting behavior toward her during their first three encounters. This was not one of them.

"Should I?" she asked.

"Yes, you should. And you would by now if you didn't look like you wanted to take my head off whenever I came near. Unless safe atop a snorting stallion—"

"*Fast* snorting stallion."

"Fast snorting stallion, you're very difficult to approach. Why is that, I wonder? Have I been that much of an ugly boor?"

"Is this a seduction?"

"What would you say if it was?"

"I'd say why don't we ask Carla? Whose thanks, I take it, I am also to accept."

"*Carla?*"

"You remember her, Tyrolean blonde, about my height, comes as a pair—along with you."

"So *that's* it. Wherever did you get that idea? Carla and I aren't lovers. We've never even held hands." Julian laughed. "But I'm flattered that you noticed."

"It was hard to miss."

"I see."

Galen said nothing, but the cat was out of the bag.

"Listen to me," Julian said. "There has never been anything between Carla and me. Not, at any rate, what you imagine. Carla and I have become especially close friends in the last few—"

"It really isn't any of my business," Galen said as a farewell gesture to an uncomplicated life.

"I'd like to change that," he said, taking a step nearer.

"I'm very clear about how I feel about Carla. And it's something very different from how I . . ."

"From how you what?"

The smile deepened the lines at the corners of his mouth, and he reached to touch her face. "When I first saw you through the screen door of the beach house, you looked like a drowned rat, albeit a disturbingly attractive one. I was very angry at the time and, to make matters worse, for the next three weeks I could not get you out of my mind. By the time I found you on my father's porch with that silly turban and white nose, and you looked at me as if you wanted to kill me, all I could think about was what it would feel like to kiss those beautiful lips. That, my dear, was two months ago. If I go one more minute without doing so, I think I shall scream."

As he spoke he leaned slowly toward her and now lightly pressed her lips with his. His skin was warm and his touch surprisingly gentle. A shiver raced the length of Galen's spine, and with an inner moan she closed her eyes. With that his arms came around her, and as he pulled her body to him he covered her mouth with his. Galen, whose knees felt as if they were about to give way, did her best to kiss him back, but it was at this point that they heard someone on the path. By the time Carla came into view— or they did—Julian had put three feet between them.

"What are you *doing*, darling? Dinner is on," Carla said. Her voice could not have sounded less accusatory, although Galen was sure she had seen them. Her eyes went to Galen and back without so much as a flicker. The woman, Galen thought, had style. "Good evening, Galen."

"I took advantage of Galen's frog-hunting expedition to speak with her alone." He was as innocent sounding as she.

"Of course, well," Carla said pleasantly, hooking Galen's arm with her own and starting the group up the path, "the rest will have to wait. Mae has laid out an absolutely gorgeous spread. She'll kill you if you let it get cold."

By the time they were at the steps of the terrace, Carla had released Galen and had taken Julian's arm. Nobody but William noticed the threesome enter by the side door and slip back into the commerce of the evening.

It seemed an eternity, but shortly after eleven the party had wound down enough for Galen to get away. On returning to the house—and its gossipy flock of friends—she had been afraid Julian would try to talk to her. She was not sure whether she was more relieved or disappointed that he did not. When their paths crossed—invariably surrounded by guests—he was formal and politely conversational; in saying good night—surrounded by Carla—he said only that he was pleased she had come. She could tell from the way he looked at her, however, that it was not the last she would see of him.

Galen was only vaguely aware that a warm rain had begun to fall at some point during the evening. She was unprepared, on opening the front door, for the torrent of drops that were pelting the foliage and bouncing off the steaming ground. Turning back inside, Galen caught Carla crossing the hall and asked her if she might borrow an umbrella.

"Oh, of course," she said solicitously, rummaging through the hall closet. "But will a mack do?" She produced a woman's trenchcoat, obviously a spare, twenty years out of style. "It will at least protect your lovely dress. I'm afraid it's all I've got. You do have your car, don't you? Good."

By the time she arrived home, Galen's hair was wet, but her shoes, which she had carried, and her clothes were dry. As she draped the dripping coat on a hanger on her porch, her eyes fell on a name tag sewn inside the collar. The legend leapt up at her in the mildly shocking way a familiar face jumps out of a crowd. JOHANNA FAIRCHILD. Judging from the style, it was probably hers in college, perhaps before then, Galen thought. A tall, thin teenager with shiny red hair and creamy skin appeared with unnerving clarity before her eyes. Musing on the various possibilities of William's mother as a girl, it took a minute before Galen made the connection. While it carried no real surprise, the moment of recognition still came with a jolt. *Of course,* she whispered out loud. The initials in the book of verse—CB and JF: To Colin Baugh, ever your love, Johanna Fairchild.

9

"Are you in love?"

"What!" Galen's head whipped around with a start.

"Or are you troubled by something?" Henry asked, looking across his bifocals at her like a teacher at an errant pupil. He placed a thick smooth hand on the back of hers.

"No, not at all. My mind just wandered. It's nothing, really."

"We don't have to finish this today, my dear. Not if you're not up to it."

"I'm fine. Honestly."

"Hmm" was all he said, replaced his pipe and went back to the page of manuscript that Galen and he were editing. They had been working on a chapter for most of the morning, and Galen had to struggle to keep her eyes from the blues and yellows of the gleaming day framed by the French windows of Henry's study. Her mind was on the news William had told her upon returning from Boston the day before. He had been enrolled in school in Stover, and he and his father were moving back to the States permanently. Henry had confirmed the story and said that Julian was expected back at the Winds in three to four weeks.

In the week since the party, Galen had not seen Julian. The morning after she had found a note he had slid under the door of the bungalow when she got back from having breakfast in the village.

G.

I'm sorry to have missed seeing you before being called away. I would not have, had it not been quite so urgent. Our parting last night was somewhat less personal than I had hoped. Perhaps our reunion will be more so.

I'm afraid I can't yet say when that will be. Will call as soon as I know for sure. Will call regardless.

If I never got the chance to tell you, last night, however brief, was worth the wait.

J.

It was neither long nor torrid, but judging from the scrawl, Galen was willing to believe Julian had had little time to write it. He had left William behind, which suggested to her that he had made his decision to move back before he had left. If this was the case, why, she wondered, had he said nothing to her? It was perhaps even stranger that he had said nothing to Henry, that the news did not come until the following weekend. Whether Julian had tried to telephone the bungalow, Galen had no way of knowing, as she had spent the weekend with Mara in the city.

Whatever the timing, it had not come as bad news to Galen that Julian Baugh was taking up permanent residence at the Winds. She had thought about him almost constantly in the week since he had followed her into the sunken garden. She would have denied being in love (her own word would have been "intrigued"), but her desire for him, fueled in his absence by the memory of his brief embrace, had grown in leaps and bounds. As to whatever else there was, on either side, there would be ample time, she had told herself, to find it out. In the meantime, it was after all just a kiss. Just a kiss. A kiss that had turned her knees into jelly and her brain into mush.

"Back, I'm pleased to say, for good." This was the extent of Henry's emotional display, but Galen had been able to tell by the light that danced in his pale eyes and touched his features with an almost rejuvenating glow that he was elated by the announcement of Julian's plans. However, he had been the only one who seemed at all surprised. Franny, who had stopped in briefly at the house, had appeared to Galen curiously unimpressed. "Imagine that," he had remarked as if Henry were pointing out a grease spot on his tie. Mae, who had been serving them coffee at the time, had grunted, "It's aboot time he brought thut boy back whar he belongs."

Carla had seemed the least surprised of all. In fact, Galen was sure she had known for some time. Whether it was in any way connected to Julian's news (Galen suspected it was), there had been a transformation in the woman's manner toward her. Ever since the Bowdoins' party she had gone out of her way to draw Galen in. After spending the week at her gallery in New York, Carla had flown back for the weekend and stayed on through Monday, making a point of seeking her out. She had corraled Galen into joining her for lunch. It was the day Galen had first heard of Julian's plan to move. It was also the day Galen had belatedly returned the raincoat she had borrowed.

"That was Johanna's," Carla had said, closing the hall closet door and hooking Galen's arm to lead her through the house. Galen's eyebrows had shot involuntarily up. No one but Caetano had so much as uttered the dead woman's name. "You know about Johanna."

"William's mother."

"I knew her when she used to wear that thing." Carla's manner was abrupt and the words she did not stretch she clipped. "That's how far we go back. I keep meaning to throw it out but somehow I can't bear to. We were in boarding school together—oh, I don't want to say *how* long ago. She was my best friend, you know. You heard what happened to her. I only feel sorry for that poor child." She had spoken with the nonchalance of someone ordering a meal.

"He's suffered a lot for a child his age."

"Oh, Galen dear, you've no *idea*. Let's sit here, in the sun. I know it's *horrendous* for your skin and we'll all look like raisins when we're fifty, but I'm vain and I'm weak." She had flashed a quick brilliant smile. "You know he was almost killed on the day his mother deserted him—he climbed into the stall of a horrible horse." Like Mara, Carla's comments often ran together with little apparent thought to transition or theme.

"Mars."

"You know, then." Carla had not seemed surprised. "I'd been searching for him for an hour. I thought he'd fallen down a well. Do you take sugar? Of course not. I've never been so frightened in all my life. That's good enough reason *never* to have kids."

"I understand he's still afraid of horses."

"Terrified. But it's Julian I feel sorry for. I mean, *imagine*." Carla's pause had seemed to assume Galen shared the same mental image. "You don't have any?"

"Children? No."

"Ever married?"

"No."

"I'm sure you've been asked." The compliment may

have been gratuitous but the question implied in it was not. Carla had wanted to know.

"A proposal of marriage is to a wedding what clean living is to a long life," Galen had said. "It may turn out to have nothing to do with it at all."

Carla had an infectious cackle of a laugh. She had let one go here.

"Men are such pigs, aren't they!"

"In this case, I changed my mind."

"Good for you!" Carla had cackled again, but before it had died she had picked up the thread once more.

"So are you entertaining one now? It's hard to imagine someone with your brains, let alone *looks*, my God (I suppose you do *nothing* to your hair, I do hate women like you!) doesn't have the cream of the Dewar's-ad crop to choose from. Don't grin at me, tell me who he is."

"I'm sorry to disappoint you, Carla, but I am not weighing any proposals of marriage. I am not even weighing an invitation for the movies this Saturday night."

"I thought you lived with someone?"

"A woman. You know her in fact. Mara James, formerly with the MOMA, now the BMFA."

"For heaven's sake! Yes, I do! I think. Oh, Mae, no thank you, unless Galen you want some more?"

"No. As my great-aunt used to say, I am replete."

"You! I feel like the python that ate the pig. So you're unattached. Julian and I will have to see what we can do. We'll have to get some of our friends up here and introduce you. I have a cousin you *must* meet."

"I didn't say I was friendless."

"No, of course not, but it's a perfect excuse for a party. We haven't had a really good party at the Winds in—well, in a long time. I'm so glad Jule has finally made up his mind to move back," she had added in the same breath. "I hate Paris."

* * *

"I love it."

"What?"

"The chapter, what you've done to it," Henry was saying. "You're worth every penny I pay you. You've certainly earned your lunch." He stood up and slipped the manuscript back into its folder.

"No, thank you, Henry," said Galen, trying to guess how long she had been daydreaming. "I think I'll just have something at home. Mae's cooking is making me fat."

"That's been our plan."

"I also have some calls to make. I'll be back at two."

William intercepted Galen in the front hall and asked if he could walk her home through the woods.

"You'll miss your lunch."

"I had a sandwich in the kitchen already."

"All right then."

"Lemme get my gun!" he cried back over his shoulder as he bolted toward the stairs. "I'll meet you around."

"Okay, but no live ammunition— *Oh, my!*" Galen's hand had been on the doorknob as she spoke, and as she went to pull it, the door flew open toward her under a power of its own. With it came a smartly dressed six-foot-plus man who all but fell into her arms.

"Ah, hello," he said, straightening with a quick broad smile. Galen looked up into shockingly blue eyes that moved leisurely under half-closed lids. "Is H. L. in?"

He sounded British.

"Yes, in his study, I think. Shall I call him for you?"

"That's quite all right," he said over his shoulder. "I know my way." Galen watched the tall figure stride away and in a moment heard Henry's voice rise with delight.

"John-ny! My *boy*! You missed Carla by a day!"

William was waiting at the edge of the lawn, a shiny plastic AK-47 slung over his shoulder. The Bowdoins' visit had effectively transformed Galen and William's walks into military escorts. William's toy "liberator" was a hotly contested gift from Uncle Dick, who insisted a child's natural obsession with instruments of death was primordial but temporary and had nothing to do with form.

"Look at you and Colin and your epic toy-soldier wars," he had argued in challenge to Julian's prohibition on guns. "Leave a child alone and the thing plays itself out."

"Is that why Katie is a mercenary?" had been Julian's reply.

"Rubbish! My niece is not a mercenary!" Dick Bowdoin had roared back. "She organizes humanitarian aid and *only* for the good guys." (Which good guys, Galen had wondered at the time, were these?) The point, however, had become moot as William and the gun had already disappeared.

Galen ate and made her calls while her latter-day Little Prince turned the lilac border around the bungalow into a free-fire zone. Listening to the wet stutter of a machine gun and fading whistle of falling bombs outside her windows, Galen began to think Julian was right that toy guns were not a good idea. What, she wondered, would Johanna Fairchild have thought? Would she even know her son?

"Hey, Rambini," she called, taking a last swallow of coffee. "Get your men together and let's move out."

"The sun parch," Mae grunted on meeting Galen at the door of Henry's empty study. The woman hissed by her with a palm-sized silver tray propped on her shoulder as if it were a seventy-five-pound sack of grain.

"Thank you, Mae," Galen murmured after her.

She and William could hear voices before they got to the screened porch that ran off the southern wall of the living room. One was English. Henry's visitor was still here.

Galen smiled with recognition at the blue-eyed man who stood when she entered. William was less restrained.

"Uncle Johnny!" he shrieked, and leapt into his arms.

"William, my little toad, my *God* what an elephant you've become, I can barely *arggghhh* lift you. Give me a look." He kissed him, set the boy down and held him at arm's length. *"Ça va bien, mon petit chou?"*

"Oui, Oncle."

"Dits-moi, qui est ton amie?"

"Mademoiselle Shaw. Elle est très gentile et très jolie, non?"

"Si jolie. Mamselle." The man extended a hand toward Galen. He was slender with longish, unevenly brown hair that was probably blond when he was a child, a ruddy tan, and a smile that revealed perfect teeth and no small measure of confidence. He was nothing if not strikingly handsome. Galen, who was rarely impressed by good looks, could not help smiling back.

Henry, who had risen to his feet, completed the introduction.

"You passed each other coming in, I gather. Galen, this is Johnny Foote. Carla's cousin and a member of the family in his own right. I was just telling him about our project."

"H. L. reports you've done a superb job," he said, indicating that she should take his chair and moving himself to another. "Sounds grand. We've all been looking forward to reading it for some time."

Johnny Foote's luminescent azure eye was not lewd but so penetrating it almost made Galen blush. If he noticed, he was too well bred to gloat. His manner was at once chivalrous, carefree, self-assured, and without indulgence or insult, as if he were as pleased with those around him as he was with himself. Johnny was obviously delighted to be there, but Galen was most impressed by how happy Henry was to have him. The combination was effective: she found herself quickly taken in.

"Johnny has been with us since he was William's size, or almost," Henry was saying, a mirthful grin creasing his cheeks and narrowing his eyes to puffy slits. "You weren't much older than that when you and Colin blew up the greenhouse."

It was only the second time Galen had heard Henry mention his dead son's name.

"Something for which I have never been forgiven," Johnny cut in, addressing Galen with a throaty laugh. "Next he'll start up about Phoebe's windshield, which in this case I had *nothing* to do with. But I was always the whipping boy for—"

"This one here," Henry interrupted, jerking a playful thumb at Johnny, "and the two boys were out in the woods with twenty-two rifles and *someone* shot out my wife's windshield."

"Boys will be boys," Galen said, thinking about William and his gun.

"Yes, well, she was driving the car at the time."

Johnny Foote was, like his cousin, an art dealer. He had a shop in London, and, as he was just telling Henry, had big plans for opening a second in Boston. In the course of a long leisurely felicitous tea that preempted further work with Henry, Galen discovered that Johnny also flew planes, played polo, and rubbed shoulders with the Biarritz–Monte Carlo–St. Tropez crowd of tycoons, titles, and throneless royals. The yellow streaks in his hair were from the Fastnet race, which his Swan 61 *Rococo* would have won had it not been for a blown-out spinnaker. What impressed Galen the most was that for all this he managed to appear genteel and sincere and was obviously a great favorite of Henry, who seemed to bask in the younger man's presence. It was not hard to figure out that besides being Carla's cousin, he had been her husband's best friend. They parted company two and a half hours later, agreeing to meet again that evening for a ride.

* * *

"And just who is Johnny Foote?"

"A friend of Henry's. He's been staying at the house for a few days. Is this belt all right?"

"You've got to be joking. Try this." Mara slipped a red suede tie around the waist of Galen's black silk dress. It was Friday evening. Galen had returned from Stover in just enough time to shower and dress for the evening out—with the help of Mara's close attention to detail. "And he's already invited you to the theater? How old is he?"

"I don't know, thirty-eight, thirty-nine?"

"Handsome?"

"Embarrassingly so. These shoes?"

"Forget it. Rich?"

"Evidently. These?"

"Gale! No! The red sandals. Now don't be coy with me. What's going on?"

"Nothing's *going on*. He's an old friend of the family. He's an art dealer. You should know him. I really don't know how rich he is. I really don't know very much about him other than the fact he flew his private jet to Stover and has been commuting into Boston on business in a rented Mercedes. He's British. He's funny. He's sweet to William. And he rides. Well. We've ridden together a couple of times. Henry couldn't go to the play, Carla is stuck in New York, so he asked me. *C'est tout.* But he's picking me up at seven so this will have to do. How do I look?"

"I think I'll wait up."

"Forgive me for staring, but you really are extraordinarily beautiful, Galen, if you don't mind my saying so."

Galen had looked over at Johnny suddenly and caught his languorous gaze fixed on her face. He was unembarrassed and did not look away.

"Thank you."

"But you look sad, Ms. Shaw. Why is that? Have I said anything to upset you? Perhaps I've spoken out of turn."

They had seen a production of *Les Misérables* at the Shubert and were sitting now side by side in a semicircular booth in the smoky shadows of O'Malley's Bar and Grill. A bulbous middle-aged woman with fake eyelashes and bleeding lipstick was murdering Duke Ellington's "In a Mellow Tone." But Galen had not been listening. Gone was the humor she had first found in this scene. Gone was the energy and excitement she had taken away with her from the play. She had been staring mutely into space trying to absorb what Johnny had just told her about Carla and Julian.

"No, not at all," she said. "I'm a little tired, maybe, but I'm fine. Really. So when is the wedding going to be?"

"They haven't been firm on a date—it's still a state secret, you know—but Carla says they've decided on the spring. When the 'cherries are in bloom.'"

"How nice."

"I don't suppose I should have said anything to you, but I'm not very good at keeping secrets, not ones like these at any rate, and you don't strike me as a gossip." He flashed his handsome, facile smile. "It will be glorious, I've no doubt. Knowing Carla. She never does anything halfway. Her marriage to Colin was practically a coronation—Bokassa had nothing on my dear cousin—although poor Julian's not exactly the type. A little . . . taut, don't you find him?"

"I don't know him well enough to judge. For that matter I don't really know him at all."

"Are you in love with him?"

"What! Why does everybody keep asking me that?" Galen knew her cheeks had probably reddened. She hoped the lounge was too dark for Johnny to have seen.

"I'm sorry." Johnny's voice was disarmingly apologetic. "It's just that most women are."

"I should think that most women are in love with you."

"Not like Julian. Women adore a man who broods. Don't you find that so? Julian's not unsociable, exactly. Quite the opposite, especially where women are concerned—even something of a rake now and again. But he can be deliciously mysterious sometimes. Honestly now, he hasn't tried to work his charms on you? I should think he could hardly resist."

"I've only met him I think half a dozen times and half of those were less than amicable encounters."

She expected to have to elaborate but Johnny needed no explanation.

"Yes, I heard about your meeting in East Cutty. I gather he and Carla were somewhat concerned about your 'relationship' with the old man. Especially about your surprise arrival at the Winds. You gave our Julian rather a scare: I saw him in Paris and he was quite undone about it."

"I can imagine." Galen had tried to stifle her anger but could feel Johnny's sidelong glance.

"Oh, but you mustn't take it personally. I think they're a tad paranoid—but then it's not my inheritance—and there were . . . precedents. However, I'm sure they've quite gotten over *that* by now. I've heard nothing but glowing reports. H. L. is mad about you. William, of course, and even Carla, who is—shall we call her a rigorous critic, particularly of other women, is decidedly warming."

"I suppose, but I'll be glad when the book is done and I'm out of their hair."

"Nonsense. They don't want you 'out of their hair,' and I don't believe for a minute the Baughs haven't managed to intrigue you just a little. Are we all as repulsive as that?"

Johnny affected a ridiculous wounded look and Galen laughed. He ordered them another round. The singer had moved on to "Lady Be Good." When the drinks arrived, Johnny took a large swallow and, putting his glass down, began to stir it slowly. His expression had grown somber.

"I kid about Julian, but he has been through quite a lot in the last few years. You have heard, I gather."

"Yes."

"You know about Johanna and Colin."

"Yes."

"Did you know that they were—that they had been involved?" Galen stared at him. Having grown so used to the secretiveness that prevailed among the rest of the clan, Johnny's candidness caught her by surprise.

"So I gathered."

"Did you know they were running away?"

"No." Galen remembered now that Carla had said Johanna had "deserted" her son. It had struck Galen at the time as an odd choice of words.

"In fact, none of us knew where they were or even that they were together for almost two days, until the plane was found."

"You were there?"

"Yes. Well, after they found it, I came up."

"They didn't leave a note? Nothing?"

"No. They said nothing to anyone. Do you mind if I smoke? Care for one? No? Good for you." Johnny took a deep drag and blew it out in a slow blue stream. He waved the lingering smoke away from his head as he would a fly. "The plane wasn't found until almost forty-eight hours later in the mountains, near Alander. There was a fire, of course, but there was rain and it didn't spread. At any rate, somehow nobody saw the crash. Hikers found the plane later."

He drew heavily again on his cigarette. His tone remained undramatic. "The bodies, you know, were burned beyond recognition. They were later identified by dental records, but we all knew right away who it was. By then we'd discovered Colin's plane was missing. It was only later that there was this . . . second shock. As the crash site was gone over, it became obvious that they weren't planning on coming back. Not right away at any rate. They had taken clothes with them. They found money. Thousands— almost ten thousand dollars in cash, if you can believe it— why, I can't guess. Possibly so they couldn't be traced through credit card charges. Who knows? Anyway, Johanna had this case, a large attaché, in which she religiously carried her working manuscript of H. L.'s book. It was found in the rubble, but it appears she had packed it with jewelry and personal mementos. . . . Well, the inference was unavoidable."

"Which is why the family tried to keep it hushed up."

"Yes."

"No one had any idea that something was going on between them?"

"As a matter of fact, Carla told me things had never been better between her and Colin, that they were planning a trip to the Algarve. It certainly looked jolly enough between the other two, but one can never tell about those things. There was some talk that Julian might have known, but judging from his reaction, I can't imagine he did. Besides, I was involved in the examination of the crash site and sabotage was never established."

"*Sabotage!* The police thought—"

"Well, it's their job, darling, but the inquest turned up no evidence of foul play and the deaths were ruled accidental."

Johnny took another swallow of his drink. There was a long moment during which neither said anything. It was Galen who finally broke the silence.

"Johnny, why did you tell me all of this?"

Johnny regarded Galen intently for a moment. Then

suddenly he smiled, straightened his long legs out in front of him, and folded his arms over his chest in a relaxed, boyish manner.

"As I told you, I'm not good at keeping secrets," he said.

Galen waited for the rest.

"A-a-nd I want you to trust me," he continued presently. His tone was more serious now. "The Baughs are sort of an arm's-length lot. Even dear old Fran. And as things are not always exactly as they appear up there, well, one can get feeling a bit at sea. It has at least been my experience over the years, and I'd like you to feel that, if the spirit or need ever moved you, there was someone you could turn to."

"That's very sweet of you."

"Somewhat sweet. I must confess to self-interest, as well. Openness is the best way to begin a friendship, and I would like very much to be your friend."

Galen and Lily waited for Johnny in the triangle of sun that fell across the top step of her brownstone. She found herself looking forward to seeing him again, even if only to give him a lift out to the Winds. It was Monday morning. They had met for brunch at Johnny's hotel on Saturday and afterward spent several hours walking about the city. After his disturbing revelations of Friday night, they had by some sort of wordless mutual consent studiously avoided any mention of the Baugh family again. Even when they had wandered into a bookstore in the afternoon and he had chanced to pull out a volume of Swinburne poems, Galen had not mentioned the book she had found in the bungalow. She did not want to think, let alone talk, about the Baughs that day. They talked instead about sailing, places they had both been to in Africa and South America, his adolescence in London, hers in Brazil. Galen found

Johnny easy to be with: relaxed, funny, respectful, unassuming, and certainly pleasing to look at. Why, she was wondering now, had she refused his invitation to drive to Rockport with him Sunday, only to spend a gloriously sunny afternoon staring out the window of her apartment? Was it because Johnny Foote was too easy to be with? Or because she was still thinking about Julian Baugh?

"You missed a lovely afternoon, silly girl." The statement so exactly duplicated her thoughts that for a moment she was not sure whether she had not said it herself. Looking around with a hand up against the sun, Galen saw that Johnny's dashing figure had appeared in front of her. Questions about opportunities lost the day before quickly gave way to the pleasing prospects of today.

"I'm not surprised. I've never been known for my foresight."

"I somehow doubt that. Shall we be off?"

"Johnny, you wouldn't mind if we made a stop on the way, would you? I've lost my riding gloves and want to pick up another pair. I won't take a minute. If you wouldn't mind sitting in the car; that way I won't have to park."

Against all odds, a gaping space was waiting for them directly outside the door of Goode's Riding Apparel on Boylston Street and Johnny came in with her.

"I love tack shops," he said, running his fingers along the wall of bridle reins as she tried on a pair of gloves. "When I was a kid, I got to know the man in a shop near our flat and he'd let me come in and sit on the saddles." He flexed and slapped a long thin dressage whip against his calf.

Galen laughed. "A farmer gave me an old saddle when I was little and my father mounted it on a sawhorse for me. I was in heaven on that thing. I don't think I ever noticed it was bolted to the floor."

"When did you break into the real thing?"

"Oh, I *was* into the real thing—I mean, Shetland ponies and riding lessons—but it was never enough. It was also a bit safer. I seem to remember falling off a lot. How about you? Did you, like all good English aristocrats, ride before you could walk?"

"No, no. I never even tried it until my first time at the Winds. I was scared to death of horses. But Colin insisted on teaching me. . . . What a beautiful rider he was. Johanna, too. They all are, really. As are you. H. L. told me about your race with Julian. Congratulations. You knew Durometer was Colin's favorite horse."

"I do now."

"Forgive me, but are you an acquaintance of Mrs. Colin Baugh?" The little bald man who had rung up Galen's purchase had hesitated in the process of handing her the bag in which he had placed her gloves.

Reaching—not aggressively—over the counter to take the bag from him, Johnny answered, "Yes, I am. We are. Why do you ask?"

"I heard you speak of the Winds," he muttered nasally. "I—I was wondering whatever happened to her."

Johnny looked stunned. He said slowly, "Nothing whatever. She lives in New York. Why would you think something had?"

"Well," the man went on hesitatingly, a little unsure of Johnny, "I only ask because she ordered a saddle from us—oh, a long while ago. She paid for it, in advance, and never picked it up. I—we were never able to reach her, you see. She instructed the store not to telephone her, and there has never been any reply to our notices. She wouldn't have forgotten, I mean not an Hermès. I'd thought maybe she'd moved, or—"

"Is it here?" Galen asked.

"No. She ordered it through us but said she would be in Manhattan and wanted to pick it up at the New York store. But that was the last I heard from her."

Galen and Johnny looked at each other.

"How odd," Galen said. "Do you still have the order form?"

The man disappeared into his office. Galen heard the sound of a metal file cabinet being drawn open. A few minutes later he returned with a yellow receipt, which he laid down on the table. The first thing Galen's eyes saw was the signature. Johanna Baugh.

If Johnny saw it, too, he said nothing. He was looking at Galen.

"This is Johanna's, not—" Galen scanned the form, reading half out loud: "One seventeen-inch Steinkraus Jumping Saddle, Hunterdon girth, Imperial Fillis stirrups, sheepskin pad." She stopped and looked at Johnny. "Two thousand seventy-six dollars. Paid." She turned to the clerk. "When was this order placed?"

"The date is on here I believe—there, July twentieth, 1986." It was three weeks before the accident.

"Do you have a date on delivery?"

"I told you, she was going to pick it up herself. I don't have a date, but unless there was a problem at the New York store, it would have been available that day. If they had to special order—two, maybe three weeks tops."

"Where is it now?"

"I presume in New York, still."

"Thank you."

"Will you have her call?"

"Yes. Of course."

Galen and Johnny had ridden a few blocks before either spoke. Galen was regretting having been so aggressive in the store and was determined to avoid a further display of just how interesting she really did find the whole affair. When he finally broke the silence, Johnny seemed again to be reading her mind.

"You're the reporter. What do you think?"

"Johnny, it's not really my business."

At this he laughed out loud. "I think it's a little late for that. Furthermore, my dear Lois Lane, coyness doesn't suit you. It's clear this whole thing has piqued your interest, as it has mine, and it's also clear that you think there's something out of place here." Looking over at him, Galen saw that he was smiling at her. "Now let's have it. I think it's fair to say I've been candid with you."

"Yes, you have. Okay. First, she did not buy that saddle for herself."

"How can you tell."

"Seventeen inches. That's a man's saddle."

"Okay," he said slowly. "Which man?"

"You tell me."

"Well, unless for some strange reason she decided I deserved one, it can only be one of three people. Henry. Julian. Or Colin. Henry's unlikely; that leaves her husband or her lover. If she was running away with her lover, would she go through the trouble of special ordering a two thousand-dollar Hermès saddle for her husband? That's a lot of guilt. And given the fact she'd have to bring it back from New York to give it to him, I don't think so."

"Neither do I. And why else the secrecy, the insistence that she not be telephoned? And why use the name Mrs. Colin Baugh for the order?"

"Unless it was a gift for Colin, who would, of course, appreciate something like an Hermès saddle more than anybody I know."

"Exactly. Which is why he already had one."

Galen felt rather than saw Johnny's quick look.

"Are you positive?"

"I think so. I remember on my first day in the barn I was in the main-floor tack room looking around for a bit for one of the horses and I saw Hermès—a man's Steinkraus—in one of the tack trunks, the big black one with the gold lettering."

"CCB."

"Yes, that one. The rest of the saddles are on racks on the walls. Julian and Henry ride in Crosby's, so it must have been Colin's."

"You're very good, Ms. Shaw" was all he said. They drove again in silence. Looking over at him, Galen saw that he was deep in thought. It was not until they were almost in Stover that either spoke of the matter again. The conversation in the interval had been mostly neutral, but it now swung back to the topic that was on both their minds.

"Johnny," Galen said as they neared the covered bridge. "What kind of woman was Johanna?"

"What do you mean?"

They were at the Swift River. Galen slowed for the nasty turn at the far bank.

"I just find it hard to believe that she would have done things quite in this way. Regardless of the state of her marriage, how does any mother leave a child behind, especially a vulnerable little boy like William?"

"That's simple. Julian would never have let her take his son. He would never have stopped looking until he found them."

"I suppose."

"You don't sound convinced." Johnny's sky-blue eyes narrowed.

"You say she took jewelry, some mementos. Did you know she had a gold locket with a picture of herself and William and a lock of his hair in it?"

"No, why?"

"William says she always took it with her for good luck when she traveled. She told him it was her way of taking him with her. She kept it in some box in her drawer when she was at home. He told me he used to sneak looks at it."

"It may have been among the things destroyed in the crash—not much survived, you know."

"No. William has it. He showed it to me the other

night. He keeps it under his pillow. Johnny, why wouldn't she take it with her? Even William thinks it's strange."

"Perhaps all the evidence is circumstantial. Perhaps Johanna and Colin weren't even having an affair." Something in his voice made Galen look over.

"No, that I believe . . . I found something in the bungalow. I don't know how long it's been there, but I think it's a gift from Johanna to Colin. It's a book of poetry. It's inscribed to CB from JF."

Johnny looked at her blankly.

"JF?"

"Fairchild. Her maiden—"

"Oh, of course."

"I don't quite know what to do with it. You see, William plays in the house sometimes."

"Give it to me if you want. In fact, it's something I'd like to have."

10

"So tell me—how have you found our Johnny? God damn it!" Dick Bowdoin missed his putt. Galen smiled. Her father had also loved to play golf.

"He's charming, Dick. He's like a third son to Henry, isn't he?"

"*Is* he!" Margaret Bowdoin appeared from the great stone house they called Westerly with a tray of sandwiches. The Bowdoins had invited Galen to lunch. Though September was almost over, the day was one of those hot muggy throwbacks to summer that usually preceded a cold snap, and the three visited in shorts and polo shirts among the big yellow chestnut leaves that littered the huge walled back lawn. Johnny had been back in New York since Monday—it was now Thursday—but his name seemed to be on everyone's lips. Henry had asked her that morning whether she did not find him a "simply delightful fellow."

"H. L. is positively delirious whenever the boy comes around," Margaret went on. "Which until you arrived, my dear, was only very rarely—since the accident, that is. Before that he and Colin were practically inseparable."

She set the tray down on the glass-top table beside Galen. The flesh on her bare arms was loose and mottled, and her large hands were knurled with thick blue veins. She had probably been athletic in her youth, Galen thought.

"Dick, come and eat," she called.

"I come anon," he called back, and lined up another putt.

"Yes, I hear he's taken a shine to you, dear," Margaret went on, smiling slowly without looking at Galen. Like Carla, Margaret Bowdoin seemed to have spontaneously warmed to Galen. She was now as serene in her hospitality as she had earlier been in her condescension. Galen hoped the Stover initiation rites were through.

"I don't suppose it would do any good to deny it," Galen said, pouring iced tea into three tall glasses hand-painted with cock pheasants and bird dogs. "Stover has to have something to talk about."

"That's enough, Peg," Dick said, dropping heavily into a chair and wiping his beaded forehead with a linen napkin. "If the girl says she doesn't find this rich, clever, suave, annoyingly handsome bachelor—who is clearly enchanted with her—up to snuff, why on earth shouldn't we believe her?"

"Do you mind?" Galen let her glass land hard on the tabletop.

"We're kidding you, my dear." Dick spoke through a mouthful of chicken salad. "I'm not especially in love with him either, though Peg is."

"Nonsense, I find him a dear attractive boy, that's all, and just wish he'd find the right girl. He's never had anyone . . . *steady* as far as I can tell, and he's not so young anymore. Have you ever been married?"

"Peggy, that's none of your business," her husband broke in.

"No, I don't mind," Galen said quickly. "The answer is no."

"Why not?"

"Peg!"

"I don't know. I came close. Twice, in fact. But it didn't work out. How long have you two been married?" Galen asked in an effort to shift the focus off herself.

"Forty-one years," Margaret said, looking at her husband, who was tearing at one of her sandwiches as if he had a plane to catch. "We took a chance and we were lucky. Some people aren't. Things happen. Awful things. But that is life, isn't it? You can't stop taking chances. I was worried Julian never would again. But I think maybe now he's ready again. What do you think?"

Galen who had been staring at her cup looked sharply up. "About what?"

"Taking chances. Your heart hasn't become too hard, has it? Do you still want to, someday?"

"I suppose. When the right guy comes along." All three spoke the last sentence at the same time and laughed. Dick drained his glass, wiped his mouth, and waddled on his long skinny white legs that toed out back to his hand-mowed putting green.

"Do you have children?" Galen asked Margaret tentatively. Nothing in Westerly indicated they ever had.

"One, a son, David," she said, looking down.

"He was killed in Vietnam," Dick called back over his shoulder.

"Oh. I'm sorry."

"It feels like ages ago," Margaret said generously. "Of course, it seemed like the end for us at the time. It might have been different had we had others—not less painful but life maybe wouldn't have seemed so meaningless—but I wasn't able." She began to collect the plates. "It makes me worry about Julian," she went on in a different voice. "A child should have brothers and sisters. You know Carla can't have children."

"No, I didn't know that," Galen said, absently sweeping crumbs onto the lawn.

"Yes, poor dear. And poor Colin was *desperate* to have a family. They tried so hard—you've no *idea* what that can be like. I suppose they could have adopted, but you know how impossible that is today—unless you go Cambodian."

"Yes, well . . ."

"Poor Colin. Poor Carla. Poor Julian. Goodness, poor *all* of them. It's a blessing Phoebe wasn't around to see it."

Johnny had said the saddle was not there when he looked for it Monday while Galen and Henry were at work, but she could not help opening Colin's black-and-silver tack box that afternoon to see for herself. Of course she saw just what Johnny had said he had found: a Hunterdon, close in color and style to an Hermès, but not the saddle Galen said she had seen. "Could you have been mistaken?" he had asked later during tea while Henry was out of the room. No, she had said then. I don't know, she said to herself now.

"Have you lost something?" a voice asked just behind her.

Galen started and with an ear-splitting crack the box lid slammed shut. How long she had been standing there staring into the trunk she hated to think.

"Oh! Caètano. Hello. Yes—I mean no." They both laughed—Galen out of a kind of nervous relief; Caetano at her fear.

"We have to stop meeting this way," he said with a grin, his beautiful light eyes gleaming innocently, then he turned to go. Galen stopped him.

"Actually, I *am* looking for something. Do you remember seeing an Hermès saddle in one of these trunks?"

"I dunno. Let's see, that's a Hunterdon."

"Yes, I know, but I'm looking for an Hermès, and I was just wondering—"

"The boys did all the tack a couple of days ago, they probably moved things around," he said, raising the lids of some of the other tack boxes. Then turning away from the line of trunks, he added with a shrug, "Maybe it's one of these."

Galen looked up and with a wave of something between alarm and embarrassment counted not one but three Hermès cantles among the fifteen or so saddles on the wall. "Yes," she said slowly. "Maybe." Why hadn't she seen these before? Or had she? "Sorry to trouble you, Caetano."

"No trouble." The smooth dark face broke in a winsome smile. "Is there something wrong with Durometer's saddle?"

Galen looked down to realize she had it propped on her hip.

"Oh, no. It's fine. Will you pass me that martingale there? Thanks. I haven't had him out in a week and you can be sure he'll try to tear me another—" Galen did not have to finish her sentence; the young man let out a school-boy giggle.

"I lunged him Monday and Wednesday so he shouldn't be too bad," he said. "No Mr. Baugh?"

"He had work to do in his studio. Why don't you come? It's a perfect night for a ride."

"I wish I could. The farrier was supposed to be here at noon and it would be just my luck to miss him. He won't go near Mars unless I twitch him."

The image of William flashed briefly before her eyes. "I don't blame him," she said. "Another time then. *Até logo.*"

"*Ciao.*"

The temperature had dropped steadily since midafternoon and a crisp wind had come up. Galen pulled a black turtleneck sweater over her head and tugged it down over the belt of her yellow britches. Her spurs clinked lightly against each other as she strode back to the annex. She was right. It was a spectacular night for a ride.

The gust of sweet-smelling breath Durometer blew at

her was warm and soft but the black horse's movements were tense. Lunging or no, he would be a handful. Galen's heart quickened a little in her chest.

Tossing his head, Durometer half walked, half jogged out of the stable yard and onto the driveway. The hollow *clops* of his hooves sounded like gunshots and she imagined them carrying for miles. Lily tore herself away from the leftovers Caetano had put out for the barn cats and ran to join them. Galen rode back up the driveway, as far as the turnoff to the cottage. Here they turned right, leapt an irrigation ditch as if it were a three-foot wall, and jogged into the woods.

This was no summer day. The dry leaves that still clung to their branches roared in the trees; those that had fallen crackled loudly underfoot. The air was so clear that the sun, even at five-fifteen, was blinding. Excited but loose, Galen let Durometer yank playfully at her hands. In the intoxicating motion of the big horse's ranging strides, everything began to slip away. Julian, Carla, Johanna. Henry and his book. She was aware only that her britches were slippery against the still-cold saddle leather and of the feel of Durometer's satiny sides against her leather-wrapped calves. The wind tossed her hair. She squinted against the sun and had only one thought in her mind: that there was nothing in the world quite like a new pair of riding gloves.

Galen drove her heels down and the horse practically catapulted her into a post as he broke into a long-strided trot, releasing a gravelly snort with every other step. He sounded like a train. It was almost the only sound they made as they sailed over a soft carpet of yellow pine needles.

They were soon at the Well Gate and broke into a collected canter back across the Ice Pond Meadows, which had been the final stretch of Galen's race against Julian. After passing through a break in the wall, they cantered up through the apple orchard and back along the bridle trail she had led Julian down. Durometer cleared the fallen log without effort and they were soon crossing the Ox Bow Meadow where the riding party had ended its race. Here Galen pulled Durometer off the path and rode him toward the stone wall separating the Ox Bow from the Long Field. It was the only other jump she would ask him to do today. She could feel his muscles bunch; he fought her for his head. Galen checked his burst of speed and counted him in. One. Two. Three. It was not a big jump but wide and the slope was away from them. It must have been the added pressure of the incline that snapped the stirrup catch when they landed.

Galen dreamed she was falling, from a great height, toward the distant tops of trees as if she had fallen out of an airplane, only slower. Johnny was flying a plane, perhaps the one she had fallen out of, a silent glider with an open cockpit, and she could see him looping in a great arching turn to come back to rescue her. She tried to call out to him but the wind was rushing in her ears and she could not hear her voice. She could see Durometer, a small black speck, running wildly, soundlessly, riderless across a field. She kept falling until the treetops were upon her. Johnny had swept just over her head. She tried to call out again. Crashing through the branches, she wanted to put out her hands to try to slow or break her fall, but her arms would not work. The ground rushed up suddenly and she closed her eyes. There was a horrible sound, a jolt, a moment of oblivion.

She opened her eyes. A face was leaning close to hers. Black eyes were searching her own. Julian was holding her wrists in his hands. He was saying something to her in a low, soothing voice. She was not yet aware of pain.

"You're all right," she heard him say. "Don't be afraid."

"I had a dream," she said breathlessly. The terror was passing only gradually.

Julian smiled. "I know."

"I was falling."

"I know. Don't move now."

The stab of pain that shot through her shoulder cleared her mind, and it gradually dawned on her that she was in a bed in Henry's house and that she was hurt. She became aware of a bandage on her head.

"What's happened to me? What am I doing here?"

Her eyes must have flashed panic because Julian put his hand on hers.

"You had a fall," he said gently. "You've had a concussion and suffered some pretty nasty bruises. Dr. Hubbard says you're going to be fine. You're just not to move for a while."

Based on the tone he used, Galen had to assume she had been acting less than rationally. She stared at him for a moment. She could remember nothing but cantering across a field.

"Durometer."

"He's all right."

"Lily."

"Caetano has her."

"What happened?"

"We don't know." Julian got up, went to the door, was out of the room for a few seconds, then returned and took a chair beside the bed. "Durometer appeared in the barnyard in a full lather at about six o'clock. Caetano called the house and we went out looking for you. We eventually found you semiconscious at the top of the Long Field. We might have missed you had Lily not suddenly appeared. You weren't exactly looking for us."

"Like Lassie," Galen said with a weak smile.

"Well, no." Julian smiled back. "You couldn't say she led us to you precisely, but we knew you had to be somewhere nearby."

She looked out the window. It was daylight. "How long—"

"You've been in and out for almost thirteen hours. It's Friday morning. You don't remember the ride home in the Jeep?"

"No."

"Or Hubbard's visit?"

"No."

"Or mine?"

Galen stared at him for a moment. Then suddenly her expression changed. The fragments of reality that had splintered under the force of her fall were gradually reassembling themselves. She had no recollection of her rescue, or anything between this moment and the moment before her fall. But something from before—a piece she would have liked to have lost for good—had just dropped back into place. It came to her as an image; one that pierced the dense haze clouding her brain with a kind of sleepy confusion. It registered in a dull pain in her chest. The picture was of Julian and Carla's wedding.

"What are you doing here?" she asked coldly.

He gave her a curious, almost sheepish smile. "You were calling my name."

"But I thought you were in France."

"I got back yesterday evening. Just before five. Evidently just before you went out."

Galen put a hand to her head. She remembered her dream. "I was calling your name?"

The door swung open before he could answer and Henry appeared, smiling broadly. Julian must have sent word to him that she was awake. He came over to the bed and squeezed her hand.

"You gave us quite a scare, my dear. How are you feeling?"

"I don't know." She tried to move again. Her head began to hurt. She slumped back into the pillows and closed her eyes, feeling suddenly tired.

Mae must have come in behind him because Galen heard her voice now.

"The doctor said to let har sleep," she was saying. "I'll sit with har now."

Julian murmured something to her but Galen could not make it out. The three figures near her bed, the bed, the room, the house, began to swirl as if caught in a giant whirlpool and slipped out of sight.

Galen woke up at about midday, unsure of what she had dreamed and what had really taken place in the last eighteen hours. Most unclear was whether she had imagined that Julian was back at the Winds or if in fact he was. It was a week before he was expected. She pushed back the blankets and swung her legs carefully over the side of the bed. The answer came in the form of a question from the door.

"And just where do you think you're going?" Julian was smiling, as he crossed the room.

"I think I should get up," she answered coolly but he had his hand on her shoulders and was pushing her gently back down against the pillows. He lifted her feet back onto the bed and drew the blankets up over her.

"I'm sorry, doctor's orders. As galling as this may be for you, you are our prisoner for the next two days, and it will be much easier on you if you behave."

"You seem to be enjoying yourself," she said.

Missing, or misunderstanding, the acidity in her voice, Julian answered with a grin. "Then be considerate enough not to wreck my fun."

Galen leaned slowly back against her pillows, and met his bright gaze with an icy stare.

"You've had your fun. Riding by yourself in the dark on a horse like Durometer. And now you must pay the piper. Don't make me resort to Draconian measures."

"Acting up, is she?"

To Galen's relief, Henry had come in and joined his son at the side of her bed. Arms folded, they looked like a pair of mad scientists considering an experiment. At another time she would have laughed at their pose.

"Yes, Father. I'm afraid we're going to have to bring the shackles down from the attic after all."

"How are you, dear?"

"I'm *fine*." Galen tried to smile back at the creased face that grinned down at her with such obvious concern. He ignored her self-diagnosis.

"Julian, a woman named Mara Jones just telephoned and gave us license to use whatever force necessary to restrain the patient. Apparently she has had some experience in this matter."

"James," Galen mumbled, and watched her plans of escape fade away.

"Just so. Now, Julian, I think it's time we get some food into our patient before she blows away on the next good breeze. Hubbard said he'd be by sometime this afternoon. He'll think we've been remiss if there's no color in her cheeks."

Julian lingered after Henry left the room. His joviality was gone.

"I'm so relieved you're all right," he said softly. "I almost went out of my mind when Durometer came back alone." Moving close to her bed, he reached for her hand. It was a long moment, when Galen pulled it back, before Julian withdrew his own. Just how he took it, she did not know. Refusing to raise her eyes to him, she had looked away. She would not make a federal case of a garden-path kiss, she told herself, but neither would she be treated lightly. As far as she was concerned, Julian and his polished manner and his—what had Johnny called him, a rake?—silken touch could go to hell.

"Are you in a lot of pain?" he asked now in a different voice. He was finally beginning to catch on.

"Just a little sore," she said, studying the patterns of the quilt.

"I wish there was something I could do," he said after a pause.

She said nothing.

"I'm afraid I have business this afternoon that won't wait," he continued a little stiffly. "I have to leave soon, right away in fact. But I hope to be back by six at the latest. May I check on you then?"

"I'd just as soon you didn't. I understand I need a lot of sleep." It was a sad excuse, but in lieu of an out-and-out brawl it was the best she could do.

"I see . . . There's nothing I can do for you now?"

"No, thank you."

"Galen?"

Only now did she look at him. This time she did not try to stifle her anger. Her emerald eyes burned with it. In what felt for an instant like a test of wills, Julian stared back at her with a surprising intensity of his own. He does not, Galen noted, take rejection well.

"What?" she asked without averting her gaze.

His black eyes narrowed, but before he could say anything there was a commotion at the door and William burst into the room with a fistful of daisies and dandelions in one hand, and Lily tugging at the end of a leash in the other. In a bound the dog was across the floor and on the bed. The boy seemed about to follow suit but a sharp word from his father froze him in the act.

"It's perfectly all right, William," Galen said quickly, making room for him and flashing Julian a warning look. "Are these for me?"

"Yes, I picked them myself," the boy said, planting himself beside her pillow and holding out the virtually stemless bouquet, which fell instantly apart as Galen tried to take it from his hand. "Grandpa said they would make you feel better."

"They're beautiful," she said and kissed the boy on the side of his damp orange head. He and Lily had obviously been running. She began to ask him where he had picked the flowers when Julian's voice broke softly across her own.

"Did you get my note?"

"Yes, I did."

"I tried to call you from Europe—three times."

"It hardly matters, Julian. In any case now's not the time."

"Very well," he said after a long pause and with a last look Galen did not try to read, he turned and left them alone.

"Ga-len! Ga-len!" Carla scolded mockingly as she glided toward the bed. "I can't stand it. What have you done to yourself? You look like something out of a Hemingway novel. How are you feeling? Hi, Mae, how are you? Galen, are you in pain?"

"No, not really." She touched cheeks with the handsome woman who raised a sleek hip to rest it on the mattress. It was four o'clock and Mae had just brought her tea.

"Julian phoned me. I came up as soon as I heard. What can I do? Are you bored out of your mind? I *hate* to be in bed."

Galen smiled at her. There was something deliciously 1930s about Carla. There was also something sometimes rather kind.

"I haven't been conscious long enough. I will, though, I'm sure. Dr. Hubble—"

"Hubbard—he's *wonderful,* I simply adore this man, he's the only doctor on earth who'll still make a house call."

"Right, said I wasn't supposed to move for three days. He says I'll be prone to dizziness for a week as it is. But I don't think I'll serve my whole term."

"Just try getting past Mae, my dear," Carla said with a backward glance. Mae, who to Galen's surprise had not left but had arranged herself in a chair across the room and begun sewing something, looked up. A look about as toasty as permafrost passed between the two women.

"Being sick in this house is a major event—they practically sell tickets—but you should try to enjoy it: crust off the toast, straws that bend, Jell-O, ginger ale, hot milk. Oh! And *don't* miss a back massage—Mae's got the hands of a merchant marine. If she doesn't snap a vertebra you'll feel ten years younger."

"Yes, well, maybe—"

"I'm going to go down to get some coffee," Carla said, slithering off the bed and turning her back to Galen. "I'll bring it up and we'll *chat*." (Carla said it like a dirty word.) "My cousin, who I understand you've met—isn't he *divine?*—is on his way up." She was halfway to the door. "He's *most* concerned about your health." Turning back, Carla arched her eyebrows, dropped her chin, and made an O with her mouth, as if registering a shocking piece of news. Then, with a wink and a cackle, she disappeared out the door in what Galen, for an instant, imagined to be a puff of smoke.

She was still looking absently after her when Mae heaved herself to her feet and lumbered over to remove her tray. Galen had thought it unusual that the woman had remained in the room and guessed that she had something to say. Nothing, however, could have prepared her for what it was.

"Ya be carful, dearie," the orange-haired woman muttered, lifting the tray off the bed.

"Pardon me?"

"Don' ya trust thut woman as far as ya cun throw har."

Galen was flabbergasted, at first as much for the fact of the woman's speech as for its content. It was more words than she had spoken to Galen in all of their encounters combined.

"I'm sorry?" she asked.

"Carryin' on like thus un thut, carryin' on like she cars for William. She never carred a whit about him, she never carred for children period! Hated 'em! Lard. It's no wonder she's so hot un Dr. Hubbard. Jes' pult the wool over Master Colin's eyes jes' like she's doin' with his brother."

It was bad enough that Mae was slandering a member of the Baugh family without Galen's aiding and abetting in this gross breach of propriety, but in this case her reporter's curiosity, which some time in the last few weeks had shifted into high gear, easily overpowered her sense of decorum.

"I don't understand," Galen prompted as delicately as she could. She need not have bothered. Mae was already continuing with a quiet viciousness that had Galen looking guiltily toward the door. Her gun-metal blue eyes dove at Galen's accusingly.

"I'll tell ya something," she said, leaning menacingly close, "thut woman loved har son more thun anythin' else in th' wurld. She'd never a' left him behind. Und I don' car whut anyone says, thar was nuthin' wrong with thut marriage. Anyone'd be lucky to have such a marriage. She was planning har son's birthday party when she died."

"What happened, then?" Galen whispered.

"To have thut child growing up thinkin' his mother desarted him is the biggest crime of all."

"What are the other crimes?"

"Look, honey, you jes' watch yarself. I know about you en yar questions aroun' here en ya watch yarself, thut's all I ken say."

"What other crimes, Mae?"

But the woman had already turned away and was halfway to the door. Watching her go, Galen knew that this extraordinary exchange would be the first and the last of its kind with Mae. Which was probably just as well, she quickly told herself. She could hardly account for the woman's veracity, let alone motivation for her sudden, uncharacteristic candidness with a virtual stranger. There was no love lost between Carla and Mae, and unquestionably the latter had an ax to grind. Had not Peggy Bowdoin just today—or was it yesterday—testified to Carla's desire for children? Who, after all, was in a better position to know? And no one could say that Carla, for all her flamboyant self-involvement, was inattentive to William. But at the same time, Galen had trouble dismissing Mae's loyalty to Johanna. Wasn't this, she asked herself, because it was precisely what she wanted to hear? Because it supported her nagging sense that there was something missing from the picture of a woman abandoning her husband and child on the eve of their birthdays? Beware of gossip that confirms a hunch, a voice spoke from the recesses of the reporter's brain. But don't ignore it either, another answered.

It was about eleven o'clock that night when Galen heard a plaintive wail from William's room. She listened for footfalls in the hall but none came. The cry was gone and she wondered whether she had heard it at all. The house was as quiet as a tomb. But then it came again, and Galen was out of bed and slipping her arms into the crimson satin robe Carla had draped on the chair.

In a wedge of light from the hall, she found William in a tangle of sheets, struggling and whimpering in his sleep. His skin was burning and his hair was wet. Sitting on his bed, she put a hand on his damp cheek and gently rocked his head.

"You're having a nightmare, little one. William? William?"

His watery eyes flashed open and stared blankly at her. She was not sure whether he was still asleep.

"You okay?"

"Where were you?" His voice was tiny.

"Right across the hall. I heard you cry. You were having a bad dream."

"But you said you'd come right back."

"I'm here now, sweetheart. I'll sit with you as long as you want."

"Why did you leave me? You said you'd be right back."

With a hollow thud of her heart Galen realized who William thought she was.

"William, honey." She leaned her face close to his. "It's Galen. You were having a dream but now it's over and you're awake."

"Mommy?"

"No, sweetheart. Mommy's not here." Galen was reluctant to turn on the bedside lamp for fear that he would see the tears that were threatening to spill onto her cheeks.

"Mommy's dead."

"Yes, lamb. She is."

He said nothing after this, but accepted her arms around him and leaned stiffly against her while she rocked him. When she was no longer afraid of sobbing, she hummed "London Bridge Is Falling Down." If not exactly soothing it was the only children's song she could think of.

Much later his body relaxed. His breathing grew heavier and finally he was asleep. Galen's shoulder had begun to hurt terribly and she lowered him onto his pillow. She sat for a moment longer, looking at the white face against the white pillow, then painfully raised herself to go.

Crossing his room, she felt a wave of dizziness and nausea. She reached the threshold but had to hold herself tightly against the door frame to keep from falling. Her temples began to throb and she pressed her forehead against the cold paint. The hissing roar in her ears was so loud she did not realize someone had come down the hall behind her until she felt a hand clutch each of her arms.

"What are you doing out of bed?" Julian whispered almost angrily. After pulling William's door closed, he led her back to her room and put her in bed. It was a minute before the room stopped spinning. Sitting beside her on the edge, he laid a dry palm against her forehead, flipped it over, and pressed its back against her cheek. His hands were cold and Galen noticed that he was wearing a coat. The sheepskin collar was still turned up.

"You're hot."

"Just a little dizzy. But I'm okay, really."

"Don't move," he said, and left the room, but almost immediately was back, this time cradling a large brandy snifter in his hand.

"Take a sip of this," he insisted. In answer to her surprised look, he explained that he had been carrying it to his room when he found her in the hall and had put it down just outside the door. Galen sat up against the headboard, pulling her knees up under the blankets, and rested her swimming head on her arms. She did not accept the glass.

"I won't go until you've had just a little," he said, adding simply, "You look terrible." He was not smiling but neither was he stern. He looked if anything tired—his hair was unkempt, she could see the blue shadow of his beard.

She did not have the energy to resist. Reluctantly she took the glass from him and raised it to her lips. After taking a swallow of what turned out to be Calvados, Galen gasped as the burning, bittersweet liquid scorched a path deep into her abdomen. She gave a single, appreciative cough. Its effects were immediate. Her head was instantly clear.

"Better?"

"Yes. Thank you," she said, handing back the glass.

Instead of getting up, Julian poured half its topaz contents into an empty teacup on the bedside stand and offered it to her. She hesitated before taking it.

"Julian—"

"Don't worry, I won't stay," he said, his voice quiet

and noticeably reserved. "But will you please answer me just two questions."

"What are they?"

"What were you doing out of bed?"

"William was having a nightmare."

There was a pause. Julian looked troubled. "I see" was all he said. He did not look at her as he took a drink from the snifter, which lingered at his lips as he stared, unfocused, over its rim. Glancing away, Galen raised the china cup to her lips. The cognac exploded inside her mouth and radiated a slow penetrating heat on its way down. In a moment she could feel the soothing effects of its afterglow.

"Is he all right now?"

"He's asleep."

"Did he say anything?"

"He thought I was his mother."

"Yes, I can see why he might," Julian said, touching the sleeve of her satin robe. "This was hers. For an instant I wasn't sure myself when I first saw you outside William's door."

Galen's eyes flew open and she sat bolt upright. "Oh, God, Julian, I didn't know! I'm so sorry. Carla left it—"

"There's nothing at all to be sorry for," he said quickly, laying a hand on her arm but then withdrawing it. "I'm sure you didn't know, and even if you did . . . Far more painful reminders come in much more discreet ways. As I'm sure you know."

"But how awful for William, to think, to really believe, even for a moment . . ." Her voice trailed off as she remembered his ghostly white face.

"Is that what made you cry?"

"What?"

"You've been crying."

"No, I haven't."

"Yes, my dear, you have. Your tears have only just

dried. If I had not earlier fought the impulse to run my
finger under your eye—like this"—Julian reached out and
touched her face—"the tear that was caught in these lashes
would have traced a silvery line on my skin. There, you
see, even now . . ."

His words were slow and tender. He was studying her
face without looking into her eyes. Despite all the sensible
words in her brain, Galen's heart began to thud. Julian's
elixir had done more than clear her head. Listening to the
hypnotic tone of his words, a dreamy, desirous state was
overtaking her. It conspired with the dark stillness of the
night to spin them in a cocoon where reason and caution,
and the rest of the world, were shut out like winter chill.

"You're shivering," he said.

"I know I am."

"Do I frighten you?"

"No."

"Does my being this close make you nervous?"

"Yes."

"Do you want me to move away?"

"No," she said.

When Julian reached again to touch her face, his fingers came this time to her lips. Slowly, then, they traced
the line of her jaw, her neck, her collarbone, and the swell
of her breasts, which all at once ached unbearably for his
touch.

"Julian," she said huskily, "are you and Carla getting
married in the spring?"

"Is *that* why you've been angry with me?" he asked
with a surprised look. It was followed by a smile. "Who
told you that?"

When she said nothing he took her hand and spoke in
a tone of quiet earnest. "Galen, listen to me. You have to be
very careful who you get your information from where it
concerns this family. There's an army of rumors and half-
truths to choose from. Especially about me. Whoever it was

in this case was simply not telling you the truth—I trust out of ignorance rather than design. Carla and I are a highly celebrated noncouple. There are plenty of people who would like to see us married—there's a certain irresistible symmetry about it—and plenty of people who will be very quick to say that we're engaged. I've told you the truth, but you must decide now whom you're going to believe. . . . Does that answer your question?"

It was, at any rate, what Galen wanted to hear.

"Yes. It does. I'm sorry," she said a little awkwardly. "It's just that—"

"I know, sweet girl, but please let's not talk about it anymore. You've warded me off like the plague ever since I got back and I want very much to make up for lost time . . . starting with a proper hello."

With that his arms slipped around her shoulders with a gentle strength that took her breath away. His kiss was not so gentle. It was hungry and penetrating, and her body molded to his embrace with as much abandon as her wounds would allow. With a thrill that obliterated any lingering sense of why she had ever resisted him before, Galen was suddenly aware of a surge of sexual passion pushing up against the surface of Julian's restraint. Her only thought was This I must know, and she told him so with her kiss.

"I am drunk on your brandy, Mr. Baugh," she whispered truthfully with a slow delirious smile when she could breathe again. "But don't let that stop you." However, Julian was letting her fall gently against the pillows and leaning back away from her. He pushed her yellow hair off her forehead with the flat of his large smooth hand.

"I don't imagine this is what the doctor meant when he ordered bed rest," he said with a sheepish grin. "You do need your sleep. I'll be in in the morning."

A long while later Galen had barely closed her eyes. She could not stop thinking about the feel of Julian's body against hers: a thought which still made her insides shudder. She could not stop asking herself whether he could be falling in love with her, a state in which Galen now happily admitted to being herself. She saw him again in the darkened walled garden and felt his kiss, saw the way he looked at her at the Well Gate, recalled in every detail how his voice and manner had changed toward her since his first weekend at the Winds. She knew that he was. She closed her ears to Carla's confident, gleeful laugh and to Johnny's inadvertent warning, and pushed away the doubt that had come painfully to rest like a boulder on her chest. She thought, instead, of his kiss.

After what seemed like several hours of sleeplessness, she kicked the blankets aside and eased herself out of bed. There was not a sound in the great house as she crossed the hall, not a sound from William's room when she pressed her ear against the door. She opened it and went in. Kneeling at his bedside, she heard his regular breathing, felt that his skin was cool. Johanna's locket, which he slipped under his pillow each night, had fallen to the floor. After scooping it up, Galen carried it to the French windows through which cuts of silver-blue moonlight streamed, and opened it. She knew the woman in the tiny oval frame was smiling—she had seen the picture before—but distorted in the faint light, she now looked helpless and pleading, like a face from the dead.

A cold draft billowed the lace curtains and Galen went to latch the window. Here her hand froze on the knob, and her heart seemed to freeze in her chest. She caught her breath. On the lawn below, two figures were visible in the filmy moonlight. They were walking slowly together, heads inclined, arms around each other. They were turned away from her, but Carla's sardonic laughter rose on the wind to reach Galen's ears. She also knew at once who the man was. His face was hidden but she could see clearly the sheepskin collar of his coat turned up against the cold.

*   *   *

Collapsing on her bed, Galen felt nothing at first but a burning sensation in her cheeks and a dull emptiness in the pit of her stomach. This soon gave way to a sense of violation accompanied by a murderous screaming in her head. The bastard! The miserable lying bastard! How dare he! How *could* he? He hadn't even had the good taste to be *vague* about his relationship with Carla: He'd categorically *denied* any romantic involvement at all! What kind of man seduces a woman under such pretenses? What *kind* of man seduces a woman *within virtual earshot of his fiancée?* Then rushes back to her side? And *why?* To boast that conquest was assured?! Like something out of a de Laclos novel? And the motivation? A simple objective matter of sexual greed? Or something with less ephemeral gain—to undermine her relationship with his father? Out of simple Oedipal competition, or lingering fears about the soft underbelly of the Baugh inheritance? Or was it some irresistible combination of all these things?

The outrage that welled in her was monumental, to be sure but not all-consuming. Periodically it would ebb far enough for embarrassment to take its place. Julian's behavior was vile and unconscionable but she had let herself be fooled. She believed only what she had wanted to believe. Hadn't Johnny *told* her of Julian's engagement to Carla? (Why would Carla lie to Johnny? Why would Johnny lie to her?) But even if he had not, she should have at least suspected it on her own as the signs were everywhere for her to see. Brandy or no, she had simply chosen not to see, to believe instead in the false enticing promises of those beautiful black eyes, in which she thought she had seen tenderness and, yes, affection. If he had been a cad, she had been a dreamer. It is only natural that you feel vulnerable and exposed, she told herself in a reflective moment, but there is only just so much space for righteous

indignation. You knew, she chastised herself. Deep down
you knew, you knew, you knew.

To Galen's immeasurable relief, it was not Julian who came
to her room in the morning. (Mae, bringing breakfast, had
volunteered that Julian had business with Franny and had
left the estate early.) Her first—and last—visitor in Henry's
house was Johnny.

"How is my fallen angel?" he said with a handsome
grin as he took her hand and kissed it. He did not let it go.
"You look like Gunga Din."

"You look like the Angel Gabriel. Oh, Johnny, I am so
glad you're here."

"What is it, darling?"

"You have to do me a favor."

"Anything."

"Drive me back to the bungalow."

"My lord, why? What's wrong? Aren't they treating
you well?"

"No, it's not that. I just need to be by myself at home.
They're making much too much of me, and—"

"But you understand, you've really had quite a—"

"I know, and I'll stay in bed, but I desperately need to
sleep and I can't here. *Please*, Johnny." Galen looked so
distressed he began mechanically to pat her hand.

"You're really upset, aren't you? All right, I'll tell
H. L.—"

"Johnny, take me home first, then tell Henry. You
know what he'll say."

He hesitated.

"I'm going to go on my own anyway," she said, sliding her legs over the side of the bed. "I just thought maybe
you'd give me a lift."

"Of course I'll swing for this, but all right, my pet.
Where are your clothes?"

At the bungalow, Johnny made another concession by allowing her to lie on her living-room couch rather than her bed without a fuss. He went into the kitchen to make tea. Galen called Lily, whom they had found waiting hungrily on the front porch, and began stroking the dog's ears. She felt drained and miserably depressed.

"Something happened up at the house," Johnny called from the other room. "What was it?"

"Nothing, really. I just don't like so much of a fuss being made over me."

"You're lying," he said, appearing at the door with a mug of tea in his hand and an exaggerated look of skepticism on his face. "Everyone likes being made a fuss over. And whether you do or not, it wouldn't be your style to be ungracious about it. It's Julian, isn't it? The old boy made a pass at you."

"No, he didn't!" Galen snapped, aware of the color rising in her cheeks. "Johnny, please—I'm so tired, I'm irritable, I'm not a good patient. Don't make matters worse."

He looked at her for a moment, then flashed his dashing smile and said in a gentler tone, "Don't you think you ought at least to call H. L. and tell him where you've run off to? Shall I?"

"If you wouldn't mind."

Based on the laughter coming presently from the kitchen, Henry did not seem to take the news too badly.

"You've wounded him deeply, of course," Johnny said as he reappeared with a cup of tea for himself, "but he's willing to overlook it this time. He insists you let Mae bring you meals, however, and that he can call you from Franny's tonight. Fair? Good, now that I'm off the hook, move your feet and let me sit down. This is an old family remedy that cures everything from bleeding ulcers to beriberi."

Placing her feet on his lap, he began to massage the soles with his thumbs.

"Better?"

Galen closed her eyes. "Oh, God.

"Johnny," she said after a pause.

"Yes?"

"Thank you."

"You're welcome."

"I mean, you're a sweet friend."

"I know." His hand moved to her ankle and then slowly to her calf. She glanced up to meet the gaze of his languid blue eyes. There was a smile at the corners of his mouth. An ambiguous smile started at the corners of hers and she slowly parted her lips to speak. Even if she was sure of just what she was going to say, she never got the chance.

They had missed the approach of the car, but they both now heard the steps on the porch and then someone coming quickly across the kitchen floor. Neither moved. Looking back on it, Galen thought how comical they must have looked, cups suspended halfway to their mouths. Julian, who had stopped at the living-room door, however, failed to see the humor in the cozy little scene. Galen recognized the coldly set mouth and flashing eyes she had seen at the door of Henry's cottage in East Cutty and she felt herself flush with fresh rage.

"Didn't anyone in the Baugh family ever learn to knock?" she asked him, setting her mug on the coffee table. Johnny shot Galen a surprised look. If he was aware of the menacing gaze that Julian had trained on him, Johnny did not let on. Setting his own mug down with one hand and sliding the other slowly back down to her foot, he resumed his massage. His tone was cheerful.

"Julian, old boy, I'm afraid your patient didn't like your cooking."

"Yes, I can see that."

The looks exchanged by the two men were not something Galen had been prepared for. The animosity between them was as palpable as ice water. Galen realized this was the first time she had seen them together and understood at once that they hated each other. She was afraid Johnny would break a bone in her foot.

"As it doesn't matter where I get my bed rest," she said stiffly, "I think I will be more comfortable here."

Julian looked at her for the first time only now.

"As you wish." The man's anger was obvious, but Galen was not sure now how much of it was directed at her. "I am going to Paris this evening," he said stiffly. "I've come only to wish you a speedy recovery. As my father will be away for the night, perhaps John will see to your needs."

"When are you planning on leaving, Julian?" Johnny asked.

"Why?"

"I'm flying out myself; I thought I might give you a lift to the airport."

"Not necessary, but thanks" was the curt reply, and he was gone.

They sat and listened to the whine of the Jaguar engine quickly fade as it sped away. Galen expected Johnny to needle about whatever it was that had obviously gone on between her and Julian to precipitate such a visit and exchange. But he surprised her by lifting her feet off his lap and getting up from the couch.

"In fact," he said, collecting the mugs, "I have some business to attend to before I'm off myself." The encounter with Julian had obviously troubled him and he now seemed distracted. "But I'll be by to check on you before I leave. I've got something that will tame that nasty head and make you sleep."

"That would be wonderful. And thanks for the rub, Johnny, it was marvelous. Particularly now that you've stopped."

Galen smiled when she said this but Johnny seemed barely to have heard.

11

Galen alternately read and stared at the ceiling for the rest of the afternoon. Her mood had gone from bad to worse. She was still furious with Julian—and angry with herself for allowing him such a free hand with her heart—but more depressing was the idea that she had turned the whole thing into a public spectacle. She should not have provoked him in Johnny's presence. Not because it was beneath her to be snide, but because it so utterly exposed her. She probably should not have left Henry's house at all. At the very least not in the fashion she chose.

To console herself, Galen tried to redraw the picture of her flight, making a case for no one's having noticed anything extraordinary about her behavior. She was on the verge of believing it when Franny rattled the screen door. It was around five. Even more nattily dressed than usual, he announced that he was picking Henry up for an affair that was expected to run late. As it was not far from Franny's house, Henry would spend the night there. No one encouraged Henry to be on the road after dark.

"In fact, if ever you hear he is, by all means remain in the safety of your home," Franny told her. "The solution has been to deprive him of a car by luring him back to my house with Napoleon brandy I keep hidden in the cellar. We've had great success so far: He hasn't had an accident in over a year. Now as for you, my dear, H. L. insists—"

"Tell him not to worry about me, *please*. I'm feeling much better. I got entirely too much attention."

"So I understand. Based on H. L.'s report, I rather think you hurt Julian's feelings." Franny regarded her with a gently accusatory look. "He's gone away in something of a rage."

"I assure you that had nothing to do with me."

Galen must have sounded defensive because Franny's eyebrows arched. "Forgive me for prying, child, but—"

"But what, Fran?"

"Let me put it this way." He paused and looked at the ceiling. "Julian and Johnny Foote are not the closest of friends. It would not take much to set the two at each other's throats."

"You're not suggesting that I'm playing them off against each other?" Galen answered a little too hotly. "Between you and me, though I hardly know him I have found Johnny to be a very likable man. I'm sure you've heard, as it appears to be public domain, that we've ridden together a few times, been to the theater once and to dinner. That's the size of it. But whatever it is, my friendship with Johnny is hardly Julian's concern. If it's not already clear to you, let me point out that Julian has other things on his mind. Whatever his problem with Johnny, it has nothing to do with me."

"Quite right, my dear, quite right," Franny said but a frown still creased his brow. "So, do you expect to be seeing Johnny again?" he asked with an attempt at a smile.

Galen stared incredulously at him.

"I mean, will he be visiting you while you recupe?"

"Actually no. He's leaving tonight. He said he had business out of town. Why?"

"No reason. I just think it would be a good idea if someone was taking care of you."

"Thank you, Fran, but I assure you I'm fine."

Franny rose to leave. Galen asked him to stay a minute longer.

"Fran," she said in a cautious tone, "will you tell me something? This may sound odd to you but—did Carla and Johanna get along?"

She might have flung her book at him. He swung around to her with an expression of utter surprise on his pale creased face. His recovery was immediate, but a little overdone, and when he spoke his tone was unnaturally casual.

"Why ever do you ask?"

"If you think it's improper of me, I'm sorry—"

"No, I'm just—you see the thing's been buried for so long. But, well, yes. They were very close, in fact. They did most everything together, went everywhere together. Peggy Bowdoin used to call them the twins. The joke was that they even had matching luggage . . . Can there be some reason for your asking?"

"Oh, not really, it was just something that Mae said."

"Mae? Whatever did she say?"

"Well, nothing specific. It's just that she's so protective of Johanna's memory and seems—well, openly hostile toward Carla."

Franny's laugh was a little too loud. "Oh, well, there you see, that's Mae. That's just Mae. If you hadn't noticed, my dear, Mae is openly hostile to everybody and was just as wicked and miserable to Johanna when she was alive as she is to the rest of us now. Now I suggest you not worry about these things and get some rest. We'll call in the morning."

Half an hour later Johnny pushed the kitchen door

open and, calling something Galen could not make out, got himself a glass, filled it with water, and marched it ceremoniously out to her. He slowly unwrapped a closed palm to reveal two shiny blood-red pills.

"As promised," he announced with a self-satisfied air. "There is yet to be a headache made that can stand up to these. Also good for pain due to hangnail, heart attack, appendicitis, bullet wound, and broken leg. I recommend two." Between her pounding head and throbbing shoulder, Johnny did not have to insist.

Johnny had not only recovered his good humor but seemed almost elated, flirting shamelessly and making her laugh. He explained his manic state as a function of the fact he had decided against better judgment on a "horribly big" acquisition and was meeting with a dealer in New York that night. He was in fact late getting away and had time only to administer his miracle drug, kiss her full on the mouth, and fly out the door. He said he probably could not make it back for two or three days but would call.

It took only twenty minutes for the pills to kick in. First the pain went away; then a deep relaxation swept over her like a wave of warm water. The sofa began to undulate gently. The book she was reading wobbled and dropped on her chest. As she gazed through drooping lids at the creeping dusk outside the window, a pleasant heaviness overcame her and at some point she closed her eyes.

Galen dreamed that William was having a birthday party. A long white table was strewn with brightly colored streamers, blowers, miniature gifts, and party hats. The room was filled with balloons. William was sitting at one end of the table, with ten or so children down each side. They were in highchairs, though they all seemed too old for that. Someone was taking pictures with a flashbulb, which turned the children's eyes translucent pink, like rabbits'. Then Galen is in the kitchen where Johanna, Carla, and Colin are lighting candles on a huge flat cake with elaborate glazed writing on it like the kind one sees at a retirement party. Carla is for some reason dressed completely in black with a mourning veil. Johanna, who appears elated and whose auburn hair flies wildly about her each time she turns her head, asks Galen to finish the candles for her and sails back into the dining room where the children are hooting on their horns, popping balloons, and laughing. Colin and Carla have stopped what they are doing and are staring, though not unkindly, at Galen. She is not sure whether to keep lighting the candles. There are so many that some have already burned down and gone out. It seems to be taking forever, and she can hear the children beginning to cry. Galen looks around and Colin and Carla are gone and there is no one to help her with the candles. They have all burned out. She hears suddenly that the children have stopped crying. She listens and there is a terrifying unnatural silence from the dining room. Galen walks through the pantry, which has become a long hall packed with Henry's paintings, toward the room. Lily begins to bark and the barks echo down the hall. Galen's heart begins to pound so loudly that it, too, echoes in the hall. She stands outside the swinging door and listens and hears nothing but barking and the beat of her heart. When she opens the door she sees that all the children are gone. Just Carla is there, sitting in a highchair in her veil and black lace gloves. She is smiling but from under her veil black tears are dropping like ink onto the white tablecloth.

12

Galen had been listening absently to the chorus of barking and banging for almost a minute before she realized that someone was pounding on the kitchen door. Judging from the light streaming in the bay window, it was at least eleven o'clock. The trip back to full consciousness, however, was something on the order of a sprint up a sand dune. What did you do to me, Johnny? she mumbled to herself as she spilled off the couch in the wrinkled clothes she had slept in and stumbled into the kitchen. She peered through the glass. There were two men in blue uniforms. Police.

Sitting on the couch again trying to keep her eyes heading straight, it took a moment for what they were telling her to penetrate her narcoleptic fog. Two local cops right out of Central Casting—one tall and skinny with bad skin, undoubtedly the rookie; the other old and barrely with a face like a bull dog—were sitting on the edge of their chairs, arms resting on their knees. Galen could not get over the size of the rookie's feet; they looked like they might be size sixteens. Do they make a size sixteen? She struggled to concentrate.

"We put it at between nine and eleven," the fat one was saying.

"Between nine and eleven?"

"Yes, ma'am. Can you tell us where you were last night?" He looked meaningfully at Galen's clothes.

"Here, I think. Yes, of course. I took some pills. I mean painkillers—sleeping pills—I've had this accident, you see. I only just woke up."

"I see, and you saw no one last night?"

"Henry's *house* was robbed?"

"Yes, ma'am," the older cop said a little impatiently. "You were here and you saw no one last night?"

"Yes—I mean, no. Yes, I was here, and no, I saw no one. You said his *paintings* were stolen?"

"Some silver, a few manageable antiques, but he was definitely after the paintings." This was from the rookie.

"He?"

"The perp—ah, burglar. We think it was a professional job."

"Henry's paintings."

"Yes, ten."

"I'm sorry," Galen said. "I can't tell you any more than I already have. Mr. Baugh's grandson and the house-keeper were the only people at home as far as I know."

"No, the grandson was at the—" The rookie took out his note pad. "Richard Bowdoins'?"

"Yes, friends of the family—"

"For the night and the housekeeper had the night off."

"What about Carla Baugh?"

"She was in New York."

"Oh, well, then . . ."

"Mind if we look around?" The bulldog got to his feet.

"No, go right ahead, please. It's not really my house. Lily, *get down*. I'm sorry."

"That's okay. Hi ya, fella. This place have an attic?"

"I don't think so."

"A basement?"

"No. Do you think I did it and hid the paintings here?" Galen was smiling but the officers did not seem to be amused.

"Just a routine check."

Galen was beginning to feel as if she had awakened in the middle of a television show, but the sensation did not last. *Ten of Henry's paintings had been stolen.*

"I wish I could tell you more," she said, "but I think I would have slept through an atomic blast."

The cops looked at her blankly. The phone rang.

"Excuse me," she said, and went to answer it in the kitchen. Mara was calling from New York.

"I thought you were sick in bed at Henry's house. What are you doing there? You make a run for it?"

"Actually yes, but I can't talk now. I'll have to call you back."

"This won't take a sec." Galen knew the voice: It would take several secs. "I've got a twelve o'clock in a couple of minutes so I can't stay on, but guess who I just saw?"

"Mara I don't have time for this. I've got the pol—"

"Carla and Joo-lian. You weren't sure they were an item?"

"I am now."

"Let me tell you, honey, we're talking about *The Young and the Restless*."

"*Julian?*"

"Put it this way, he was not fighting her off."

"No, I mean Julian's in Europe." Galen threw an involuntary glance toward the living room.

"Well, I saw them climb into a limo outside Nigel White's office five minutes ago. That's where I am now."

"You don't even know what he looks like."

"You've described him to me: tall, dark, handsome, Savile Row suit, Burberry raincoat, Rudolf Schnieder shoes . . . Tell me, who else would have a hand up Carla's dress? And I know her personally."

"I don't know but I'm sure it wasn't Julian."

"You still think they're not in amorado."

"On the contrary I'm sure they are, it's just that he left for France last night. Listen, Mara, I really can't talk now, the police are here. Can I call you back?"

"The *police*? What did you do?"

"*I* didn't do anything, Henry was robbed, someone broke in and took ten of his paintings."

"You're kidding."

"No, I'll tell you la—"

"Who do they think did it?"

"They don't know. I'll have to—"

"Who could it have been?"

"Anybody. No one was here. Except me, and I was asleep."

"Do they think it was an inside job?"

"*Mara.*"

"Okay, okay. Call me tonight. I'll be at Serge's."

The chilly afternoon air was rich with the smell of rotting leaves and homey traces of woodsmoke from someone's chimney or brushpile a long way off. The distant whine of chain saws made the world seem comfortingly simple and small. Galen walked slowly along the overgrown path that led away from the back of the bungalow. She breathed in deeply and let out a long sigh. She could see her breath. She blew out again. Her head was finally beginning to clear.

Lily waited for her at the point where the trail intercepted one of the broad bridle paths that laced the woods of the southern half of the estate. Galen turned west and followed the wider path through a stand of slender young silver beeches, most of whose yellow-white leaves had flown. The forest was thick on all sides, but after a short while she could sense by the subtle glow of reflected light the nearness of a large clearing to the north. She walked a little farther. It was the great field behind Henry's house. The path had arced gradually northwest and was tracing the edge of the grounds. Galen stopped at a point where the trees had thinned out and looked across at the majestic house. She had never seen it from this vantage point. It looked more imposing and severe than ever. She gave a little shiver. What had happened there last night?

Galen was still standing and staring when a figure emerged from the house. It descended the terrace steps and began making its way across the field directly for her. She could tell by the walk and misshapen County Donegal hat that it was Henry. She was not sure whether to wait or to avoid an encounter. She had telephoned earlier, and he had sounded distracted and as much as said he had rather not have to see anyone else right away. She had heard voices in the background.

The decision was made for her by Lily, who on seeing the old man had bolted into the open and was bounding toward him, appearing intermittently over the top of the long grass, like a miniature kangaroo.

"Hello there," Henry hailed Galen when he finally made out her figure through the trees. His voice sounded cheerful and he smiled at her as he approached. He seemed more concerned about how she was feeling than what had taken place at the Winds.

"Are you supposed to be out of bed?" he asked cheerily.

"My three days are up."

"No, they're not."

"I'm counting Thursday."

"So I see. I won't tell. You're sure you're feeling better?"

"Much. A bit drowsy. How about you?"

"Oh, I'm all right. It's always disturbing to think of someone in white gloves, black leotards, and a ski mask creeping about your house, but I suppose I should be flattered he'd go to all that trouble for my pictures. I presume this means I've finally arrived."

"No one was at home?"

"No."

"Isn't that odd?"

"How do you mean?"

"Well, how would he know? The house is rarely empty, isn't it?" It was a nasty implication and Galen immediately regretted having made it.

"These days, I suppose" was all he said. Galen quickly changed the subject. She asked him what would happen next.

"To be honest, I'm not altogether sure. You see, dear Carla, who's always handled the business side, has been running interference for me. (I'm playing hooky now.) She came up as soon as she heard, and the darling handled the statements to the police, estimated value of the pictures and so on, and has started in on the insurance claim."

"Have you been able to reach Julian?"

"Oh, yes, he's at the house now."

"This house?"

"Yes."

"I thought— He said he was leaving for Europe."

"No, he changed his plans. He evidently had business in New York and flew up with Carla this morning."

The Baughs may have managed to keep the plane crash quiet, but poor Henry was less effective this time around in keeping the news media out of his personal affairs. Monday morning's *Boston Globe* ran the story on its front page under the headline:

BAUGH PAINTINGS STOLEN FROM ARTIST'S HOUSE

Ten Works Worth Almost $750,000
Removed From Berkshire Mansion

By Diane Lang
Globe Staff Writer

STOVER—Ten H. L. Baugh paintings valued at nearly three-quarters of a million dollars were stolen Saturday night from the artist's mansion here, according to police.

Mr. Baugh was not at home at the time. His housekeeper and grandson were also away for the night, police said. According to Stover Police Sgt. Craig Stebbens, who is heading the investigation, there are no suspects in the case but the robbery was believed to have been a professional job committed by a single individual.

"He knew what he was after and he knew where everything was," Sgt. Stebbens said. "There are no prints, no evidence of forced entry. The alarm system was disconnected. It was a very clean job. We're not dealing with kids or some second-story man."

Asked about the chances of recovering the works, Sgt. Stebbens said, "With something like this, they're probably out of the country by now." Asked about any leads, he said only that "the investigation is continuing."

The artist is best known for his portraits and rural landscapes. His most recent work, which was exhibited following a two-year hiatus during which time it was widely believed he had retired, is a dramatic departure from his traditional work in both style and subject matter. His critically acclaimed show of seascapes this summer at the Boston Museum of Fine Arts stunned the art world.

Police would not say which paintings were stolen or whether they were older or more recent works. Mr. Baugh was not available for comment.

(continued on Page A12)

Galen was just turning to the jump page when the smell of smoke catapulted her out of her chair. In a single fluid motion she was across the kitchen and whacking the lever that opened the blackened glass door of the ancient toaster oven, which, regardless of the setting, cooked whatever was in it until it was gone. This was not the first time she had burned the toast. Swearing emphatically, she threw two slivers of charcoal into the trash and headed for the pantry, which ran off between the kitchen and the living room, to get two more pieces of bread.

Here she found Lily, nose pressed into the corner, wobbling her lump of a tail and emitting short grunts. "Cut that out and get in here," Galen said authoritatively. Not only did the grunts continue but the dog did not even look around. Galen had seen this kind of thing before, although not in this setting. Lily had cornered a cockroach: second to cats, her favorite prey. Taking a broom in hand, Galen swept the dog out of the way and poised for the kill. But there was no bug.

"Sorry, girl, looks like he got away," Galen murmured, only slowly remembering that she had never seen a roach in the bungalow. But the dog pushed her way back into the corner and started her grunts anew. It was not until Galen bent down to pull the animal away again that she saw it. It was funny how she had never noticed it before. The darkly stained walls of the pantry were ribbed with raised narrow panels, four inches wide. She crouched to study the floorline again then slowly stood up, tracing with her finger the discreet line of a hidden door, which sealed almost invisibly along the crack between two of the panels. The grandfather of one of Galen's childhood friends had had a hidden wine cellar, out of which her friend, as a teenager, used to lift terrifically rare bottles of wine for sloshing down at pajama parties. The key to access to his cellar had been a latch located somewhere else in the room. Galen was looking for such a device when she heard a rap on the door and Johnny's voice calling her name.

"Johnny, Johnny, you'll never guess what I've found," she cried, rushing across the kitchen to let him in. "Lily found it actu— What is it? You look upset."

"I'm afraid I've got bad news, dear. Sit down." Johnny looked haggard. Galen felt the tingle of alarm.

"Henry—"

"No, no. He's fine. Everyone's fine. It's nothing like that. The police have a primary suspect in the case."

"But that's wonderful, isn't it?"

"They have an arrest warrant out for Caetano."

"*Caetano?* That's impossible."

"I'm afraid it's not. They've done it."

"But, that's *insane.* Caetano would no more steal one of Henry's paintings than you or I would. There must be a mistake. What evidence could they have possibly found?"

"He was seen entering the property at about the time the police think the theft occurred."

"By whom?"

"By Julian."

"*What?*"

Johnny told her that according to Julian's statement to the police, he had left the Winds at about five o'clock Saturday night and driven into Boston before realizing that he had left behind some papers that were essential to business he was conducting that night in New York. He telephoned his appointment, rescheduled it for the next morning, moved back his plane reservation, and had a leisurely meal with a friend in town before returning to Stover to pick up his papers. He arrived at the Winds at about 11 P.M. After leaving the driveway five or ten minutes later, he passed a van, which he identified as Caetano's, on the River Road. Looking in his rearview mirror just before the road swung into the trees, he saw the van pull into the Winds driveway and start up the hill toward the house.

"The police are looking for him now," Johnny said. "The problem is he seems to have skipped."

"Skipped? What do you mean *skipped*?"

"His apartment is empty and he appears to have taken some clothes with him. Apparently he was due at the barn yesterday morning and no one has seen him since."

"I don't believe it."

"It's hard to accept, I know."

"Johnny! *Do you?*"

"I don't know, Galen. I mean, I agree with you it's *so* unlikely. I've known him for years. But someone had to know the house was empty. They had to know about the alarm system. And of course where all the paintings were. He was in and out very fast."

"Exactly. And I would hardly characterize Caetano as a professional art thief."

"It was either professional *or* an inside job, that's what the police said. And . . . Julian left no doubt in their minds that it was Caetano's van he saw."

"You really believe he did it," Galen said incredulously.

"That's not what I said," Johnny said, taking her hand. "I said I didn't know what to believe. But Caetano's disappeared and I can't believe Julian would lie."

"Why not? You two seem ready to believe anything about each other."

"What about you? The look you gave him the other day would have stopped a train."

The phone rang. It was Alex Taylor, Galen's former boss and good friend at the *Post*. She had called him as soon as Johnny had left and asked him for two favors: First, to find out what he could about the police investigation into the robbery. Second, to pull the clips on the deaths of Colin and Johanna Baugh.

"We miss you, Gale," Alex said. It was four-thirty, just over an hour to go before the metropolitan reporters' first-edition deadline. Galen could feel the energy and tension of the city desk pulse over the line. The AP and Reuters wires crackled like static in the background. She felt a mix of nostalgia and relief.

"Heavy news day?"

No sooner had she asked than she heard a familiar voice come over the newsroom intercom: "We must have all metropolitan copy by five o'clock, please, early deadline tonight, all metropolitan copy by five o'clock."

"Must be," Galen answered herself.

"Iran-Iraq, big drop in the dollar, *big* drop in the Dow, presidential press conference, and an Air France crash."

"You want to talk another time?"

"No. I'm afraid this won't take long. On the robbery suspect, we know nothing that you don't. But it's not looking very good for this Brazilian kid. His disappearance is pretty incriminating. He's going to have to have one hell of an alibi if he does show up. I understand they've staked out his family's place in Rhode Island."

"No other suspects, of course."

"Nope. I'm sorry, Gale, I can only let you know as soon as we hear. You conducting a little investigation of your own?"

"Not really. He's just a friend."

"Sure, sure." Alex knew Galen too well.

"What about the other?"

"I'm afraid I have even less on that. There are no stories about a plane crash on August tenth that year or *anything* about *any* plane crash in western Mass. in the next month. As for the obits, Colin Baugh's is a four-incher that says he died in a hunting accident. There is nothing on a Johanna Baugh, but Johanna *Fairchild*'s appears a week later and does not mention a cause of death. You know of course how they died."

"Yes. But if you do, why didn't the *Post* or the *Globe* run the story?"

"You know, Gale, the Baughs are a very old, very well-connected Massachusetts family. The son—"

"Julian."

"—is a very powerful man. I can't speak for Ross at the *Globe*, but the man upstairs here has always been chummy with that crowd. He's got an H. L. Baugh in his office."

"Probably a print," Galen said sourly. Alex chuckled.

"That's not a very satisfactory explanation," she went on after a pause.

"I know."

"What's going on?"

"It happens all the time."

"That doesn't wash either, Alex."

"I'm sorry, Gale. It's the best I can do."

"I know, I know. Will you call me if you turn something up?"

"Only if you promise to do the same."

She heard the Jaguar engine long before it got to the bungalow. Between her accident and the robbery, work on Henry's manuscript, at least for the coming week, was deemed out of the question, and it was agreed Galen would return to Boston until both Henry and she felt up to resuming. In truth, she no longer seemed to be suffering any ill effects from her fall—her shoulder was still a little sore, but the dizzy spells seemed to have passed. However, she had other reasons for wishing to be away, and it was with a keen sense of relief that she had been packing her suitcase for the trip home. But now she froze with her hand on its open lid as she listened to the car's long approach. It was coming fast. In a few moments its headlights were sweeping the house and came to rest on the kitchen door. It seemed forever before the engine died. But then almost immediately she heard Julian's hurried step on the wooden porch and an impatient rap on the glass.

Galen walked slowly through the house and into the kitchen. She swung the door open but did not step aside. She could not read Julian's expression, but he could evidently read hers and, acknowledging it and that she was not inviting him in, took a half step back. If his gesture was respectful, it was less than meek. Even meeting him eye to eye from the vantage of the kitchen step, Galen felt uncertain of her ability to control the situation. Her own calm was a precarious enough affair.

"Galen," Julian began stiffly, "I've come to apologize for my behavior here last week." It was with surprise that she heard something like irritation under the decorous tone. It registered like a slow insult. "I was concerned and at first confused by your sudden flight. I believe I overreacted. I assure you it was never my intent to take liberties with you."

"Oh, no?" was Galen's acid reply to what sounded to her like a gratuitous and unimaginative disclaimer for the offense of his lies. Not until much later would it occur to her that Julian had meant to apologize only for storming into the bungalow two days before without knocking. For now, her judgment was not what it might have been. It had been a horrible three days. Except for the one induced by Johnny's red pills, she had not had a decent night's sleep since the accident. Not at any rate since she had discovered the truth about Julian. It had wounded her deeply and left her bitterly angry and massively depressed. The problem was she really had begun to fall in love with the man—the man who was going to marry Carla when the goddamn cherries came into bloom.

As for the state of that love now, it had been exploded by his deception, and the bits swept away by a healthy rage. She had briefly blamed herself for having been so willingly deceived, even perhaps for having invited it. However, by the time Julian was facing her on the front porch of the bungalow with the steely gaze and cool politesse he wielded like a spear, Galen had long since come full circle: She glared back at him with undiminished fury.

On top of everything else there was the matter of Caetano, who Julian, of all people, had implicated. Galen was convinced that the boy was hiding out of fear, and the more she had thought about his having been betrayed by the Baughs, who—in the most charitable view—did nothing to protect him, the more enraged she had become. She would have thought Julian incapable of such a thing; certainly no one could believe Caetano would rob Henry. But then, she would not have thought him capable of so abusing her own trust either.

Galen struggled to control herself. "Let's just forget it, shall we? Now if you'll excuse—"

"But I *have* offended you," Julian said, a hand shooting out to stop the door. "Deeply. I will certainly endeavor never to do so again. But in fairness, I would remind you that it was not entirely without provocation."

"*Provocation?*" Galen was ready to scream.

"You were not exactly subtle," Julian went on, his inflection clearly accusatory. Galen's jaw hung open. The man had the audacity to sound angry! "Am I deluded to think your behavior had something to do with me? Or perhaps I have been naïve. Could it all along have had more to do with John Foote?"

"That's none of your damn business!"

"Perhaps not, but I must advise you—"

"You will do *no such thing*! I am not interested in your advice! I have seen enough of your self-serving, paranoid, Machiavellian worldview, Julian Baugh! First it's your father, now Johnny. Who do you think you are? The height and breadth of your ego is truly astounding! It belongs in a goddamn museum! Right next to the totem of the pagan god who oversees the comings and goings of its minuscule creations! Well, I am *not* one of your creations, and I will *not* be observed or manipulated or controlled by you. I have had it with your arrogant disregard for other people's feelings!"

To her great annoyance she felt a tear splash on her cheek, and Julian took a step toward her.

"Galen—" he began, but she would not let him speak.

"You steamroll your way through people's lives, taking—let *go* of me—taking what you want out of some perverted notion of what's your due, as if suffering has somehow entitled you to give other people pain!"

"Galen, please, you're dis—"

"I think of him hiding out somewhere, trying to understand. The one person he trusted, the one person who he would have expected to help him. He *loved* you."

"Galen, dear—"

"What could Caetano have possibly done to you that you would betray him like that?"

This got through. In his attempt to soothe her, Julian's voice had softened and an infuriating gentle expression had come over his face. But at this last remark, he looked at her as if she had pulled out a gun.

After a long moment in which recognition seemed at

last to take hold, he said with even, ominous quiet, "Is that what you believe? That I lied?"

"It wouldn't be the first time."

"Why would I lie?"

She brushed her tears off her face with an angry sweep of her hand and met his dark look squarely.

"To—suit—your—needs."

13

Caetano's absence hung over the great house like a dark cloud. Galen had returned to the Winds the following Monday, and she and Henry had tried to go back to work. The next five days had been less than productive. There was an almost funereal air about the place, everyone speaking in hushed tones, the rooms where Henry's paintings had hung—the library, the parlor off the living room, Phoebe's study—being avoided.

Carla, who had helped Henry in the first days of the investigation, had returned to New York halfway through that first week and had stayed away since. Johnny also seemed to have found the place too depressing to take, and left the day after the police began looking for Caetano. Galen suspected that Henry had also let it be known that he was not in the mood for company. Even Franny seemed to be avoiding the house. As for Julian, he had left the Winds the night of his stormy encounter with Galen and had remained away on business in Europe and New York for the last week and a half.

The cast, however, was about to reassemble.

The only one who seemed to have found any joy in the whole affair was William. He appeared in fact delighted to have had a break-in, and was clearly thrilled by the presence of police detectives endlessly peering, poking, and measuring things about the house and grounds. (He had not been told that Caetano was their primary suspect.) Two weeks after the robbery his language was laced with expressions like "M.O.," "alibi," "priors," "plainclothes," and "perp." Just whether his sympathies lay with the detectives or the perpetrator was, however, not so clear. Both Henry and Galen had seen him on separate occasions playing imaginary games in which he seemed to have cast himself in the role of the thief.

"I'm beginning to wonder about William," Henry said wearily from the window of his study where he and Galen were finishing up their work for the week. It was Friday and Galen was delighted to be leaving Stover for the weekend. Henry was watching his grandson crawl commando-style through the shrubs at the back of the house. "He asked me over breakfast whether I wouldn't 'fence' some marbles for him. I'm not sure what that means but I gathered from the way he said it that it wasn't legal."

"It's just a phase," Galen said, sliding the manuscript into her briefcase and getting up from Henry's desk. "Tell Mugsy I'll be at my crib."

"I beg your pardon."

"Inform your grandson, with whom I have a walking engagement, that I will meet him at the bungalow."

"Quite. Have a good weekend, my dear. Give John my best and I shall see you Monday morning?"

Galen was just wondering how Henry had known that she would be seeing Johnny in Boston that weekend when she heard William scuffling across her kitchen floor. His cheeks were pink from running and his trouser knees were smeared with mud and grass. He found her in the bedroom, lacing up her hiking boots.

"Ready?" he asked.

"Ready."

She had promised to go with him to the ice pond to look for frogs. Located at the northern end of the estate on the other side of the stable yard, it would be a long walk. Galen was eager to get away, as Henry said Carla and Julian were due at the Winds sometime that evening, but she knew William would be disappointed if she put it off again. As it was, he shadowed her every move until they were out of the house.

"I'm coming, I'm coming. Let's take some apples. Here you go . . . Let me get my coat . . . Hold on. Hold on. All right. Here I come. Where's Lily? Okay, we're off. You lead."

It was a clear windy fall afternoon and dead leaves flew all around them like huge brown flakes of snow. William was, as usual, talking about the robbery.

"I think I know how he got in the house," he was saying as they followed a wide trail that circled the stables to the east.

"And how's that?"

"Through my room. You never saw it before but there's a secret way to get into my room from the balcony. There's a ladder right under my window. Hidden in the flowers. Uncle Colin showed me."

Galen considered it. The back side of the house was literally crawling with trumpet vines, which presumably clung to a trellis.

"Perhaps, but the burglar disconnected the alarm system," she said. "Why would he do that?"

"So it *looked* like he came in the door, of course."

"Of course."

Galen and William had had a version of this conversation ten times in the last two weeks and she had begun to believe his obsession with the thief was rooted in anxiety.

"You know he's not going to come back, William . . . the burglar, I mean."

"I know." He said this with a sigh that sounded so let down that Galen wondered suddenly whether she was not wrong.

"William, how much television do you watch?"

"I don't get to cause we don't have one. Grandpa says it turns your brain into cat food. Mae lets me sometimes but"—he glanced at Galen cautiously—"I'm not suppose to tell."

"Your secret's safe with me."

"Hardly ever really."

"Right, I know."

They crossed River Road and climbed the gate that opened into a long low hayfield that an early frost had begun to turn stiff and white. On the other side the trail crossed a noisily rushing stream and led back into woods. William and Lily ran ahead and Galen followed in distracted silence. She was looking forward to a weekend in Boston. She regretted missing Mara again but relished the notion of being in the city. Since the robbery, she had found herself not entirely at ease in the bungalow. More than once in the last two weeks she had imagined that she had heard footsteps outside late at night. Several times she had also awakened from a sound sleep in the middle of the night for no apparent reason and found her heart pounding. To Lily's unbridled delight, Galen had started letting the dog sleep on her bed with her. But whatever had awakened Galen had not managed to rouse her sentry, who in each case had continued to snore lightly through her moments of dread.

"William."

"What?" Boy and dog had returned to her side.

"You said your mother used to stay in the bungalow."

"When Daddy was away sometimes. I did, too."

"You know the pantry, where the cereal and the soup cans are kept?"

"Yah, there's a secret door there."

"You *know* about it? How does it work? I mean, how do you open it?"

"There's a switch. Underneath, on the side."

"What's behind the door?"

"Some stairs that go down and a room with shelves in it."

"You're kidding! A wine cellar? A *hidden* wine cellar? In a little house like that? Whatever for?"

If the boy knew, he would have to tell her another time.

"There it is!" he cried now and broke into a run.

They had stepped out of the woods at the top of a sloping clearing of scrubby grass overrun with exploded milkweeds and blazing red chokecherry shrubs. At the base of the gentle hill, protected from the gusting wind by a tangle of trees on three sides, lay the ice pond, as still as if it were frozen. The black water was barely visible under a mosaic of floating leaves. Where the cover was broken, it was so clean that they could see the junkyard of branches, logs, and leaves ten feet down as clearly as if they were looking through a pane of glass. The pool was swollen from recent rain and overflowed across a stone dam on the far side. The artificial banks on either side were grassy; the rest of the shore was mud, moss, and lichen-stained ledge.

William was already in position on the grassy part of the bank, stooped at the waist with his hands on his knees, when Galen caught up. She joined him in his search and with glacial gradualness they sidestepped their way toward the waterfall, scanning the tangle of twigs, grass, and leaves at water's edge for the giveaway bulge of a submerged frog's nose.

"Are you sure there's some here?" William asked after several minutes.

"No."

He straightened. "No!"

"I never said I'd actually seen any," Galen said, taking another sidestep along the bank. "I only said that I *thought* it would be a good place to look. Remember?"

"Oh," he said skeptically, and stooped slowly back over.

After several minutes of this they had had no luck, and Galen suggested they might do better if they split up. She instructed William to continue to work his bank while she circled around to the far side.

For several minutes she backtracked up the full, clamorous stream that fed the pond in search of a place to cross. The surging water sparkled as it cascaded between two banks of emerald-green moss. The sun-dappled woods of the bog were like something out of a fairy story about damsels, knights, and magicians. Galen walked slowly, watching the water bulge and fall, here like ice, there like a column of cut glass. She stopped to stare in silence. It was so uncomplicated. She wished she could sit down and think of nothing for a while. She wished she could stop thinking about Caetano. She wished even more that she could stop thinking about Julian.

The spell, which was fragile to begin with, did not, however, last. Glancing up, she was surprised to see that she was out of sight of the pond. Looking down at the now-narrow stream, she also realized that she had wandered much deeper into the woods than she had needed to go to cross it. She took a deep breath. Another day she might have kept going. But today there was William and the long trek home.

She was just turning to head back when she noticed something else. On the other side of the brook, cradled in a curve in the cliff that rose behind the pond and ran west

like a great wall for almost a hundred yards, was a dilapi-
dated building. A snarl of leafless vines covered it so completely that they all but obscured a small solitary window
that faced in the direction of the pond. The broad side,
which faced Galen, appeared to have neither windows nor
a door. Whatever entrance there was must lie on the far
side. Too utilitarian-looking for a cabin, it had to have been
the old icehouse. Something to explore with William,
Galen thought. Another time.

She had not gone ten feet back the way she had come
before she heard the loud *crack* of a door slamming shut.
She froze. The wind was gusting through the trees but
something definitive about the solitary report told her that
it was not a door swinging free on its hinges. She listened,
but she somehow knew that she would not hear it again.
Someone had entered or left the building. And in the next
second she realized who it was.

Teenagers had been a problem off and on throughout
the summer, riding their dirt bikes over young grass in un-
cut hayfields, sneaking onto the estate property at night,
sometimes to camp, and leaving a trail of beer cans and
bottles behind them. Trespassing was not the problem.
Damage to the fields was not that severe and their litter
was really only an irritant. Henry's great fear was fire.

Galen wondered how long they had been using the
icehouse for their parties. There was one good way to find
out, she told herself, and started to make her way through
the brush around to the door. But almost immediately she
stopped. There was no point in being incautious. Teenagers,
she reminded herself, came in all sizes. Galen headed toward the window.

She pressed her way through the vines as quietly as
she could. It was not until she virtually had her face to the
glass that she heard the sound of a human voice. The rushing wind had until now obscured it—as it had, fortunately,
also covered her own clumsy approach.

The glass itself was clouded by a veil of cobwebs and decades of dirt, but there was a corner missing from the pane. Looking through it, Galen could see only the solid-looking beams of light that streaked through the dust from a matching window on the opposite wall. It illuminated four small rectangles of dirty wooden floor and seemed to leave the rest of the room in darkness. The voice she had heard was silent now, and for a moment it appeared as if there was no one there. Then, with the slight movement of an arm, a figure in the corner took form. It was sitting on a stool, bent over something in its lap. Suddenly it raised its head and seemed to look right at her. Galen could not see the face clearly but she knew who it was.

Caetano.

She was in the act of raising her hand to rap on the glass when something in the tilt of his head made her stop. He was not looking at her. He was looking at someone else. Someone she could not see. A voice only a few feet from her ear now spoke. It was barely audible over the rushing wind but it was a voice she knew. Her heart gave a violent jerk.

"Any more trouble with the local kids?" it asked.

"No, just that one time. I think I scared them so badly they'll never come back."

"You've been warm enough? If not I'll get you another blanket."

"No, I'm okay."

"There's more ham here. Also cheese . . . milk . . . Coke . . ."

"That's great, Julian. Thanks a lot. I was getting a little sick of tuna."

"I'm sorry about that. I also brought some more bread—just in case. Chicken . . . more rolls . . . and a pie."

"What kind?"

"Blueberry."

"Fantastic."

There was a pause. "No ice cream, though."

Caetano laughed. "That's okay."

He said something else but the wind, which swelled suddenly to a roar, drowned out his words. But Galen heard Julian's reply.

"It's the least I can do. You're bearing the brunt of this whole thing."

"It's worth it." Another pause. "How much longer, though?"

"I don't know. Not much, I promise. We're very close . . ."

The wind rose again and Julian's words were lost. When it died again she heard him say: ". . . getting her to agree to go along with us, but I'm confident she will. By tonight I hope, then we can move. Then it should be all over."

"You think she'll do it?"

"Yes, Caetano, I do." Julian's voice, however, sounded strained. "It's a big step for her and she needs to think it over before she makes the decision, but she will and it'll be the right one. Trust me."

"Did she know about the crash?" Caetano asked.

"Yes."

"What about William's. . . ?" He had glanced up and Galen quickly ducked her head, missing the rest of what he said. She heard only Julian's answer.

"No. I don't think so."

Caetano asked something else she could not make out.

"Well, she's afraid of the police . . . Naturally."

". . ."

"Stebbens still has it and sends you a message saying he's taking good care of it for you . . . he knew you'd be worried."

". . ."

"He has no choice. He owes us . . . what else you need . . . I'll come tomorrow, early . . ."

Julian's voice faded as Galen leaned back against the icehouse wall. She had begun to shiver from deep down inside, though she was not cold. Neither was she afraid, exactly, although her heart was pounding and her breathing was coming hard. She was more confused than anything else. What was she hearing? It did not make sense. Caetano was hiding in the woods of the estate. Julian, who had implicated him, was bringing him food and blankets. What could this mean? Surely Caetano and Julian had not plotted together? Galen took a deep breath and heard it quiver as she let it slowly out. She felt suddenly, disturbingly, like a spy.

This was ridiculous, she told herself quickly, pushing herself off the wall. There was some explanation, surely. And it was simply a matter of asking for one.

It would not, however, be as simple as all that. She was just turning to go around to find the door when Galen heard her name. It came as clear as a bell in a lull in the wind and stopped her dead. Caetano had spoken it.

"What about Galen?" he had asked.

Galen pressed closer to the crack in the window.

"She's right on the verge of figuring all this out," he was saying. "She's asked so many questions. She knows about . . ." Galen strained to hear but the wind muffled his words. Then, in another lull, came: "I'm surprised she hasn't found out about the stirrup catch."

"I know," Julian said. "But . . . our last encounter was . . . She thinks I lied about you."

"That could be very bad for us, couldn't it?"

Julian answered him with an edge in his voice that made Galen's insides turn.

"That could be very bad for her," he said.

Caetano said something she could not make out.

Julian's reply was curt. "My real fear is that if she does, the first person she'll go to is Foote."

"You sure he doesn't suspect anything now?"

"It depends on what she has told him already, but I don't think so. He wouldn't be coming back to Boston this weekend if he did."

"Julian—"

"Don't worry, I'll take care of her . . ." The rest was gone except for the one word: "Tonight."

Galen leaned back against the wall. Without it she would hardly have been able to stand. She had to fight for breath as her body began reacting to something her brain had yet to grasp. Still, it could not seem to move. As fear warred fiercely with disbelief, she was for a moment rooted to that spot on the ground in the Baugh woods in the shadow of a falling-down icehouse. This is not happening, she told herself. None of this is real.

But then suddenly the war was over and she was pushing her way back through the vines out of the line of sight of the window. When she was free of them she began to run. She was still running when she reached the pond. Crashing breathlessly through the brush into the clearing, she was almost startled to see a boy and a dog at the water's edge, staring quizzically up at her.

William! She had almost forgotten. What was she going to say to him? She made an effort to compose herself.

"Hey, we found one!" he called, waving his arm.

"William—honey—I just remembered something." She was gasping for air and wracking her brain for an excuse to leave, quickly. She had to get him back and it had to be fast.

"I have to get back to the bungalow—at once," she said, attempting a smile, "but I have a fun game we can play on the way home. You want to play?"

"What is it?"

"We are the robbers," she said, breathing deeply, improvising as she went along. "We steal paintings like your granddad's. But the police are on our trail and we have to sneak through the woods and not get caught."

It was lame, but the best she could do on such short notice. He looked at her dubiously. She was not exactly in character.

"Sure," he said tentatively, with a disappointed look toward the pond. "Let's go this way . . ."

"*No!* I mean, we have to be getting back anyway so we'll pretend our hideout is back at the house. And we have to get there quickly and quietly and then not tell anybody that we were here . . ."

Whether William thought this strange or not, he seemed willing to go along with it. They set off at a jog down the trail by which they had come. Galen looked back over her shoulder as the pond slipped out of sight. There was no view of the icehouse from here. She prayed the icehouse had no view of them. There was, at least, no sign of pursuit.

William talked as they ran along but Galen heard almost nothing of what he said. A voice in her head crowded out the boy's chatter. It said just one thing over and over again. *I'll take care of her.*

What could Julian have meant by that? she asked herself repeatedly, as disbelief began pushing its way back inside her head. Surely he did not intend to harm her. The notion was too wild to consider. This was not some made-for-TV movie. But what was he doing hiding Caetano in the woods? They had to be somehow involved in the robbery, but how? And why? It did not make sense. Who was Julian trying to get to "go along" with them? Carla? And with what? Why would she be afraid of the police? What were they afraid she, Galen, would find out? What would Johnny suspect?

Galen abruptly slowed to a walk. They were at the edge of the pines now and the stables were visible through the trees. What had Caetano asked? *Did she know about the crash?* Then what did he say about William? An image entered Galen's mind but it was expunged almost as soon as it appeared. She would not—could not—believe that

Caetano was in any way involved in Johanna and Colin's deaths. Or that he would try to harm William. That was impossible. And for whatever else Galen thought of him, it was just as impossible that Julian was involved in their deaths, or that he would try to kill his own son. It was, for that matter, impossible that either of them would rob Henry Baugh.

Galen made a conscious effort to calm herself. You are overreacting, she told herself, as they were at last crossing River Road, and the sight of Henry's house in the distance lent her a momentary sense of safety and hope. There was an explanation. Henry would have it, or would help her find one. In any case, she needed now just to get to him. Until then none of the answers to these questions really mattered.

Then suddenly a piece of the conversation that she had forgotten dropped into her brain like an unexploded bomb. It was something Caetano had said, it was about the stirrup catch. *I'm surprised she hasn't found out about the stirrup catch.* Galen stopped in her tracks and stared blindly ahead. William came back to her side but she did not see him. *The stirrup catch.* The catch that had given way over the big wall at the top of the Long Field. Galen let out a little gasp. The bomb went off. The implication was unavoidable. Someone had tampered with it, knowing that she would be jumping Durometer, knowing that the pressure would surely snap it and that a fall would surely follow.

"My God," she whispered out loud, "I could have been killed."

"They'll never get us."

Galen looked down with a start.

"What? Who will never get us?"

William was staring at her uncertainly.

"The police," he said. Then he added tentatively. "Our game."

"Oh, William. No—not if we're quick. Let's hurry. No!

Not to the house. We—we'll go there later. To the bungalow.''

William was chatting again but that other voice was back, drowning out all of her other senses. *I'll take care of her . . . Tonight.*

William and Galen arrived at the bungalow winded. She had not dared take him back to Henry's house for fear Julian might already have returned. She would give him a glass of juice then send him on his way alone while she called Henry and, if need be, the police.

The phone was ringing as they came in the kitchen door. Before she could stop him, William lifted the receiver. He handed it to her. She had no choice. Praying it was not Julian, Galen held it, eyes closed, to her ear. With a deep, unsteady sigh of relief, the distant static told her at once who it was.

"Oh, Mara, thank God it's you.'' To Galen's surprise, something like a sob welled suddenly in her throat. Wheeling quickly away from William, she choked it back.

"Gale! I'm so glad I finally got you. I've been trying to reach you all night.''

Something in Mara's tone told Galen this was more than just another one of her personal crises. It also told her that it had something to do with her.

"Mara, what is it? It must be three o'clock in the morning there. Are you all right?''

"I'm okay. It's you I'm worried about.''

Galen's heart felt like it skipped a beat. "What do you mean?''

"Is anyone there?''

"Yes,'' she said quickly, her eyes on William, who was gazing intently at her. She struggled with her voice, trying to communicate something to Mara while at the same time not alarming the boy. "Can I call you right back?''

"It can't wait. Can you just listen?''

"Yes, but hurry, I—I really can't stay on.''

"You know I've been doing some authentication work for a private collector—the Greek shipping magnate. I told you, you remember—the one with the incredible collection—"

"Korikus, he never sells anything, keeps it all in an underground bunker or something. Right. Mara, *let me call you back.*"

"No, listen, this is important." Mara, who talked quickly to begin with, was speaking almost unintelligibly fast. "It's Koriskos, and it's a gallery actually. In any case, I was there today, in one part of it anyway. He's got a complete laboratory where we've been doing the tests. It's a long story as to why, but I ended up somewhere I wasn't supposed to be. I was trying to find a painting I'd been looking at last week and was walking around the place on my own. It's like a honeycomb down there, all these passageways winding around huge vaultlike storage rooms. I found out later this is a gross breach of security: access to this place is extremely limited. Anyway, I ended up—I was lost essentially—but I thought I'd found the room I'd been in the week before and started looking for the painting, going through storage crates. It may in fact have been the same room, I never found out. I never found the painting, but you won't believe what I did find."

"Mara, *please.*"

"*You.*"

"What?"

"You, your face."

"What are you talking about?"

"Your picture, H. L. Baugh's portrait, tacked on a some kind of temporary frame, in a shipping crate."

Galen's eyes, which had been peeled on the crest of the driveway, flew back to William. She tried to sound calm. "Are you sure?"

"I'd know it anywhere. Even in a split second. I'm positive."

Galen was silent.

"Hello?"

"It was stolen," Galen finally said. "It's one of the paintings that was taken from the house."

"I know."

"Those crates. They must all be there, the nine others."

"Possibly. I don't know, but your portrait definitely is. Why he would buy them hot, I don't know. He's certainly rich enough to have bought them all easily enough legitimately."

"No, he couldn't. They weren't for sale. None of the ones in the house were."

"I see."

"So do I." Galen looked again at William who was playing with a pen on the kitchen table. "Listen, I've got to call you back."

"Wait, Gale, there's more. Do you remember I called you two weeks ago, the day after the robbery, from New York and said I saw Carla and Julian Baugh on the street?"

"Yes. And you were right, by the way, it was J—. . . it was him."

"Do you remember where I said I was?"

"At some dealer's."

"Nigel White's."

"Okay."

"Nigel White got me the job with Koriskos. He's his personal buyer. I've always thought he was a shade sleazy, but he's sent me interesting and—up to now—always legitimate work, so I've maintained a business relationship with him."

"So."

"So the reason I saw the Baughs that day was because they were coming out of Nigel's gallery. Gale, honey, I think Carla and Julian ripped the old man off."

Galen took a long, deep breath. She whispered simply, "I know."

14

"You know!"

As if on cue, William got up and, with a last glance at Galen through white-gold eyelashes, walked deliberately from the room. Galen swung back to the window and, with her eyes riveted on the spot where she would first see an approaching car, spoke urgently into the receiver.

"I found Caetano."

"You did! Where?"

"Here on the estate. He's in a shack in the woods."

"Did you ask him—"

"Julian was there."

"Julian?"

"Mara, listen to me now. I don't know what's happening, but I'm a little frightened and I think I should tell you everything I know, just in case. I'm going to try to get to Henry but it wouldn't hurt if you knew, too."

"Galen, honey, aren't you being a bit melodramatic? I mean, it isn't as if—"

"Just listen. I don't have much time. I'm afraid—I

overheard Julian and Caetano talking. I didn't catch everything they said, but Julian was talking about some woman, presumably Carla, who he was waiting to decide to agree to come in on something with them before they could 'move.'"

"Move what? The paintings? Come in on. . . ? But she had to be in on the robbery already. I mean, if they were both at Nigel's—"

"That's not important. Caetano asked him whether she knew about the 'crash.' Then about what happened to William in the barn."

"I don't understand."

"Mara, the plane crash that killed Colin and Johanna, William's falling into Mars's stall. I could tell by the way they were talking about it . . . and I think I knew already . . . that these weren't accidents."

"Galen! You don't think—"

"I don't know, but please just listen, there's more." A new sensation was grabbing at her heart.

"Are you crying?"

"No, but I'm shaking like a leaf."

"But there's no—"

"Mara, listen to me. Caetano said he was afraid that I would find them out and that if I did that it would be 'bad' for them. Then Julian said"—Galen glanced back at the living room where she could hear William playing with Lily—"that it would be bad for *me*, and that he would . . . 'take care of me tonight.'"

"Ga-len, ho-ney, you *don't* think . . . Oh, come on, this is *not* some B picture. Real-life people like Julian Baugh don't say things like that and mean it the way *you're* thinking. I mean, I think it wouldn't hurt to call the police, there's obviously some kind of conspiracy going on, but I don't think you have to be afraid of—"

"Mara, Caetano said he was surprised that I hadn't found out about the stirrup catch."

"What's that supposed to mean?"

Galen took a deep breath. "I think someone loosened the catch so that I would be thrown."

There was a long static-filled silence at the other end of the line.

"Galen," Mara finally said, "call the police. *Now.*"

Galen dropped heavily onto the kitchen chair, her hand still on the receiver. For all that had gone on between her and Julian, the idea that he would steal his own father's paintings—let alone murder his wife and brother—itself still required an enormous mental leap. The idea that he would endanger her life was almost impossible to believe. But listening first to Mara's story, then to herself tell her friend what she had overheard, brought it into a brutal, razor-edged focus Galen had until now not seen.

It was perhaps shock, it was perhaps because a small part of her was still holding on to the hope that Julian was not involved, but she had not wanted to see. How could she have been that wrong about him? It was true that she had not thought him the type of man to lie about his engagement to another woman in order to get her into bed, but that he would try to harm her . . .

The full force of his threat, however, was now slowly beginning to make itself felt.

Galen was light-headed and short of breath as she squatted in front of William. A voice she barely recognized told him in a cheerful tone:

"William, sweetheart, I can't come back to the house with you right now but that doesn't mean our little game is over. Do you want to keep playing? Good. This is how we'll do it, even though we're not together. When you go back to the house you must remember that you're still a robber."

"Call me Jack."

"Jack?" She could have hugged him. "Okay, Jack, you can't tell anybody where we were or what we did. It's a secret. Not your dad, not your granddad. Understand? It'll be our secret game. Just go back and say we visited at the bungalow and that I've gone back to Boston. You got that? And then on"—Galen wondered when it would be and under what circumstances—"Monday we'll be robbers together again. Let's shake on it."

The first thing to do was call Henry, Galen told herself as she watched William disappear into the woods that lay between the bungalow and the great house. If there is any other conceivable explanation, he will have it.

Her hands were shaking as she dialed the number. It seemed to ring forever. Finally someone answered. It was not Henry.

"Mae, hi, this is Galen, is Henry there?" She tried to sound brisk, but Mae's hesitation told her she had not done a good job.

"Er—no, Miss Shaw, he's jes' left far the Bowdoins' far supper." Another hesitation. "Mr. Mole is, however, ya can speak with—"

"Yes, yes, please . . . Oh, Franny, I'm glad you're there, I have to talk to Henry, it's urgent."

"Galen, dear, where are you?"

The question in and of itself was perfectly innocent, but it stopped her as surely as if he had cut the line. She was not even at first certain why. Something unidentifiable in his tone. It was as if he had already known what she was calling about. He had not even bothered to ask. Why would his first question be where was she?

Galen was just telling herself that she was becoming paranoid when she heard the sound of Franny's hand come over the mouthpiece. Then the sound of muffled voices. Whom was he talking to? Mae? No. As he took his hand off, Galen heard a man's voice in the background. It was

unintelligible, barely a syllable, but there it was. It came
over the wires like a bolt of electricity.

"Hello? Galen? Are you all right?"

"Yes, Fran, I am," she said calmly. "It's nothing. I'll—
I'll talk to him later."

"Are you at the bungalow?"

"No. No, I'm in town, on my way to Boston. But it'll
keep."

"Hang on a sec, dear. I need—"

"I can't now, Franny, but I'll call you as soon as I get
to my apartment. Bye."

He was still speaking as she laid the receiver back in its
cradle.

Could it be possible that Franny was in on it, too? Was
she losing her mind?

Galen's heart was slamming against the walls of her
chest as she fumbled with the telephone book. With one
eye on the driveway, she dialed the Stover Police Department. In a minute she heard the singsong voice of a man
with other things on his mind.

"Headquarters, Sergeant Stebbens speaking, how can I
help you?"

Galen opened her mouth to speak but nothing came
out.

"You've reached the Stover Police, go ahead please."

Stebbens. An alarm sounded in the back of Galen's
brain but she could not immediately think why.

"Hel-lo, anyone there?"

She replaced the receiver with a slow movement. Stebbens. *Stebbens.* First she saw the name in print. The *Globe*
article on the robbery. Sgt. Craig Stebbens, the officer heading up the investigation into the theft. Then she heard it
spoken. But not in her own voice. In Julian's. *Stebbens still
has it and sends you a message saying he's taking good care of
it* . . . There was more. What had Julian said? *He has no
choice . . . he owes us.*

In the next instant Galen was on her feet and looking wildly around for her briefcase, which she found at once, and her handbag, which she did not. She ran into the bedroom and, not finding it, rushed back to the kitchen, which she began frantically to search. At this point she was incapable of fully accepting the idea that someone, let alone a man she had thought she loved, could actually want to murder her. It was still no more than a wild, cinematic notion, a theory too fantastic to absorb. But the fear that gripped her chest was very real and, for whatever reason she would later decipher, she was getting out of Stover as fast as she could.

She was not going anywhere, however, if she could not find her bag. She could do without her wallet, but not without her keys. She was in the process of tearing the room apart when the phone rang again. Hoping for no good reason that it might be Henry, she answered it.

Johnny's voice washed through the wires like a tonic.

"Gale, darling, you sound a bit nervy, you all right?"

"Oh, God, Johnny. No. No. Everything's— Oh, Johnny, I'm so glad you've called. I know where Henry's paintings are and I know who did it, but I can't talk, I have to get out of here *now*. God damn it! *Where are my keys!*"

"My lord, dear girl, settle down. You're making no sense at all. You sound completely over the edge. Now take a deep breath and start at the beginning and tell me what you've found out."

"I can't tell you everything now but I've found one of the paintings and I think Carla and Julian are behind the robbery. They've sold the pictures to a Greek collector in France. I'll tell you all about it but I have to get out of here. I'm afraid that Julian—Johnny, where are you?"

"As a matter of fact, that's why I'm calling. I'm at the airport—"

"Logan?"

"No, Stover. I decided to fly up myself. I was hoping to catch you and hitch a ride with you into the city."

"Can you get a car?"

"I . . . if it's an emergency you know I can."

"I can't find my keys! Will you come here right away?"

"Of course, Gale, but don't you—"

"Never mind!" she practically shouted. "I found them! Thank God! Listen, I'm leaving right now. I'll come right there. I shouldn't be more than twenty minutes."

"Okay. But listen to me—why haven't you called the police?"

"I think the man in charge of the investigation is somehow in on it. I can't talk about it now. I'm really afraid that—"

"Have you talked to Henry or Franny?" Johnny's tone, at first a bit overwhelmed, was suddenly assertive and assuring.

"No, no, I haven't talked to anybody. I don't dare. This whole thing is—"

"Listen, my dear, I doubt there's really any need for such panic, but if you feel better about it, come straight here. We'll sort everything out, I'm sure. But, Gale, you've got to calm down."

"I'm calm."

"And drive carefully."

"All right. Good-bye."

"See you soon."

Galen called Lily and tore out to the car. It was dark. She started the engine, flipped on the headlights, and flew down the driveway, hitting the main road to the great house at about sixty miles per hour. She drove the rest of the way to River Road with her eyes glued to the rearview mirror. There were no signs of pursuit.

It was not until she had started down River Road that she realized she was out of breath and that her heart was racing. It felt suddenly as if it would burst. She took a long deep breath. Can this really be happening? she asked herself as she watched the hulking shadow of the stable disappear into the darkness behind her. She was shivering with cold, but her hands were wet on the wheel. She saw the lights of the mansion flicker once through a break in the maples, then nothing but blackness as the road passed into the trees.

Galen did not want to think about what she was doing, but questions boiled feverishly up in her brain. Perhaps she should have tried to talk to someone else at the police station. Or to reach Henry at the Bowdoins'? Poor Henry. What would she have said to him? Your son and your trusted stableboy of ten years killed Colin and Johanna and then robbed you? What's more, they tried to kill your grandson and they tried to kill me? William. What would become of him? Even as she considered it all, it was with a sense of unreality. Caetano's involvement gave it an absurd quality. It would have seemed almost funny, if two people had not died and two others had not come close. No, it was not funny. It was horrifyingly serious.

What made it so difficult a notion to grasp was the larger question that hovered at the edge of all these others like a distant storm. It was this: What if she was mistaken? Is it possible that somehow she had put the pieces together wrong? That she had gotten the wrong picture? Julian's face appeared dimly in front of her the way she had first seen it, in the photograph with Colin at Henry's beach house, grinning handsomely and passionately. She had started to love that face. You are certifiably insane, she thought, but part of you still does. Then it was gone . . . She heard only the cold voice over the sound of the high wind, *I'll take care of her . . . Tonight,* and a violent spasm of fear convulsed through her. Even if there was a chance, she told herself, you could not afford to take it.

Galen looked down at the speedometer and realized

she was going almost seventy. She was sweating and cold. She took her foot off the gas and tried to relax. You're safe now, she said out loud. Safer with every mile you put between yourself and the Winds and heading for the bustling crowded haven of the city. Heading for Johnny. You are safe.

Galen checked the rearview mirror for signs that someone had followed her, but all she saw was blackness. She flipped on the radio. The smoky sound of Astrud Gilberto's voice broke incongruously, if not without a little irony, across her nightmare. *Tall and tan and young and lovely, the girl from Ipanema goes walking . . .* Galen gave a short nervous laugh. Palm trees. Pretty girls. A turquoise sea. Brazil.

But suddenly the image was gone as a little sound escaped her. Twin specks of light had appeared as if out of nowhere in her mirror. There was someone on the road behind her. Galen made herself take a deep breath. It could be anybody, she told herself. If someone had come down from the big house behind you you would have seen them before now. It could even be the police. Galen checked her speed; she was going sixty-five on a back road. She slowed to fifty and narrowed her eyes at the mirror. Was he gaining? At this angle it was impossible to tell, but he did not appear to be coming that fast. No, she told herself, not quite believing it, you are not being followed. She was, nevertheless, comforted by the sight of a second car pulling out of a driveway onto the road just behind her, and in front of the first.

Both sets of headlights disappeared now as she started around a long gradual bend in the road. Galen was irrationally comforted by the blank darkness in the mirror. The road straightened out finally and there was a moment of stillness and almost peace.

Oh, but he watches so sadly, how can he tell her he loves her? . . .

The second car was obviously moving along at a good

clip because there was a splash of light sooner than she had expected. In fact, he seemed to be moving very fast and was soon right behind her. From where the car had turned onto the road, it could not be Julian, she reminded herself. And from the height of the lights, it had to be a van or a pickup truck—not the police. By the way he was now hanging right on her tail, the driver was probably a teenager and probably drunk.

Galen downshifted and pulled quickly away. The headlights disappeared around a curve but, to her annoyance, she discovered when the road straightened out that he had increased his speed and was closing in again. He came within four or five lengths of her car and held there, his lights reflecting into her eyes, but making no move to pass. She turned her mirror down to kill the blinding glare but could do nothing about his relentless pestering presence, which was beginning to anger her. The old Alfa was still a fast car and she knew how to drive it, but the hairpin switchbacks of the plateau's steep escarpment were coming up soon and there was no way to lose him until they had descended into the valley and crossed the bridge. She turned her eyes ahead and tried not to think about her tormentor.

But each day when she walks to the sea, she looks straight ahead not at him . . .

As she approached the first set of curves at the crest of the escarpment her tailgater was still there, and she touched her brakes several times to warn him that she was going to slow. He pulled back for the first two bends but was back behind her again as they straightened out for the next series of turns. In fact, he was suddenly so close that she was afraid if she hit her brakes again he would run into her. The road had narrowed and there was no shoulder onto which she could pull over.

"Goddamn drunk!" she growled between clenched teeth as she dropped the car into second gear and shot forward. She knew she had the steering and tires to push her speed through the last set of turns, and that a van or pickup truck probably did not. "Hold on," she said to Lily, who, with a nose for excitement if nothing else, had raised herself to a sitting position. The Alfa's rear end broke away for a moment as Galen drove through a forty-five-degree turn at about forty miles per hour. The tires grabbed the road at the end of the slide with a violent shake. She changed gears and put her foot to the floor for the short straightaway.

There was a moment of quiet as she shot through the night. Then everything exploded and Galen's fragile sense of calm shattered like a crystal glass dropped on a brick floor. For a few seconds there had been nothing but darkness behind her, but suddenly he was there again, and in the moment that his lights swept the night to train on her back once more, it became suddenly, belatedly clear what was happening.

He had cleared the corner in a full slide—it was a van—straightened out, and was bearing down rapidly. Galen's anger dissolved under the wave of fear that finally crashed over her as she took the next corner at a terrifying speed, breaking into a marginally controlled four-wheel drift and only barely pulling out of the violent reverse slide. Her eyes flew to the rearview mirror. The van was still with her and closing. He was not drunk. He was trying to run her off the road. He was trying to kill her.

And he would surely succeed, she told herself, if she did not do something fast. The adrenaline that flooded her body as she screeched very nearly out of control around the last corner would be of no use: There was simply nothing she *could* do. There was no shoulder on which to pull off, no more corners from which to borrow distance from her pursuer. They were on the last straightaway and he was closing, four car lengths, three, two, driving her toward the bridge and the river. With a sickening twist in her stomach, Galen knew in the elongated seconds during which everything would now come to an end that no car on earth could make the ninety-degree turn onto the bridge at this speed. She also knew if she did not make it into that tunnel, there was no place else but the river, twenty feet beyond, fifty feet below. She stepped on the brakes and heard more than felt the impact of the van smashing into her bumper. She braked again, and again he hit her, this time so hard the car skidded and threatened to twist sideways to him. And then she was almost at the turn.

There was a moment, even before he hit her again, when she understood clearly and without hysteria that she was going over the edge. It came to her as a matter-of-fact thought: something like "Oh, this is it." It came with resignation, but not, however, with surrender. If she wanted to, Galen could not have let go of the steering wheel and rushed to the end of her nightmare. A side of her she did not know took over: a voice she did not know told her there would have to be a moment between her attacker's last hit and the flimsy guardrail during which he would have to brake to avoid going over the edge himself.

She heard a crunch, her head snapped back and the voice told her *Now!* Galen stood on the brake pedal and yanked the steering wheel right, turning the nose away from the bridge and slamming it into the steep wall-like embankment. Things happened so fast at this point that she had no sense of their sequence or speed. She was barely aware of the front end of the Alfa bouncing off the bank and whipping around in a 360-degree spin. It smashed into the side of the van, which was braking hard and sliding toward the bridge. The broadside collision violently changed the direction of the car's slide and in so doing checked the forward momentum that was hurtling it toward the cliff.

The car must have been perpendicular to the road— that is, dead on the bridge tunnel—when it slid off the pavement and onto the gravel. Galen felt the impact of the guardrail and at this point closed her eyes. It was time for surrender. The voice, the adrenaline, the struggle were all gone. And now there was only stillness and silence and Galen saw herself arcing through space over the river. She waited for the final crash.

It never came.

She heard first the screech of the van's tires in the tunnel of the covered bridge. Then the sound of sand and stones cascading down the cliff to the river, then the feverish ticking of the hot, stalled engine and the smoky cool voice of Astrud Gilberto singing about Brazil.

. . . Tall and tan and young and lovely, the girl from Ipanema goes walking . . .

Galen slowly opened her eyes. The headlamps shone off into hazy blue space. She had no sense of the world around her. She could see no ground or trees, nothing, just filmy emptiness as if she were careening through air. Lily! She looked over quickly at the empty seat. "Lily!" There was a rustling sound on the floor and the cold wet touch of Lily's nose on her shaking hand.

Galen was aware of the precipice more by feel than by sight or sound. Listening now she could hear the murmur of the river below. After easing up the emergency brake, she opened the door slowly and slid out a foot, both feet, and pulled herself out of the car. She could see that they were on the other side of what was left of the guardrail, literally hanging on the edge. The front driver's-side tire was off the ground, turning slowly, in eerie silence, on its own. Galen took a step back and called Lily. When the dog leapt free of the car, Galen's legs buckled from under her. She collapsed onto the ground and threw her arms around Lily's neck. She struggled but Galen clung to her. "Oh, God, oh, God, oh, God," she whispered, rocking slightly and shaking violently with each breath.

It was probably less than a minute before she heard the car coming fast toward them across the bridge. She could not tell what kind of car it was from two beams of light that streaked the night air ahead of it. She held her breath. With an explosion of light, it cleared the tunnel and Galen could see it was the van. It screeched to a stop, beams trained on them like the beacon eyes of some blood-less, maniacal predator.

Scrambling to her feet, Galen made one unsuccessful attempt at flight, but the headlights blinded her and she stumbled to her knees on the invisible uneven ground. With the river at her back there was nowhere for her to go. Getting slowly to her feet, she turned to face her attacker. She heard the door of the van, which she vaguely recog-nized as Caetano's, and saw a silhouette dart in front of the headlights toward her.

She threw up her arms to shield herself from him and tried to scream, but heard nothing but a crackly wheeze. His hands were on her and she flailed blindly, hysterically. She hit something hard and heard Julian curse. He said something else, but in her panicked struggle, Galen did not hear. Despite the second rush of adrenaline that surged through her veins, the contest did not last long. Julian had her wrists in his hands and gave her a violent shake. It did the trick. She stopped her struggle and just looked at him.

Whatever he had had in mind to do with her then, Julian was forced to change it as a second set of lights swept the wreckage and stopped on his back. It must have been the car that she had first seen on the road behind her. Then a blue light flashed. No, it was, by some miracle, the police.

Galen yanked at Julian's hands and with his dark eyes still on her face he let her go. He spoke her name but Galen barely heard. Gasping for air she staggered toward the lights, saying something about having been run off the road. She did not, however, make it. She stumbled and would have fallen had someone not caught her. She was vaguely aware of Julian's hands on her. She heard voices but they sounded a long way away.

"Jesus Christ, Mr. Baugh, what happened? Is she hurt?"

"I don't think so."

Someone had lain her down on the bank and was pushing her hair off her face.

"I'm all right, I'm all right," Galen cried, struggling to get up, but for a moment she was held there.

"Are you sure you're okay, Miss Shaw?" asked a voice she did not recognize. A large, round face loomed close to hers but it was in shadow. Then it was gone and Julian was speaking to someone in a low, urgent tone.

"I'll radio for an ambulance," another, younger voice was saying.

"No, Mike, I don't think that's necessary. I think she's just shaken up. Let's just get her into the car."

"If you say so, Sarge."

"Mr. Baugh, you want to ride with us?"

"I'd better not leave the van here. I'll follow you."

And then, just like that, it was all over. Galen was in the backseat of a police cruiser, the siren was on, and they were flying away from the river's edge. She even had Lily's head on her lap. She sensed the rhythmic flash of the blue light through her closed lids. She was safe. Incredibly, at last, she was safe.

She opened her eyes.

"How you feeling?" The younger cop had turned around in his seat and was watching her. He was smiling broadly. She had seen his face before.

"Okay," she said shakily, not bothering to try to place it.

"You didn't hit your head or anything?"

Galen put a hand automatically to her forehead. "N-no, I don't think so."

"You seemed for a minute like you were gonna faint."

Galen remembered Dr. Hubbard's warning. He would not have called this taking it easy.

"I just tripped," she said.

"It's no wonder," he said, as if he hadn't heard. "You almost ran right over that cliff into the river. You could have been killed."

Galen stared at him for a moment then sat bolt upright. "Where's Julian, what have you done with him?"

"Done with him?"

"He's the one who—"

Galen looked beyond him at the road ahead. Something was wrong. "Why are you taking me this way? Aren't we going to the station?"

"There'll be plenty of time for that tomorrow, ma'am." The face was still smiling pleasantly. "You look like you could stand to lie down for a bit. That was some accident you had."

"But that was not an accident," Galen said, her voice rising. "You don't understand! Julian Baugh tried to run me off the road!"

"Calm down now," the officer said soothingly. "Why would he want to do that?" There was laughter in his voice. There was the edge of panic in Galen's.

"It was no accident!" she shouted.

This had the effect at least of wiping the smile off the young face. He looked at her dumbfounded, then at his partner.

It was his partner who now spoke. "You're just a little shaken up now, that's all, honey. It'll all come clear again as soon as we get you home."

"*Home?* Where are you taking me?"

"You live at the Winds estate, don't you?"

"You can't take me back there! He tried to kill me!"

"Julian Baugh tried to kill you," the older cop repeated in the mild, patronizing tone reserved for lunatics.

"Yes, he did! *Twice!* Listen to me! He killed his wife and his brother and stole those pictures from his father! I can prove it. Caetano da Silva is in the icehouse in the woods. I'll show you! *You have to believe me.*"

Her hands were gripping the wire mesh that separated them and she was shouting at the back of the older cop's head.

A new nightmare had started. The kind when you try to flee but your legs move only in slow motion. Or you try to make yourself understood but no one is willing to listen. Most terrifying of all was that in the middle of this nightmare there was a pinpoint of calm in which Galen understood perfectly well why they would refuse to believe her. She must sound completely out of her mind. She stopped and leaned her head against the metal cage. There had to be a way to get them to listen.

"Sarge?" she heard the younger cop say tentatively, but whether out of concern about what she was saying or the hysterical nature of her claims, she could not tell.

The sergeant ignored him.

"Look, honey," he said calmly back over his shoulder without taking his eyes off the road, "you've been through a rough time and you're probably in shock. It'll pass. You just sit yourself back—"

"I am *not* in shock," she said. Gone was the hysteria. In its place came a surge of anger. Her voice was low now and she spoke slowly through her teeth. "I am perfectly lucid. I have a criminal complaint and I demand to be taken to the police station."

The car slowed; but with a gasp Galen realized they were at the entrance of the Winds and that they were actually going to turn in. Her anger was short-lived. In its wake came desperation. She felt quickly for door handles. In the backseat of a police cruiser, of course, there were none.

"*Please,* listen to me," she said feebly.

The younger officer's mouth was hanging open. "Gee, Sarge, she sounds—"

"Heh, Mike," the older cop said simply, and they flew up the driveway in silence. At the top the older man got out and opened Galen's door. He extended a hand, not, she discovered, to help her out but to secure a grip on her arm. In a flash of light that swept them now, Galen saw him clearly for the first time. She knew instantly where she had seen the younger officer before. It was the day of Henry's robbery. He had come to the bungalow to ask her questions. He had come with the sergeant, whose name she remembered now, too. Craig Stebbens.

The lights were from Caetano's van, which Julian had just driven into the turnaround. He was standing now at Stebbens's side. Galen leaned back into the car but Stebbens held her fast. She felt a flush of heat sweep over her body. Her breath was suddenly short and there was a muffled roaring in her ears.

"Sweetheart," Julian said in a strange quiet voice, and reached for her.

"Julian, please," she said weakly as she was pulled to her feet and fainted dead away into his arms.

15

Galen was not out for very long. She came to inside Henry's house. She was being carried—by Julian—up the front hall stairs.

A barely audible "Put me down" was as much of a struggle as she could muster as her arms and legs still felt weak.

He said nothing.

The last thing she saw before he turned into William's room at the top of the stairs was the mystified face of the young cop looking up at her from the foyer. Then there was a shout from outside. He turned and, with a last glance, pulled the door closed behind him.

Julian had just put her down on William's bed when there was another shout from downstairs. He glanced at the door and then turned back to her. She could not read his expression but, while hushed, his voice was pitched with tension.

"I don't want you to move," he said slowly.

There was another shout. She did not recognize the voice but it was calling Julian's name.

"I'll be right back," he said to her. "I have to speak with the police, then I'm going to call Dr. Hubbard. Promise me you'll just lie still for a moment? Please?"

His attempt at a smile was strained. Galen said nothing. He stared at her darkly for a moment then got up and crossed the room. From the door he glanced briefly back at her. His eyes had taken on an expression she had never seen before, but all at once she knew, with a sudden choking certainty, that Julian Baugh was fully capable of violence.

He started to say something but stopped and instead turned, closed the door behind him, and started down the hall. Then she heard him coming back. He stood for what seemed like an eternity outside the door, then there was a light *click* as the lock turned and he was gone.

At this point Galen's head, which she dropped between her knees, began to clear very fast. She was sweating and her whole body shook as if she were deeply chilled, but her arms and her legs were at last becoming her own. She pressed her eyes with icy wet hands and looked around her. The austere room was as neat as a pin, with nothing but the castle and Johanna's picture to give its occupant away. Galen felt under the pillow. Her fingers found the locket and drew it out into the light. She did not look at it, rather worried it with her fingers as her eyes flew about the room. In a minute she was up and pacing it end to end.

Her state of mind at this point bordered on some kind of shock reaction as her fear underwent a second transformation. She was no longer feeling faint. Indeed, to her own surprise, quite the opposite. Her heart was thudding, her body was tense, and her brain was racing, but methodically, not with hysteria. There was something she could do, a voice was saying to her, it was simply a matter of figuring out what. Back now in Henry's house, where she had spent a day like any other with Henry and William, she only half believed that the events of the last two hours had taken place at all. Henry and William. Where were they? And Mae. Surely Julian would not have dared bring her back here if there was anybody in the house. If it had not been for the young cop, Galen wondered almost incidentally, would he have brought her here at all? Was he only waiting for the innocent to leave?

Galen jumped up and pressed her ear against the door. Silence. Then voices, but whose? Pieces of a muffled conversation rose in irregular waves from somewhere downstairs. She could not make out what they were saying or who was speaking, but there was an unmistakable urgency in the tenor. Galen sat back down on the bed. A second later she was up again, crossing the room, turning, pacing back. He would surely return. Soon. She went back to the door, listened, turned and walked to the window. The window. Something scratched eerily against the glass. A branch. The trumpet vine. *The trumpet vine.*

In an instant Galen's hand was on the latch and she was on the balcony, leaning against the stone railing and looking over into the leafy knot of vine. Somewhere in the tangle was a trellis, or was two and a half years ago, when Colin had impressed William by scaling the wall to his room. But that was a long time ago; the vine would have been half as dense, and the feat was probably accomplished in the light of day. Also, Galen thought as she leaned farther out and peered down into the darkness, he had climbed up, not down.

She lay across the wide flat railing, hooked her fingers around the inside edge, and swung her legs over the side. She searched the vine with her feet, feeling for something that did not give, as she slowly inched herself down. The benchlike slab of stone ran atop a long row of hourglass pillars. Galen maneuvered herself lower so that she could wrap her arms around one of these.

It occurred to her only as an afterthought that in one ill-conceived move she had gone beyond the point of safe return. Raising herself back up to the railing would be impossible. Still she could find nothing solid with her toe. A rash of perspiration exploded across her face. Her shoulder was beginning to ache. She tried standing on something firm but it gave way with a snap. It had to be here, she told herself, but she did not dare lower herself to the point where she was holding on with only her hands. Even without the hot pain that was shooting through her shoulder, she would not be strong enough to cling for more than a few seconds.

In a last desperate move she heaved herself to the next pillar, which put her more deeply into the vine. If she could not find the trellis, she would have to take her chances with the vine itself. By kicking at it she could feel that the trunk was thicker here. As she reached for it with her hand, she felt the solid, angular edge of a slender wooden beam. The trellis!

She scratched her arms and her face on the way down but the structure held, and in a few minutes Galen was tiptoeing across the terrace and rushing out into the concealing darkness of the back lawn. The light emanating from the house followed all the way to the edge of the woods, but it was diffuse and she knew she was invisible to anyone within.

In the thick roaring blackness of the wind-torn trees she stopped running for the first time since she had left the bungalow—how long ago? She had lost all sense of time. Galen dropped to her knees on the rough bed of dry leaves and gasped for air. Her heart was hammering painfully in her chest. The wind felt icy against her skin and through her clothes: She realized only now that she was dripping with sweat. Putting the back of a hand to her scratched cheek, she wiped away warm liquid—blood or perspiration, she could not tell which.

Leaning back against a tree now, she listened to the cacophony of the dead leaves being whipped by the wind.

She paid a silent tribute to the darkness, which had embraced and would now shield her. The wind, however, which had covered her descent and flight, was a mixed blessing, as in its chorus of myriad voices she repeatedly heard the sound of someone approaching from behind. Even after several false alarms, she could not keep from jumping up and looking wildly around. Even if he is here in the woods, she tried to tell herself, he cannot see you without a flashlight and you will see its beam long before you're in its range.

Galen had just begun to believe this when she felt the press of live flesh on her bare arm. Her heart stopped and she let out an ear-splitting scream. It was not, however, answered by a shout or a blow, rather an equally terrified bark. She realized long before her own shock had subsided that it was Lily. She had forgotten all about her. After being let out of the cruiser, the dog must have been waiting for her outside Henry's house. She had picked up her trail and followed her into the woods.

"Oh, Lily!" Galen cried, burying her face for a second time in the little dog's short thick fur. "Oh, girl, you're all right! And you found me. What a *good* girl you are. We're all right now, we're safe, we're safe."

No sooner had the words come out of her mouth than she was on her feet and scanning the field for the silhouette of someone who might have heard her scream. She had no way of knowing how far her voice had carried against the wind but could not risk waiting to find out. She had to make her way back to the bungalow on William's footpath. But where was that? Even as her eyes had adjusted to the dark, it would be impossible to find, let alone follow.

But this seeming impasse had, as it turned out, a rather simple solution. Lily.

Galen pulled off her belt and slid it under the dog's collar. "Do you want your *supper*?" she asked doubtfully. To Galen's profound gratitude, Lily responded with a tug.

Prodded by the repetition of the word *supper* and with no more than the expected number of mishaps with low-hung branches, protruding roots, and patches of mud, the little dog towed her blinded mistress through the dark. It was surprisingly soon after the lights of the mansion had become invisible that the solitary porch light of the bungalow came into view.

Preoccupied with the task of navigating a dense forest in the pitch dark, Galen had felt safe during her passage. The sight of the little house brought a fresh shiver of fear. As soon as he found her missing, Julian would doubtless come straight here. But so, it now occurred to her, would Johnny. She should have been at the airport by now, and he would have begun to worry. He would have given her an extra half hour then rented or borrowed a car. Johnny would not have waited around, not after what she had told him. He would come looking for her. But when would that be? Galen had no sense of elapsed time. It seemed like yesterday that she had driven out of the driveway in the Alfa Romeo that now lay in a wreck on the edge of the Swift River.

Galen leaned against the rough trunk of a pine tree at the rim of the clearing around the bungalow, warring with another thought: Julian could have discovered that she was gone right away and already be lying in wait inside the house. She went over in her mind the sequence of events since she had slipped over the balcony and tried to guess how long it had taken her to get here. Trying to get up the nerve to dart across the lawn, she told herself that she could not be sure that he was here, but she could be sure of something else: If he had not come already, he definitely would. She had to get to a telephone and call Henry—she had to take that chance. It would mean being in the house for only two, maybe three minutes; then she could run back out and hide in the woods. She stood up and listened, straining to filter the sound of a car engine out of the roar of the wind. Hearing nothing, and seeing no dance of lights in the blackness to the west, she made her move.

Galen was at the kitchen door when she realized that the house keys were of course swinging from the ignition of the Alfa. She leapt off the porch and began to circle the cottage in the tunnel of space between the wall and arching lilacs. William's war zone, she thought, taking little pleasure from the irony. One window after another was bolted shut. Preparing for the weekend in Boston, she had done it before setting out on her walk with William. It was not until she was three-quarters of the way around that she remembered which one she had left open and why: the high, narrow kitchen window over the sink, the smallest and hardest to reach, the least likely, if not impossible, port of entry for a burglar. She ran around to the porch again, grabbed a stool, and pushed her way with it through the bushes on the other side of the house. With a Herculean struggle she hiked herself up and, after several false starts, managed to squeeze her body through the narrow space, sending a row of spices flying across the floor and an African violet into the sink. Lily, who had come all this way with one idea in mind, began to bark. Galen ran to the door and let her in. As she closed the door, her heart almost exploded in her chest. Something had flickered against the velvet drape of blackness that dropped behind the porch light's diffuse yellow glow. She peered into the dark but saw nothing. Then suddenly it was there again, clearly this time. A flash of light coming through the trees. A car.

But was it Julian or Johnny? Galen had only seconds before he, whichever one he was, would reach the end of the driveway. She bolted the door and darted back across the kitchen, slamming shut the window, scooping up what was left of the plant's shattered pot. Of course she had left the trash bin outside, as she always did when she closed the house for the weekend. She dumped the debris in the silverware drawer, turned on the water to try to wash the spilled soil down the drain and went to gather up the spices. It was dark and impossible to know if she had them all, or if all the dirt was out of the sink, but it was impossible, too, to turn on the kitchen light: the car had come over the crest. Cradling half a dozen small glass jars in her sweater, she ran out of the kitchen, Lily at her heels. She got as far as the pantry. A fraction of a second behind her, car lights flashed into the house. They swept back and forth through the windows then came to rest dead on the kitchen door, streaking down the passageway Galen would have to cross to escape the doorless little room that offered her no place to hide.

As she fumbled at a side drawer, Galen heard the car door slam. Kneeling down, she set the bottles noiselessly, one at a time, into the drawer. She heard footsteps on the porch, the kitchen door knob being tried, then the jingle of keys. Whoever it was had a key.

Just then something unexpected happened. As Galen placed the last of the bottles into the drawer, a smooth piece of cool metal brushed the back of her hand. She explored it with her fingers. A lever. She pushed against it. It gave with a *click*—not inside the drawer so much as behind her.

A breath of cold, damp air touched her when the cellar door swung ajar. Galen wasted no time in pulling it wide and dragging Lily into the envelope of black chill. Whoever had let himself into the bungalow flipped on the light just as she pulled the door silently shut in front of her.

With perspiration dripping off her face, she listened as he walked slowly through the house, pausing as if to look or to listen, clicking on lights and saying nothing. In the long silences—he was in one of the back rooms for what seemed an eternity—she began to imagine he could hear her pounding heart. Galen prayed that Lily would not stir. She prayed that the intruder would either not know or not think of the wine cellar. She prayed that she would neither faint again nor rush out into the open to end the torturous suspense.

. He came back now and walked quickly past the pantry into the kitchen. She heard him lift the receiver off the wall phone and dial.

"Anything?" was all Julian said. After a long pause he went on: "I'm at the cottage—no, there's no sign she's been here . . . I don't know, I'm going there now— No, she couldn't have gotten that far . . . We're all right as long as she doesn't somehow find her way to John . . . Stebbens said that she saw Caetano at the icehouse, so William was right . . . Don't worry, her next move will be to call the police, and Stebbens has already passed the word. They'll let us know as soon as she does. Don't worry, we'll find her. Okay, Fran, good-bye."

Franny. Galen felt as if she had been punched in the stomach. She was right. But *Franny?* He simply could not be in on all of this, too. And the police? None of this was possible. The last three hours had been a bad dream. Julian Baugh could not have robbed his father, he could not have killed his wife and brother, he could not want to kill her. No, that she could be sitting in the dark in a hidden wine cellar in the middle of the woods ten feet away from a man who had tried to murder her was simply not possible.

Julian locked the door behind him on the way out and Galen heard him start the engine. What now? Not daring to come out until she was sure he had gone, she sat for a moment longer before gradually getting to her feet. Her hand groped first for the latch to open the door, then, failing that, felt the wall for a light switch. This she found and flicked on. She saw now that she was at the top of a narrow stairway that descended steeply and disappeared around a corner. She saw also that Lily was not on the stairs. Calling quietly to her and hearing nothing, Galen followed the steps down.

The "wine cellar" might better have been called a vegetable cellar. Carved out of a ledge, its walls were the rock the house was built on, its corners softened by dense dust-whitened cobwebs. Its floor was dirt, the ceiling an ugly tangle of pipe and wire running between the exposed beams that supported the bungalow's wide oak floorboards. The shelves William had spoken of were indeed wine racks, but they were filled only with dust. The room itself was cluttered with scrap and junk that nobody cared about anymore: wooden skis whose paint was gone; clay pots, some of which still contained the brittle remnants of long-dead plants; rusted garden tools; ancient lawn furniture; a jumble of old crates; a pile of wood.

Galen found Lily at the bottom of the stairs intently sniffing dirt that she had scratched up with her paw. Something dead, Galen thought, and nudged the dog with her foot. Lily returned to the spot as if drawn by a magnet. Taking her by the collar, Galen dragged the animal halfway back up the stairs. But there she stopped. Something she had seen in the room below had caught her eye, but its unlikeliness had not sunk in right away. After descending into the cellar again, she looked up at the ceiling. Slid in among the wires were several—she counted almost a dozen—new-looking cardboard tubes, the kind in which one might mail a poster, only larger, longer and of heavier material. Her pulse quickened as she dragged a crate to the center of the open area and stood on it to remove one of the cylinders. When she uncapped one end, she could see there was something inside. She knew what it was even before she slid it out into the light.

Galen had the rolled canvas halfway out when she heard the footsteps on the stairs. Julian had come back. Whether for her or for the paintings was immaterial, he had them both now. She froze, her breath caught in her chest, blood throbbing in her ears, as he stepped into the light.

16

"*Johnny!*" Galen cried, leaping off the crate and into his arms. "Oh, Johnny! I was so afraid—I thought you were Julian—he tried to kill me! He locked me in William's room—I had to climb down—I didn't know what to do—"

Johnny stared at her dumbstruck as Galen babbled incoherently on.

"I couldn't call the police—they brought me back here. I should have gone to Dick and Peggy's house— We should go to Dick's—I was so afraid you wouldn't come!"

"Galen, darling, you're not making any sense, calm down," he said, taking hold of her now and shaking her gently. There was a smile on his lips but his eyes were without mirth. "I'm here now, as you can see. Everything's going to be all right. Now settle down, and try to tell me what this is all about. What do you mean, Julian tried to kill you? And what are you doing down here?"

"Johnny, I've found Henry's paintings, they're all here, in these tubes. Julian and Carla took them and hid them down here—all but one, which is in Paris. Then Julian—"

"Slow down, slow down. What do you mean Julian and Carla took them? What are you talking about? Are you quite sure you're all right?"

"Of course I'm all right! A friend of mine saw them in New York the day after the robbery, at the gallery of a man who's the buyer—oh, I forgot, you're a dealer, you'd know him—Nigel White. He—"

"Nigel White had H. L.'s paintings at his gallery? Galen, I think—"

"*No*, not the paintings, *Julian and Carla*. She saw them coming out of the gallery. She saw *one* painting, in Paris, at the house of a Greek collector named Korikus."

"Koriskos, yes, I've heard of him, but I fail to see the connection."

"Nigel White is Koriskos's personal buyer. Don't you see it? They took the paintings, hid them down here, and are selling them one at a time through Nigel White."

Johnny looked at her. His smile was gone. "Your friend, she's sure it was H. L.'s painting?"

"Yes, of course."

"And she's sure it was Julian and Carla? Has she told the police?"

"No, she didn't dare report anything until she got back here. Even then she isn't sure whom to tell. Koriskos is a small god in the art world, and at this point it's just her word against his. Anyway, she only just saw it today—well, now yesterday there—and called me. Just before I talked to you. Johnny, I can't believe any of this is happening. Then Julian tried . . ."

Here Galen's voice seemed to die in her throat.

Johnny put his arms around her.

"I know it's difficult for you but you must tell me," he said quietly, his mouth against her hair. "Tell me about Julian."

"He followed me—in a van—and tried to—to run me into the river."

"So that *was* your car. I didn't dare believe it. Galen"—

he looked hard at her—"you're absolutely sure it was Julian?"

"Yes, he came back when he realized I hadn't gone over the edge. I don't know what he would have done, but the police came and took me back to the house. One of the cops, Stebbens, is somehow in on this with Julian . . . and Caetano. That's why they brought me back here instead of to the station." Galen took a deep breath and in a voice that was finally her own again, she finished quickly, "Julian locked me in William's room but I got away and came here. How did you find me? Did you know about this place?"

"No, I saw the light coming through the floorboards."

"How did you find the latch?"

"The door was ajar. He hasn't been here looking for you?"

"He was here just before you came. I'm surprised you didn't pass him on the road."

"Does he know that you found the paintings?"

"I don't think so. No, he couldn't. I only just found out."

"You said something about Caetano's being involved after all?"

"He's here. In the woods, in a building by the pond."

"The *icehouse*?"

"He's been hiding there. I saw Julian there with him. They said they were afraid I would figure everything out and go to you about it."

"That bastard," Johnny said slowly, adding under his breath, "And so they should be."

"That's all?" he asked.

"Yes . . . Johnny—"

"Did they see you? Do they know you saw them?"

"No, I don't think so."

"When Julian took you back to the house, what did he say to you?"

"Nothing."

"What did you say to him?"

"What would you say to someone who had just tried to kill you?"

"Galen, darling, I'm sorry. I'm just trying to figure out why he could possibly want to kill you."

"I don't know," she said weakly. "I don't know."

"You haven't called the police?"

"No, I told you, Stebbens. And then I heard him say something to Franny on the phone that suggested Stebbens isn't the only one."

Johnny did not seem to hear this last part. His eyes had been scanning the room. He looked troubled and angry, but forced a smile.

"Come on, we'd better get you out of here," he said suddenly.

There was an edge in his voice.

Galen felt it, too. The cellar had suddenly grown cold and claustrophobic and she was shivering uncontrollably. She felt all at once that she could not bear it for another minute and turned quickly, grateful to flee its musty closeness. Something stopped her, however.

Something she had been looking at without seeing had just taken shape before her eyes. It was partially hidden in the rubble. A small suitcase. As it was aged and discolored by a thick coat of gray-brown dust, she had subconsciously dismissed it as trash. Looking at it now, she realized suddenly that it was not old at all. It was a woman's valise. A Louis Vuitton. Not quite large enough for an overnight bag.

"Johnny, wait."

After pulling free of his grip, she dug the case out from the under the slats of wood.

"I really think—" he began sharply.

But, oblivious, Galen was already grabbing at the latch and stretching open the mouth of the case. A stack of typed pages slumped against the bottom. She lifted out a sheet.

Even before she read the words, so familiar to her, she knew what the document was.

In his later works, Baugh's worldview seems at first untouched by the cultural storms of the fifties and sixties, but the curious angles of his color fields, offbeat perspectives, and deceptively simple compositions reflect the influences of Surrealism and other experiments in modern design. Pictures like *Phoebe* and *Sea Stallions,* while firmly rooted in the Realist tradition, reveal a . . .

Galen looked up. When she spoke, it was just above a whisper.

"Johnny! It's Henry's biography! Johanna's working copy. It's all here. This is where she left it . . ."

Johnny stared at her. Galen leafed through the pages and began to read the last. A frown creased her brow. She turned quickly to the second-to-last page, then, with the same urgency, to the third-to-last.

"This is very strange."

"What is?"

"Why . . . would she take the trouble to hide it down here? Even if she was running away and quitting on the book, why not at least leave it out for Henry to find?"

"Perhaps he had a copy."

"Yes, in fact he did, but not this one, none so complete. I've never seen some of this. There's maybe"—Galen flipped through the last third of the manuscript—"two month's worth of work here that Henry could not have seen. Don't you think that's odd?"

"I don't know," Johnny said absently as he fished his jacket pockets for a cigarette.

"Did the police ever look in here? I mean, there *was*

no inquiry, was there? No one ever even looked into the possibility of . . ."

"Of what?" Johnny said, pulling out a cigarette case and flipping open the lid. "Of murder? Listen, I know you think Julian tried to run you off the road, and perhaps he did, but I still can't see why he would murder his brother and his wife."

Galen said nothing. Whatever expression this had brought to her face, a smile began to spread across his. He gazed at her like this for a moment then let out a laugh.

"Galen, *darling*," he said teasingly. "Look at you, you've scared yourself! And now you're beginning to scare me. You watch entirely too much television."

Thinking fleetingly of William, Galen laughed thinly. "I don't know what to think anymore. I'm afraid I'm a little off my nut . . ." She trailed off with a glance around her. "Let's get out of here."

Galen led Johnny back up the stairs, back toward the fresh air of the cold, windy night, into which she would again run to escape this awful place. The door was closed. He reached around her to lift the latch but she stopped him.

"Where's Lily?" she whispered.

"She must still be in the cellar, don't worry, she'll come."

"Not if she's found something rotten to roll in."

"Like a body?" He was smiling.

"Let me get her," Galen said, smiling faintly back at him and started down the stairs.

Lily, of course, did not come when Galen called, but she could be heard rustling something somewhere on the other side of the wine racks. Galen wound her way through the jumble and eventually found her dog. She was standing on a crumpled piece of white butcher's paper with her front feet, tearing strips off with her teeth and chewing them. The paper appeared to be stained with blood.

It was not the dark smear of the blood that alarmed

her. It was the whiteness of the paper. Tossed among film-covered odds and ends that had not been touched in years, it was so obviously new, like the cardboard tubes in which she had found Henry's paintings. Whatever the sheet had contained, it had to have been left there by the burglar. By Caetano, or by Julian. Galen looked quickly around for anything else that was not layered with the airborne silt. Seeing nothing, she leaned over to grab Lily's collar and pulled her once more toward the stairs.

Galen had gone only a few feet before she let go and slowly straightened. There, glinting in the pile of junk like a diamond in a button box, was an eighth of an inch of shining steel with not the hint of rust or tarnish on it. She had not seen it before because it was all but hidden from the sight of a standing person by an old leaf-spread. It was the edge of a stirrup. Galen tore the tarp away and let out a gasp. Under it lay Colin's saddle.

"What have you found now?" Johnny asked mildly from the bottom of the stairs. Galen glanced around. He was leaning against the wall, lighting another cigarette. She opened her mouth to speak but nothing came out. She could only stare.

Galen's mind had flown from the saddle. She was instead transfixed by what Johnny held in his hand. The silver cigarette case glinted under the bare bulb. Why had she never noticed it before? The ingraved initials, simply drawn and deeply carved, were so clearly visible now. They met her eye with a sudden brutal familiarity. *JF.* Pieces of a different picture, more nightmarish than any she had yet drawn, began to fall, one at a time, into place in her reeling brain. Each piece meaningless by itself, their collective import was not immediately plain. Rather, like a jigsaw puzzle, the larger picture was taking form only gradually, in sudden bursts of separate, staggering images. The look on Galen's face told Johnny which one it was that Galen saw now.

"Poor dear," he said almost pleasantly, "what a shock this must be for you." Then he added, with eyes narrowed as if stung by the smoke that he blew away with an irritated jerk of his head, "You don't know when to quit, do you? Or to leave well enough alone."

He leaned his head back against the wall as if settling in for the evening. "But I suppose I'm fortunate that you didn't stumble onto it before, even without finding this room."

"*You?*"

Johnny inclined his handsome head with the suggestion of a bow.

"*You* stole Henry's paintings?"

He said nothing. He did not need to.

"I can't believe it."

"What can I say?"

"*Why?*" Galen struggled to grasp the full meaning of her discovery. Delayed by the shock of it, real fear had yet to take hold.

"Mon-ey, dar-ling," he said with comic affectation. "In-sur-ance."

"*Insurance?* Henry's insur—"

"No, silly. *My* insurance, *our* insurance. Insurance against you." He smiled but it quickly faded and he took a deep drag on his cigarette. "Yes, *you.*"

"I don't understand."

"You wouldn't. Shall we just say that your touchdown in our once-merry midst all but put an end to some rather torturously laid plans."

"What are you talking about?"

"I'm talking about our security. Everyone's entitled to that. But you rather backed us into a corner."

"*Us?* You and . . ."

Johnny let the cigarette fall from his fingers and stared after it on the dirt for a moment before he spoke again.

"Perhaps you're not so smart as I thought. 'O fierce and luxurious' Carla, of course, 'Our Lady of Pain.'"

"You and *Carla*? But you're—"

"Cousins?" Johnny threw back his head and laughed loudly. "Never has so much been overlooked by so many for so long . . . on account of so small a lie."

"*You* and Carla," Galen whispered, her mind racing first to Julian then immediately to Colin. *CB.* Not Colin Baugh: *Carla* Baugh . . . ever your love, *Johnny Foote.*

"Except, unfortunately, for Colin," Johnny was saying, "who did finally find out about us."

"Colin? So *you* killed him?" Another piece crashed into place, another jolting image flashed before her eyes. "He discovered you so you *killed* him?"

Johnny looked up sharply at the condemnation in her tone.

"It's never so simple as just that." He had spoken almost with disgust, but an eerie lightness quickly returned to his voice. "If every lover killed every husband who found him out, we'd live in a world of widows, now wouldn't we? The problem was that the husband in this case reacted rather badly. He was going to divorce his wife. Now, in fairness to the old boy, he also found out about Carla's arrangement—you Americans would call it 'kickback'—with the ladies she set loose on H. L. I always told her it was risky, but the old fool hardly needed encouragement. As I'm sure you know. What's he given you in the way of baubles, pet? Or has it been just money?"

Galen could say nothing.

"As you wish. I wouldn't dream of prying. In any case, Colin found out about that and then on top of everything else the abortion, so you can understand . . ."

"The abortion? Carla had an abortion," Galen murmured. It was not a question. It was what Mae had been trying to tell her and something Galen had somehow known for some time. From something that Carla had said herself.

"Colin wanted children," Galen said quietly, "and Carla didn't. . . . But surely Colin wasn't that rich that murder was better than divorce."

"Not Colin, no, but do you have any idea how much H. L. is worth? His art constitutes only a fraction of his estate. Even without his sister's trust, it's more than he and Julian could ever hope to spend in a lifetime. But Carla would have had no claim to the will at all, even after all those years. Now that's hardly fair, is it?"

"But why Johanna?"

"She wasn't part of the original plan, but opportunity virtually beat down our doors when she came up with this secret trip to New York to buy Julian a saddle." Galen's eyes went involuntarily to the Hermès resting among the junk against the wall.

"You were right about that, my sweet," Johnny said, not kindly, lighting another cigarette and strolling over to the saddle. "Colin did have one."

Galen backed involuntarily away as he came closer. She could tell by the curl at the corners of his mouth that even without looking at her Johnny had noticed and was amused.

"We couldn't have dreamed up such a tidy little package. The Baughs would spare nothing to avoid a scandal like that, including quashing an inquiry, which, incidentally, is just what they did. So all Carla had to do was make their little trip look like a tryst and all I had to do was make sure there was no one to deny it."

As Johnny Foote stopped to look at her through narrowed eyes, Galen was feeling her first flash of real fear since his revelations had begun. She had been listening as if in a trance—at one point she had even wanted to laugh—but his silence now changed all that. The danger was suddenly very real and very near, and her stupefication was replaced by one desperate, overriding sense: that she had to keep him talking. He had told her too much already. It meant only one thing: He would have to kill her. As soon as he stopped, he would come after her. The look in his eye told her she was right, and that he knew she knew. But she also saw something in the way that he silently considered her that might give her more time, for whatever it was worth: Johnny was enjoying himself. He seemed almost to be proud of what he had done. He also seemed to relish his power over her and her mounting fear.

You must keep him talking, she told herself, taking a small step toward the door. You can't let him stop.

"So you sabotaged the plane. How?"

"It doesn't matter. Suffice it to say it was frighteningly simple."

"And undetectable."

"More or less . . . the Stover P.D. is not Scotland Yard."

"And you planted the site with money and Johanna's jewels?" Galen moved again.

"No, no. She carried those on herself. Carla asked her to pick a prescription up for Colin on her way to the airport. She phoned it in only after Johanna left so that there would be a delay at the store and I would have time to switch the bags in the pharmacy parking lot."

Galen's eyes fell on the Louis Vuitton.

"Carla and Johanna's matching luggage," she said quietly.

"Quite. You've noticed, I'm sure, that the lot is at the back of the building. And Carla had a key to her car . . . The rest happened on its own accord."

"But you missed with William," Galen said. Her tone was subdued but her nerves were about to shatter. She took another step.

"William? Nothing happened to William."

"Because he was *lucky*! He should have been stomped to death! Carla locked him in the stall, didn't she?"

The smoldering anger with which Johnny flicked his cigarette made Galen flinch. You've gone too far, she told herself bitterly. But after a pause, he continued matter-of-factly:

"H. L.'s first will was a generation-skipping will, which left the principal of his estate to his grandchildren. Barring that, it would have all gone to his immediate offspring."

"Widowed in-laws included."

"Yes, but that doesn't matter now, because after Colin's death H. L. saw that he would never have a blood grandchild on that side, so he changed it to let the principal go to the first generation, Julian and Carla—but with Julian getting the lion's share so as to provide for William and any further procreation on Julian's part. The truth is, Carla's share is nothing compared to Julian's. This, however, hardly mattered as widower and widow were brought together by the terrible tragedy—you know how death has a way of doing that. Incidentally, I didn't make up the part about a spring wedding. Carla had indeed assured me that the event, cherry blossoms and all, was decidedly in the offing. But that was before you came along—"

"*Me?*"

"—and the idiot fell in love with you."

The words fell hard.

"You look surprised, my dear. Can you really have missed it? Carla was right, you are out of your league here, aren't you? You really don't understand any of this at all."

He took a step toward her but stopped.

"Labor Day weekend I got a frantic call from my beloved 'cousin' that all her well-laid plans were going to pot because some green-eyed bitch was on the scene and her intended was threatening to fall in love with her. Her idea was for me to come and take you out of the running."

Johnny reached out suddenly and took Galen's chin roughly in his hand. She threw her hands out against his chest. He smiled.

"I confess I would have loved to do it some other way, but you were 'preoccupied.' You did fall for him, didn't you? When I told you about Carla and him, you wanted so badly not to believe it, poor thing. You tried not to care but you let him come to your room up at H. L.'s. You would have let him have anything he wanted—yes, my dear, I was there that night. And I saw you in the hall together and I saw him carry you to your bed. You didn't see me, did you?"

"Yes," she said. "I did."

Johnny was clearly taken aback. He slowly let go of her, reached again for his cigarette case and lighter, and began casually to pace. Galen took another sidestep toward the stairs.

"Later, outside, with Carla. You were wearing Julian's jacket," she said. She could tell by his amused silence that her guess had been right. "I saw you from William's bedroom window."

Johnny gave her a long shrewd look. A grin spread slowly across his face.

"But you didn't know it was me," he said tentatively. When Galen said nothing, he laughed. "So *that's* what happened that night! We couldn't for the *life* of us figure it out! We knew Julian couldn't have been that bad in the sack. *You thought I was Julian.* That's why you flew the coop the next day. And poor Julian never knew what hit him. That's truly rich! And there *we* were snuggled up together when he comes barreling in to straighten you out! (I wonder what I did to deserve that piece of luck!) And by then Carla had told him there was something going on between you and me and then you go and ask me to carry you off. You read your lines perfectly, my dear. Is there anything quite so divisive as mutual suspicion?"

If he only knew, Galen thought, seeing again Julian's terrible glance from William's door not much more than an hour ago. She had thought it was meant for her, that he had wanted to kill her. She knew now, with a knifelike stab of inner pain, that he had not been thinking about her—he had been thinking about Johnny.

Johnny's smile was fading. Galen was halfway to the stairs. Oh, please, she prayed. But finally he continued.

"The only problem was how long could it last. Had I not been here the day you fled H. L.'s house and Julian came running after you, it might have ended right there. Another attempt to get rid of you—"

"*Another . . .*"

Johnny stopped to look at her. "If your fall didn't kill you, we certainly expected it to scare you away. However, Carla was wrong on that score. Too bad for you, you don't frighten easily enough. So where did that leave us? Another 'accident' would have been too suspicious, which brings us back to our little insurance policy."

"Henry's paintings." It was barely a whisper. Galen's nerves were gradually giving out. She could not move so long as he was looking at her, and she was beginning to feel weak and vaguely disoriented. She struggled to keep her balance.

"Of course we hadn't planned for that night, but the empty house was impossible to pass up. And with you, my little Snow White, in dreamland—those pills work like a charm, don't they?—and your ridiculous little dog preoccupied with Mae's stew beef—it was entirely too easy. What I couldn't have hoped for was Julian's seeing me and thinking it was Caetano. The vehicle I chose was for that reason similar, but I never thought anyone would actually see it." Johnny began to pace again. "Though from what you've said Julian is perhaps somewhat less convinced now than then—"

"That was you, not Julian, at Nigel White's gallery."

"Brilliant deduction. Yes, that was me. And Carla, of course. If I'd only realized I looked so much like Julian . . . Yes, Nigel has agreed to find generous and discreet buyers for any painting we can bring him out of H. L.'s private collection. With Carla's scheme for all intents and purposes in ruin, it gives us a little more to work with. Or to live on if, as they say in the movies, 'our cover is blown,' which may or may not already be the—"

"You used a *van*," she whispered, mostly to herself. The last piece, the one she should have seen first but somehow had not been able to face, dropped into place. How could she have missed it? Why did it take so long? It did not matter now. The picture was complete. "That was *you*. You tried to—"

"A little slow on the uptake, but congratulations—you found me out."

Johnny spoke with sarcasm and sickening calm.

"Yes, and I might have succeeded then if Julian hadn't magically appeared, oddly enough in what looked like the real thing. (I wondered where he got Caetano's van.) I would have loved an aerial shot of us all rushing about in matching vehicles. And, of course, of your tender encounter, which I did see from across the river. Though I can't say as I understand why he was quite so rough. I suppose you hurt his feelings by trying to run away from him. Then he went and locked you in William's room, without a word, you say. That's interesting, too."

"But, Johnny, *why*?"

"Why? Why, indeed. I'm not entirely sure the idea was such a good one myself—I mean, look how it turned out. Impulse, I suppose. And again . . . irresistible opportunity. I mean, there I was and there you were on the same road . . . I'd really just driven out to see whether they'd found the van and thought I'd call—fully expecting you to have left for the city by then—and if you had, to come out and clear out the saddle and the rest of the pictures. I should have done it earlier, but we learn from our mistakes. . . . Anyway, to my infinite surprise, you greeted me with the unfortunate story of your discovery—an as-yet-unretold story, I might add—and there I was on the very road you were just about to start down. As I said, irresistible opportunity. With you so ready to think it was Julian, I

realize that I perhaps acted hastily. You see, I've always admired you. There's something so bloody bold about you,
like that horse you like so well. I was almost glad you
didn't go over the edge. I believe I would have had a
change of heart."

"Johnny—"

The smile, the affected calm, was gone. He stepped toward her again and took her face in his hands.

"After all," he whispered menacingly, "even if you've
talked to anyone else, you've only accumulated evidence
against Julian, isn't that right? Who did you tell the police
had run you off the road?

"Unfortunately . . ." He looked down at the floor,
where the saddle and the bag containing Henry's manuscript lay. "You've been too clever for your own good and
now you simply know too much."

"Julian knows," Galen said quickly, leaning away
from him and, when he did not pursue, taking another step
toward the door. "That's why he's hiding Caetano in the
woods. He—"

"Knows what? He may indeed suspect—the son of a
bitch never did like me—but he has no proof. If he did, he
and the Keystone Cops would have come after me by now.
Thanks to the diligent but not altogether accurate in-
vestigative work of you and your meddlesome friend, I
would say that the evidence is rather more incriminating of
Julian than of me. And as soon as we tip Nigel off, you, my
lovely, will be the only living soul with even a shred of
concrete proof."

Galen had inched her way almost to the stairs when
Johnny suddenly grabbed both of her wrists in his hands
and, with a quick, painful tug, pulled her close to him.

"Where *do* you think you're going?" he said between
clenched teeth.

"Johnny, listen to me!" she cried. "They all know!
Mae knows about the abortion. Julian and Franny know

about the robbery and about the crash! If I disappear the first thing the police will do is reopen the investigation—"

"Who said anything about your disappearing? I'm thinking . . . What if something were to happen to you that tied you to the theft? You were, after all, the only one near the house that night, and everyone knew how chummy you were with Caetano. The whole matter might stop right there."

"They know Caetano didn't do it! And they'll never believe—"

But Johnny was not listening to her anymore.

"Say a fire, in which you and one or two H. L. Baugh originals went up—one, I suppose would suffice—I daresay that would take care of some other incriminating evidence." He looked slowly around the horrible little room, his eyes lingering on Colin's saddle. "I doubt Julian will recover fast enough for a spring wedding after all, but I make it a habit never to underestimate my dear Carla. It's a pity to destroy art—but I've got to give the police something to go by."

"Johnny! There's no need— It doesn't make sense! You'll never get away with it! You've got the paintings, you should just try to—"

"Shut up!" he shouted, yanking hard on her arms. "It's much easier to get away with murder than one would think."

Then his voice dropped again. "But it will be a pity to destroy you, too. You're what my Scottish grandfather would call a figh-en piece of work yourself. *'Take hand and part with laughter,'*" he whispered. "*'Touch lips and part with tears.'*"

With this he pulled her roughly against him and his mouth came down over hers. She struggled but he had thrown one arm around the back of her neck and the other across her lower back and was holding her so tightly she could not move. She tried to knee him but he was pressing too hard against her.

"The problem with you," he said, leaning back now to look at her, "is you've—become—quite—impossible—to—live—with." And with that he smacked her so hard across the jaw with the back of his hand that she landed across the floor against a pile of wood.

Dazed, Galen raised herself to her knees. *"Lily!"* She cried weakly and utterly without hope. But rather than bite Galen's attacker, the dog trotted jauntily to her side. Johnny let out a laugh and began to remove the cardboard tubes from the tangle of wires on the ceiling.

Her senses coming only slowly back to her, Galen dragged herself to her feet. Absorbed in easing free a tube that was tucked behind a beam, Johnny seemed not to notice. His talking, Galen knew, was over. If he speaks to you again, she told herself, it will be the last thing you'll ever hear. And with that she made a charge for the door.

With one short lunge, Johnny caught her and pulled her to him. This time, however, she had enough room to fight back, and caught him squarely in the shin with her boot. The impact was enough to make him loosen his grip, and in an instant she was at the door and halfway up the stairs. Taking them three at a time, she was at the top now and grabbing frenziedly at the catch. It would not slide.

Had it not given way when it did, Galen might have turned to defend herself. With the advantages of the higher ground and the adrenaline that was coursing into her bloodstream, she might even have held him off, for a time. As it was the latch did give and she tried instead to escape through the door. But Johnny was close enough by then to grab her by the ankle and, with a series of violent jerks, drag her back down into the cellar. She tried to scream but heard nothing but a hollow breathy sound. He was on her now and his hands were groping at her neck. She clawed savagely at his arms, but his hands, which were quickly around her throat, were unyielding. Then suddenly they constricted and her breath was gone. A death-struggle panic took over, and she flailed and writhed uncontrollably, but Johnny did not move. She heard him growl, "That's it for you, Saint Joan."

The room, however, did not go black. It seemed instead to explode.

There was a thud and Johnny's crushing weight was off her chest, although she could still feel the pressure of his hands on her throat. She twisted around onto her stomach and began coughing and gasping for air. She was vaguely aware of Lily's barking and the noise and chaos around her. As she fought for consciousness, she was aware that something had happened, but it was a moment before she realized what it was.

Struggling to her knees, Galen looked up to see Julian, with Johnny on top of him, falling against the wine racks, sending them crashing against each other like dominoes. Galen did not lose consciousness, but everything after that happened as if in a dream. Johnny was bent over Julian's body, his hands around Julian's throat. Then somehow she was on her feet, grabbing for a board and swinging it at the back of Johnny's head. She felt a sharp stab of pain and was suddenly on the ground again. And then the two men were falling back across the room.

Galen had no sense of how much time went by before she heard it, but she would never forget the sickening crack that preceded the long eerie silence.

—17—

"Try to drink some of this," Dick Bowdoin's voice was saying through a kind of hazy numbness. Galen tried to focus. Dick was holding out an orange-juice glass about a quarter filled with something that looked like brandy. In his other hand he held another better than half full.

Galen looked around her. The bungalow was crowded with people. From the couch in the living room she could see uniformed police officers, what looked like paramedics, photographers, and a number of men in street clothes passing in and out of the pantry. She could hear Franny's voice on the phone in the kitchen.

She looked up at Dick. "What are you doing here?"

"Looking for you," he said simply. "Drink up."

"Where's Henry?"

"He's up at the house."

Galen stared blankly at two police officers talking quietly in the hallway.

"Johnny killed Johanna and Colin," she said, her eyes narrowing in almost a wince as the scene in the cellar began to come back to her.

"I know," Dick said, still holding the glass.

"He sabotaged Colin's plane. They weren't having an affair. Johnny just tried to make it look like they were. Then they robbed Henry. He and Carla—"

"I know, shhhh," he said gently. "It's over now. Now do as I say and drink some of this."

Galen took a sip and over the rim of the glass noticed Caetano for the first time sitting in a chair by the fireplace. He smiled at her.

"Como vai?" he murmured.

Caetano. Her world, which in the last few hours had burst apart, was slowly coming back together.

"Then you know" was all she could say and closed her eyes.

"That was Stebbens," Franny said, coming into the living room now. He was carrying an ice pack. "He's on his way down. Galen, my poor child, how are you feeling? Here, put this on that cheek. You gave us a horrible scare." He tried to smile. "Are you up to talking to the police?"

"Yes, of course. Where's . . . Johnny?"

No one said anything for a moment. The two men just looked at her. Caetano looked down.

"He's dead," said a voice from the door. Julian had just come up from the cellar. His face was swollen and bruised and blackened with dried blood. Galen could not suppress a gasp.

"You killed him?" she asked. The horror in her voice was not at what he had done so much as at the events of the entire night. The picture of Johnny's lifeless body, only a few feet below where they were standing, was just one in a series of grotesque images that were returning to Galen as in waves and pummeling her senses like a series of blows.

Julian misunderstood.

"I'm sorry," he said stiffly, hooded eyes meeting hers but then looking away.

Galen continued to stare.

"It's very difficult to accept, I know," Franny was saying to her.

But Galen was not thinking about Johnny anymore. Her thoughts were only of the barely recognizable man on the other side of the room who looked at her now as if from across an unbridgeable expanse. Another kind of agony gripped her. What had she done? The distance she had put between them in her fear and confusion was, she knew, insurmountably great. How could she ever apologize to him for thinking that he was capable of murdering his brother and wife, let alone son, and then of trying to kill her? How could she thank him for saving her life?

"I am so ashamed" was all she said, and looked miserably away.

"You mustn't be," Julian said wearily. "He fooled many people for a long time." His voice was utterly without warmth.

Galen began silently to weep.

The phone rang and Julian went to answer it. He returned to say something to Franny and then went quickly out the door. And, Galen knew as she listened to the Jaguar engine roar and then fade away, out of her life. If Johnny had been right that Julian had fallen in love with her, it was unquestionably over now. She had killed it. She could never explain how her heart had fought for him, had denied what all the evidence around her suggested, what Johnny had told her. She could never explain that deep down inside she had never stopped loving him, had never fully accepted that on which her fear had made her act.

Franny sat down beside Galen.

"You mustn't be too hard on yourself for being . . . drawn in," he said gently. "We all were." Then, with a glance at the door through which Julian had just left, he added, "To one degree or another. Johnny was very, very good at what he did. Even better than Carla, who was frightfully good herself. We'd been trying to find something linking him to Colin and Johanna's deaths for almost two years, but there was never so much as a trace."

"You knew all along?" Galen asked.

"We suspected."

"You knew that Johanna and Colin were not having an affair?"

"Julian did, yes, and after a time he convinced me. Which of course made the circumstances of the crash unacceptable. But we did not know about Johnny and Carla's relationship until recently. Nor could we figure out the motive. The two, as it turned out, came hand in hand."

"H. L.'s will," Galen said, drying her cheeks with Dick's handkerchief and taking a large swallow of his brandy. She straightened her back and went on in a stronger voice. "Colin found out about Johnny and Carla and threatened to divorce her."

Poor Franny seemed grateful for her poise. He gave her a weak smile.

"He found out a good deal more than that," he said. "Apparently Carla had been introducing acquaintances of hers to H. L. in the hope that they might take advantage of his generosity and she might in turn take advantage of theirs. That's who we thought you were when you first turned up at East Cutty."

"A friend of Carla's!"

There was an embarrassed, apologetic pause before Franny went on. "The problem was that there wasn't a shred of evidence to go on. Julian never believed that the crash was an accident and suspected Johnny's involvement almost immediately, but Foote's path was as pristine as virgin snow. No fingerprints, nothing to suggest sabotage, and no conceivable motive. But finally, after almost two years, we suddenly got lucky. By pure chance, Julian ran into a fellow in Paris who knew one of H. L.'s former . . . lady friends—in this case a girl named Gabriella—and had a rather startling conversation about their mutual acquaintance. I must say the whole thing surprised me, as I rather liked the woman myself. But it seems our Gabriella had been less than discreet about her intentions toward a certain 'rich and famous American painter.' There was hardly anything new in that, but she had gone so far as to mention something about an in-law's participation. It was purely gossip, of course, and years out of date, and had no ostensible connection to the crash, but it was cause enough to track Gabriella down in New York—which, I must say, wasn't easy, but that's another story.

"At any rate, Julian came back at the beginning of the summer—that would have been the weekend you met at East Cutty—and eventually found her. She was, not surprisingly, less than cooperative, denying any part in a sham. Interestingly, however, there seemed to be a bit of bad blood between Gabriella and Carla, because she was *not* averse to implicating Carla. Not at first and never directly, but Julian persisted in seeing her, and, over the course of several visits, without making any concrete accusations, of course, she let it drop that Carla had some things of her own to hide. Not the least of these being a long-standing affair with someone who fit Johnny's description. Except that she described him as a 'gigolo' and said that Carla was supporting him. This is what first led us to look into his business affairs, which we were surprised to find in virtual ruin. It seemed that despite, or maybe because of his lifestyle, John had been deeply in debt for some time. Gabriella also told Julian outright that Carla had aborted Colin's child, which came as something of a shock. It was still hearsay, but it provided the first piece of the puzzle— that things might not have been so idyllic between the Colin Baughs as we'd all been led to believe."

Franny stopped for a moment and seemed to be lost in thought.

"Johnny said Colin eventually found out about them,"

Galen said in the pause. "Also about the abortion and the plan to milk Henry, and was going to divorce her."

"Yes," Franny said with a slight shake of his head. "Thanks to Gabriella. It seems she and Carla had something of a falling out when things didn't work out with H. L. Gabriella evidently felt Carla had left her by the wayside, and took it upon herself to tell Colin all about it. She confessed this to Julian on the weekend that you, Richard, showed up."

Galen swung around. Dick had been so uncharacteristically quiet, she had all but forgotten that he was there. It occurred to her suddenly that the revelations would have to be a terrible shock for him, as well.

"She also told him about another woman, in France, with whom Carla had had a similar arrangement, although he never found her. In the meantime, you, Galen, had come to the Winds, which had brought Johnny back out of the woodwork. Your . . . interest in each other seemed, well . . . natural enough, but Julian thought there might be cause for concern and accelerated his plans to return to Stover."

"Julian announced his plans to return before I met Johnny."

"Oh, well, that may be—"

"'Cause for concern'? Concern about what?"

"That he might be planning something."

"Why didn't anyone tell me?"

"Or me?" Dick said stiffly.

"I'm dreadfully sorry. It was a difficult decision, but we were afraid of alerting him inadvertently. We didn't even dare tell H. L. I mean, could either of you have acted the same toward Johnny, knowing, or even suspecting, that he might have caused that crash? We knew we were getting close but we didn't really have anything concrete and we couldn't actually *do* anything until we were sure. By now we knew enough that *if* he did it, it had to be for the money—we figured to protect Carla's share in the estate—and that, short of killing Julian, which was never an idle consideration, we didn't think there was much more he could do. We figured he wasn't going to kill H. L. because there was still the probate business involving his sister's trust, which hadn't reverted to him yet—although by this time next year he might have been in some danger . . . But then, of course, Galen had her fall."

"Johnny tampered with my saddle."

"Yes, so we discovered."

"*And that wasn't concrete enough?*" Galen almost shouted.

"I'm sorry to say we were rather stupid about this and only just established it yesterday. It was Caetano who suggested we have the catch looked at. I'm sorry we were so slow about this, but it was the farthest thing from our minds. First it didn't make any sense that he would attack *you*—we all rather assumed that he'd fallen in love with you. In fact, the only person we could imagine wanting to see any harm come to you would be Carla, and that she would do anything was, at the time, unthinkable. Besides that, Johnny hadn't been near the place in a week. And then suddenly we were preoccupied with this robbery business, which caught us completely off guard . . . But I really don't think he was trying to kill you, my dear. I think he was just trying to scare you off. You had obviously stumbled on something that had made him nervous."

"The saddle."

"What saddle?"

"Just before the crash Johanna bought an Hermès saddle for Julian as a surprise for his birthday. Colin was flying her down to New York to pick it up."

There was a long painful silence.

"I mentioned to Johnny that I didn't think it fit the picture of an unfaithful wife."

"Perhaps," Franny said slowly, "but I can't imagine that that would be enough."

"I'd also found a book of Swinburne verse that Johnny had given Carla. Inscribed. I thought it was from Johanna to Colin. Maybe he thought I would figure it out."

"John loved Swinburne," Dick Bowdoin said. "Isn't the name of his yacht the title of one of his poems?"

"Still," Franny said dubiously. "I can't see . . ."

"And, of course, their plan was for Carla to marry Julian," Galen said finally.

It was a moment before Franny grasped her meaning.

"Oh, yes, I see," he said quietly, and after an awkward pause, went quickly on. "Not wanting to take any chances, Julian came back at once. He figured that if Johnny was up to something, he would hardly dare do anything with him hovering about. Unfortunately, with your flight from the house, you made things rather more difficult. But with John leaving that night, we didn't think we had anything to worry about. Of course, the last thing we expected was for him to go and steal H. L.'s paintings. It made no sense, coming when it did, unless he felt that we were closing in."

"He did. So the charge against Caetano was fake all along?"

"Julian actually did see the van but he knew it wasn't Caetano. He also knew Johnny might not be quite as careful if he thought he was not suspected and so got Stebbens to go along."

"They."

"They?"

"Carla helped him sell one of the pictures to a collector in Paris. My friend, my roommate Mara James, saw it there yesterday."

"Really . . . Interesting . . . Well, *we* didn't know what he'd done with the pictures and we figured if we just watched him long enough, he'd lead us to them and then at least we would have him on something. In the mean-

time—last night, in fact—Julian got lucky with our friend
Gabriella, who finally confessed to having had good reason
to suspect the crash was not an 'accident' and agreed in
principle to give evidence against John and Carla. Apparently Carla had confronted her after she'd gone to Colin
and in a fit of rage had told her that it would take more
than divorce papers to cut her out of the Baugh family fortune. She said Carla had also threatened her that if she ever
said another word about their arrangement vis à vis H. L.
that she would have Johnny kill her, 'too.'"

"'Too'?"

"Yes. We thought this would be enough for an indict-
ment. However, she wanted a little more time to think it
over."

"'It was a big step for her,'" Galen mumbled to herself. She felt Caetano's surprised look.

"How's that?" Franny asked.

"Nothing," she said a little sadly, looking up at
Caetano. She had seen him only a few hours before but it
seemed now like years ago. Could she really have thought
this boy was involved in something that endangered her
life? She could hardly remember, so insane was the notion
now. It was as if the woman running through the woods
only that afternoon had been someone else, not her. Had
they only told her. Had she only asked. Thanks to Julian
she was alive, but, thinking of him now, she almost wished
she were dead.

As if reading her thoughts, Dick reached over and
squeezed her hand. Nobody said anything.

At this point Stebbens came in. He gave Franny a look
that the older man seemed to understand.

"How's H. L. taking it?" Franny asked.

Stebbens shrugged his shoulders by way of reply. He
then looked slowly around the room, his gaze resting on
Galen. His eyes were sad and sympathetic.

"How are you, Miss Shaw?" he asked with an apologetic smile.

Galen could only nod.

"Did he. . . ?" he asked, pointing at her cheek.

"Yes," Franny said.

There was another short silence.

"Do you feel up to some questions?" Stebbens asked Galen.

She nodded again.

Stebbens took a chair and she began an abbreviated version of her story, starting with her trip to the pond with William. She left out the conflict that had raged between her head and her heart, her own private nightmare in which everything she thought she knew no longer made sense, her fear of being right, and all that was at stake if she was wrong. She told him only what she had overheard through the broken window at the icehouse and about her flight back to the bungalow. Recounting the incidents in a subdued, businesslike voice, she then told him about Mara's call.

"I was afraid of calling the police because I couldn't be sure, after what I had heard Julian say. I just didn't know what to think." Her eyes rose briefly to Franny, whom she knew now had spent the night searching for her. "It didn't make any sense, of course, but . . . Anyway, I decided to go back to Boston. Just as I was leaving Johnny called and asked me to give him a lift to the city. He said he was at the airport, which is why I never for a minute suspected . . ."

"He was at a phone booth at Poland's gas station when he called," Stebbens interjected. Galen considered it: The filling station lay on River Road about halfway between the Winds and the covered bridge. She could not even remember passing it tonight.

"Oh" was all she said. "The rest you know. I left. Someone tried to run me off the road. And failed. Barely. I thought—Julian drove up in what appeared to be the same van and I thought he was the one . . ."

Galen stopped here and looked down at her lap. She wished she had never rented the beach house in East Cutty.

"Go on," Stebbens prompted gently.

"Well, I was quite frightened at that point and when you brought me back here against my will, I thought—"

"I'm deeply sorry, Miss Shaw," he said almost tenderly. "You see, we didn't know where Foote was and couldn't take the chance of his having another go at you. Mr. Baugh planned to tell you the whole story as soon as we got you back, but . . . you didn't really give us the chance."

"No, I guess not." Galen did not try to disguise the bitterness in her voice.

"How'd you get out?"

"The trellis."

"Really!" Stebbens seemed impressed.

"Anyway, I came back here to the bungalow to call Henry at Dick and Peggy's house. I figured the whole world couldn't have gone mad. Julian arrived and . . . looking for a place to hide, I discovered the cellar, which is where I found the paintings . . . and Johnny found me."

The interview did not last much longer. Galen recited what she remembered of Johnny's "confession," which more or less confirmed what Franny had been telling her. Near the end she was interrupted by a noise on the cellar stairs. Everyone looked around to see Johnny's covered body being taken from the house on an ambulance stretcher. When they looked back at each other, it was obvious that whatever else needed to be talked about could wait until morning.

18

With a comprehending nod from Stebbens, Dick rose to leave.

"Galen, come back to Westerly with me tonight. It's late and you haven't eaten and I'm sure you don't want to sleep here. Peg will want to have a look at that leg. Did you know she was a nurse during the war? That's where we met."

Galen got stiffly to her feet. Her leg did hurt—and her throat ached. She was not hungry, but she was grateful for the chance to get away from the bungalow. The farther away the better.

Letting Dick and Franny pass ahead of her into the kitchen, Galen stopped and turned to Caetano.

"I never believed you could do anything like that," she said, and touched his hand.

"I know," he said simply, and smiled. There was not a lot else to say. The men were waiting for her, and she followed them out the kitchen door onto the porch.

Here they all spoke at once.

"H. L.!"

He looked ghostly white in the wash of light that reached him from the kitchen, but he was smiling. His eyes were on Galen. Without thinking, she pushed her way past the others and threw her arms around him.

"I'm so sorry, Henry" was all she could think of to say.

"So am I," he said, taking her two hands. "It has been quite a shock, for all of us. I suppose we'll only really begin to understand it later on. But you, my dear, what an awful ordeal. Are you sure you're quite all right? Your face . . . We have abused you terribly, haven't we?"

"She's fine, H. L.," Dick said. "In fact, I'm taking her back to Westerly with me now to get some food into her."

"You don't want to come up to the house?" Henry asked Galen, but in a tone that suggested he already knew the answer.

Dick came to her rescue. "Why don't you and Fran come along, too, H. L.? You saw how much food Peg has prepared. Bring William along—he's probably a little shaken up by all this himself."

"Perhaps it would be best to get away from here for a little."

Henry was looking directly at Galen, so that she did not know whether he was speaking for her or for all of them.

"What did they . . . Where's Carla?" Franny asked.

"They've just taken her down for questioning," he said, adding almost as an afterthought, "They've arrested her."

As if transfixed by the picture in Henry's mind—or perhaps each had his own mental image—nobody moved or said anything for a moment. The police came and went, flowing noisily around them as rushing water around a river island. The little group appeared to be in mourning. Perhaps each in his own way was. But if H. L., Dick, and Franny were mourning the past, Galen was mourning the future. She thought again bitterly of the cold empty space that she had put between her and Julian and let out a tiny groan. It was hardly a sound, more like a hum, but Henry heard it.

"Somehow I wasn't that surprised when Julian told me about Johnny," he said sadly, "although I'm sure I loved him. I even think he was somewhat fond of me. Even so, it leaves one feeling . . . quite shaken at the roots. Quite helpless. Helpless sorrow, helpless rage. I suppose I shall hate him one day but I can't seem to just now. Perhaps I just don't really believe it yet. For now there is a kind of grizzly tradeoff in it: The revelation of his guilt gives us something back of Colin and Jo." His eyes lighted briefly on Caetano's. "You know what I mean, Fran?"

"Yes, in fact, I do. It was like that for me."

Henry took Galen's hand and began to lead her slowly toward the driveway. The three followed.

"The problem," he said, "is that we have to mourn them all over again. I, at any rate, do."

There was a pause and then he went on. "The real shock was finding out about Carla. I have always looked upon her as a daughter. We had something . . . particular between us, I thought. I would never have thought her capable . . . Perhaps I should feel sorry for her. Right now, oddly enough, I feel sorry for me. As strange as this may sound—I am perhaps suffering from shock—I am sure I shall miss her. I shall miss them both."

They had stepped out into a sea of cars: Dick's, Franny's, Henry's, Caetano's van, and half a dozen police vehicles. The sound of police radios filled the night. The pulsing lights of several of the cruisers—why didn't they turn them off? Galen wondered—flashed against their haggard faces. Men in uniforms with heavy-butted guns on their hips were everywhere. The entire Stover police force seemed to be there. It was a scene out of a disaster movie.

"I'm old," Henry was saying. "I've lost many people in

my life. The thing is to know when to hold on and when to let go."

Here he stopped and turned to Galen. "I know you have had a terrible shock, too, my dear. Forgive me if I am presumptuous, but you mustn't feel embarrassed or that somehow you should have known. We can only take people at their word and if they are not as they seem, it's to our credit, not a sign of our weakness or foolishness, that we have trusted and perhaps even loved them. As painful as it is, we're better for having loved them than not. I know how you feel—"

But here Galen cut him off. She could not stand their misplaced sympathy any longer.

"No, you don't!" she said with more force than she had meant to use.

Henry was taken aback.

"I assure you, my dear, I do," he said gently. "You mustn't feel ashamed. We all loved Johnny in our own way. Dick and Franny, too—"

"But don't you see, *I* never did!" Galen said, her voice rising. "Everyone assumes that I was in love with him. Can't you see that it was *your son* I loved?"

Galen was almost shouting, and it seemed suddenly as if everyone—the three elderly men, Caetano, the entire Stover police department, even the radio dispatcher—had stopped to listen to her. She looked self-consciously around and continued in a low voice.

"I never suspected Johnny but I never loved him. So, you see, you're quite wrong, Henry. I have everything to be ashamed of. *I* suspected the man I *loved*."

"But we thought—"

"That's what Johnny wanted you to think. For the same reason he wanted me to think Julian and Carla were engaged to be married, that it was Julian not he in the garden with Carla, that Julian could not be trusted."

"I see . . . Have you told Julian, my dear?"

"Told *Julian*? Told Julian *what*? I love you but, forgive me, I thought you were a murderer?"

There was a long moment during which Henry, Dick, Franny, and Caetano just stared at her in silence. Then Galen added very quietly, "I forgot to feed Lily. I won't be long," and disappeared back into the bungalow.

In a minute she heard Franny's car start up and then begin down the driveway. He and one or two of the others had evidently gone on ahead. It was just as well, she thought. Galen filled Lily's bowl and stared absently at the dog's back for a moment. As she stooped over to give her a pat, something dropped out of her pocket onto the floor. It was William's locket. She had forgotten all about it. She picked it up, opened it, and glanced a last time at the picture of the handsome young woman whose life was already over. It had ended in a violent and surely terrifying death. Galen thought of William, then of Colin, then of Julian. She realized suddenly that she really knew nothing of what it was to suffer at Johnny Foote's hands. That her bitterness and self-pity were entirely misplaced. If she had something to be ashamed for, it was that.

Stepping back out into the parking lot, she could see the solitary outline of Henry waiting behind the wheel in his decrepit Volvo station wagon. She was glad the others had gone on ahead. She needed a chance to speak with him alone. It was Henry, not she, who needed comfort and support.

She opened the passenger door and slipped in.

"*Oh!*" was all she managed as her heart leapt into her throat.

His mouth was cut and swollen and one eye was black and half closed. He was not smiling. Galen opened her mouth to speak but nothing else came out.

"I sent my father on ahead. I hope you don't mind," Julian said in a tired voice. He was half turned in his seat, watching her as if waiting for a reply. Galen could say nothing. They looked at each other silently for a moment; then he turned back, put the car in gear, and started down the driveway. Galen looked down at her hands.

They were almost at the town road before he spoke again.

"Do you mind if we make a stop along the way?" he asked.

"No, of course not," she murmured, and with that he swung into the darkened stable yard, pulled up to the barn door, and cut the engine. He opened his door and said in the cool, businesslike voice she first knew, "There's something I want to show you." He then climbed slowly out and walked stiffly toward the barn. In a moment a dim light shone through the half-opened door. After a brief hesitation, Galen got out and followed him in.

She stopped just inside.

"This way," he said simply, and began down the main aisle ahead of her. They were greeted by soft, throaty nickers as they passed the darkened stalls. Three-quarters of the way down the barn, Julian stopped in front of a stall and slid open the door. Galen came up behind him, gave him a quizzical look, and peered in. At first she saw only the chestnut brood mare Luna, who came forward to greet them with a low, chuckling sound. But then something in the shadows behind her moved. Galen gave a little cry and went slowly into the stall. There in the corner was a tiny, newborn foal, its long nobby legs folded awkwardly under it, its velvety face hardly bigger than a dog's.

"Oh, *Julian*," she whispered, dropping to her knees and gently cupping the little head in her hands. Eleven months earlier the mare had been bred to Durometer. The foal appeared against the light shavings to be, like its sire, black, but with what looked like a small white star on its forehead.

"I didn't think she was ready yet!"

"Neither did we. She did it on her own."

"When did it happen?"

"Today. This afternoon."

"A colt?"

"A filly."

"She's so small and so delicate," Galen said, forgetting herself, forgetting the horrible events of the day, forgetting the chasm between herself and the man who was now standing just behind her. "I want to pick her up and cradle her in my arms."

She cupped the little chin in her hands.

"I've never gotten over the softness of a foal's nose," she cooed. "It's like baby's skin. And their ears and their eyes are so *big*, like a fawn . . . Look at her now, she's closing her eyes." Galen held the head in one hand and stroked it gently it with the other.

"What a lovely, perfect jewel you are," she murmured. "What a treasure . . . what a gift . . . Oh, Julian, look, she's falling asleep in my hands."

Galen leaned her face close to the foal's and touched her swollen cheek against its downy muzzle. She then let the little head drop slowly back onto the shavings, got quietly to her feet, brushed off her knees, and turned around to face Julian. He was standing very close to her and made no move to let her pass.

"What are you going to name her?" Galen asked.

"Caetano suggested Galen's Girl, but I thought I should ask you first."

"*Galen's Girl?* What an awful name. The answer is an emphatic no."

"That wasn't the question."

"Oh . . . What was?"

"Is it true?"

"Is what true?"

"What you said in the driveway."

Galen's heart gave a funny little jerk. "About my not loving Johnny?"

"No, about your loving me."

"Julian . . ."

"Is it true, Galen Shaw? Do you love me?"

"Julian, *why* didn't you try to warn me about Johnny? If you'd only told me what you and Caetano were doing, if you'd only trusted me. You can't know what it was like trying to sort through the maze of contradictions with your heart telling you one thing and your brain telling you . . ."

She looked away. "I thought it was *you* with Carla that night at Henry's, which was exactly what Johnny had been trying to get me to believe, and then Mara said she saw you with Carla in New York, and then seeing you myself in the icehouse with Caetano and hearing—"

"You haven't answered my question."

Galen stopped. She could feel more than see his eyes on her face as his was in shadow. She could hear the beginning of a smile in his voice. He leaned a little toward her and took her bruised face gently in his hands. They must look like a pair of prize fighters, she thought, and was struck suddenly with an urge to laugh. Galen closed her eyes and he kissed them.

"Julian, how did you find me?" she asked.

"I heard you scream."

"I screamed?"

"Yes, my love, like a siren."

"But you'd left. Why did you come back?"

"I'm not sure exactly, but suddenly I knew you were there. . . . Now answer me. . . . What *did* your heart tell you?" he asked.

"That I loved you."

"Then it *is* true."

"Yes, it's true."

His arms came around her and he said softly against her hair, "Then you won't run away from me again?"

"No."

"You see, we need you. H. L. and William and I.

Franny, too, for that matter. That doesn't frighten you, does it?"

"No."

"Then you'll stay with us?"

"Yes, I'll stay."

"Good, then Galen's Girl it is."

She pushed away from him.

"*No.*"

"I'm afraid so," he said with a laugh as he pulled her back to him and began to lead her slowly out of the stall and down the long aisle back toward the light, their shadows trailing long after them, their voices and their laughter echoing and eventually fading in the still darkness of the sleeping barn.

"You see, Luna's our best mare and two years ago she had a colt by Teton's brother, a stud over at—"

"I can't believe you!"

"You will train the filly, and I'll train the colt—"

"You just can't stand to lose, can you?"

"And in five years, we can have a rematch—"

"Absolutely not! Besides, a mare would be at a disadvantage to begin with."

"What about Ruffian?"

"She was one in a thousand."

"If Durometer is all that you claim, Galen's Girl should be at least that."

"Stop calling the poor thing that."

"If she wins you can change her name."

Galen stopped and looked at Julian. A smile crept slowly to her face. "She'll win."

"Yes, I suspect she will."